The Greater of Two Evils

Jane Thornley

ISBN: 1540489280
ISBN-13: 978-1540489289

*1 *

Sometimes it seemed that everything I loved conspired to kill me—deadly men, deadly family, deadly art, deadly artifacts. Why couldn't I just live an ordinary life? As I stared down at the array of ancient gold jewelry on my bedspread, it occurred to me that I may soon add my name to the mounting list of outlawed friends and relatives: Phoebe McCabe, smuggler.

On the other hand, the seventeen Etruscan pieces were gorgeous, unbelievably rare, and once treasured by women like me three thousand years before. Well, maybe not like me exactly, the original owners being wealthy, which I certainly was not. Still, artifacts this exquisite didn't deserve to be locked away or buried alive. It was my responsibility to admire them regularly and with gusto, a task I took seriously.

Today, I chose the single disc-shaped gold earring with the female head pendant flanked by long tiny beaded dangles. I held it up to eye-level, wondering if the tiny

face looking back at me was a portrait of
the original owner or some long ago goddess.
Her expression seemed stern enough for a
goddess, though any woman wearing an earring
this heavy would probably constrict her face
from effort alone.

I admired the delicate filigree, the
tiny gold dots lining the ear cuff, the
itty-bitty flowers applied strategically to
the base. How did they manage work that fine
without magnifying glasses? I shook the
earring gently so the dangles clinked
together as I imagined a woman long ago
stepping out in her robes, flowers or a gold
diadem in her hair...

The ringing phone jolted me. I dropped
the earring onto the pillow and jumped up.
Damn. The house phone. I scrambled into the
lounge and snatched the thing from its
stand. Caller ID announced Baker & Mermaid,
meaning that either Serena or Max was
calling from the gallery below. "Hello? I'm
not late." The phone clock read 11:35. I
wasn't due in until noon on Tuesdays.

"Phoebe? Good morning. No, you are not
late. You are all right, yes?"

Serena, then. "Yes, of course. Why do
you ask?"

"Your voice, it sounds frazzled."

"Frazzled, me? No, I'm fine. The phone
just startled me. Happens every time. How's
things in the gallery this morning?"

"Good, but that is not why I call. Sir
Rupert has sent another gift that he asks
that you sign for."

"Another? Will he never give up? I'm
not signing anything. Please send it away
like we did the others. I'll accept nothing
from him." The collection of rare orchids,

4

the jade carving from the Ming dynasty, the hand-tooled leather and kilim bag—all returned to sender. Did he think my forgiveness could be bought? I'd return the Etruscan gold, too, once I figured out how. Or, if I could bear to part with it.

"This time he sends this package with his chauffeur, er, mister...?"

"Evan, he only goes by Evan, and what difference does he think that will make? Please tell him to get lost. I don't want to speak to him, either." The last time I saw the muscled ex-M6 agent he was in a hospital bed in Rome only a few doors down from his employer. I hadn't laid eyes on either since my return from Italy weeks earlier, and planned to keep it that way until I was good and ready.

"But he requests that you read the note from Sir Rupert before he will leave."

"Are you serious?"

"Serious, yes. He says he will not go until you sign it. He is very nice to look at but maybe does not match the carpets? It is the bandage, I think."

Hell. Maybe we could call Diamond & Dew to have him forcibly removed. Diamond & Dew being our expensive security company, might consider that above and beyond their call of duty since bouncing services were not in our contract. Besides, with Evan's skills, who knew how he'd handle a physical eviction?

"Phoebe, Max has just arrived."

I didn't need to catch the alarm in her voice to drop the phone into its stand and scramble into my bedroom to quickly but carefully return all the pieces to their velvet pouches and the pouches into the cubbyhole under the floorboards.

5

Floorboards—such a stereotypical hiding place. I had to do better than that. This was my fourth attempt to find a suitable place. In minutes I had combed what was left of my hair and dashed from my flat down the glass stairway to the gallery floor.

My godfather and business partner, Max, stood facing Sir Rupert's chauffeur. Max may as well have been pawing the ground and snorting while Evan stood gazing at him quizzically, perhaps even a bit amused, holding a parcel in one hand and an envelope in the other. As usual, the latest temple bandage only enhanced his rugged good looks.

"I apologize for not calling in advance but I really must see Ms. McCabe," he was saying.

Rena, bright as a poppy in a rich red tunic and tights, had positioned herself between the two men. "Coffee, tea? We have special waters, too."

"The only thing this dropkick's getting from me is a knuckle sandwich if he doesn't get off my bloody premises." Max said, fixing the chauffeur with an unwavering gaze. Both stood six feet tall, both were impressively built, but one was at least thirty years older and didn't possess half the defensive maneuvers or expertise of the other. Plus his anger management training had apparently gone AWOL that morning. "I said I don't want to see so much as a bloody hair of either Sir Foxy or anyone who works for him on these premises. After what you did to Phoebe—"

I inserted myself between the men, my eyes catching Rena's, who stepped away. "Max, let me handle this."

"Look, Phoeb, this bastard and his boss have-" I held up my hand to silence him and swung around to face the chauffeur. "Evan, leave immediately. I want nothing to do with either Sir Rupert Fox or you ever again. I would have thought all the returned gifts made that clear. Go. Tell Rupert that, from hereon in, we are not on speaking terms. He knows why."

"He does?" If his confusion was an act, he made a damn good job of it. "But, Madam, I assure you Sir Rupert has no clue as to his offense. He realizes that events in Italy were very trying but thought matters resolved in Rome. He misses you terribly and factors your Wednesday knitting sessions among the highlights of his week. He hopes only that, in interests of your friendship, you will allow him a few moments of face-to-face conversation."

"No," said Max and I simultaneously. I glowered at my godfather before returning my attention to the chauffeur. "Tell him to stop the pretense. This time he's gone too far."

"But how, why?" He looked genuinely dismayed. "May we go someplace private to speak further?" He gazed pointedly at Max and Rena. The latter was at least pretending to water the potted palms on our central display table while Max stood by flexing his fists.

"The only place I want you to go at the moment is out the door," I said. "Just leave."

"But, Madam," Evan said, "Please. Sir Rupert asks only to speak with you in person so he can understand. He offers this invitation as well as a note to express his feelings."

"I care about his feelings about as much as he cares about mine." Did he care that I didn't want to constantly be plunged into activities I saw as ethically and morally wrong? I took the thick envelope and attempted to tear it in two. Of course, Rupert used the kind of heavy bond that made ripping impossible. Max plucked the envelope from my fingers and used his Swiss Army knife to scissor the note until the pieces snowed to the floor.

Without missing a beat, Evan whisked the top from the box he carried to reveal a pile of softly gleaming silk yarns coiled into little satin muffin cups like a feast of tactile candy. Cerulean blue, lapis, amethyst, topaz, and a variegated combination like a peacock's glistening tail feathers. "For you. Sir Rupert had them dyed especially to inspire your next knitting project."

I almost gasped, but to my credit, recovered in seconds. That man knew where to get me. "Stop. How many times do I have to say it? I will not be bought. He's placed me in the worst possible position. Must I call Interpol to make my point?"

The tremor of alarm may have been my imagination but his sudden pallor was not. Evan straightened and bowed. In seconds he had exited the gallery, his absence bringing relief tangled with remorse. We had shared such incredible adventures together, so many laughs, so many tears. Why did Foxy have to go and ruin everything?

"We haven't seen the last of him," Max remarked.

"Of course not." I turned and marched towards the glass steps. "I intend to talk to Rupert on my time, not his. When I'm ready." When I'd cooled down enough to be strategic rather than furious.

"Phoebe, wait."

I paused. "I have to change before the O arrives," I said, indicating my jeans and sweater. "I'll be back down in a few minutes."

"We need to talk about this, Phoebe. Can't avoid dealing with it forever."

"Maybe not forever, but at least a few more days." Or weeks. I caught Rena's gaze from across the room. She knew, of course. I kept nothing from her. Turning, I trudged upstairs with Max following behind.

"Let's deal with it now, Phoebe." Max said behind me, though he said nothing more until we were inside my flat. "This is not something we can just drag on. That agent of yours is all over this place. What if he finds the stash?"

I swung around. "In my flat? He's rummaged through our trash but I doubt even he'd come up here without an invitation. Besides, since Italy he hasn't been around much. I think he finally believes my innocence."

"Now there's an irony."

"But I am innocent," I said. So why did I feel so hellishly guilty? "I didn't knowingly smuggle Etruscan artifacts into Britain, did I?"

"No, but you kept trusting that bloody little viper over and over again. It was only a matter of time before he shafted you the way he did me."

"The difference is I was never in business with him, you were." I held up my hands. "Okay, sorry I brought that up. Let's not go through all that again. I really believed we were friends, okay? He gave me the keys to his Orvieto escape, and put Noel and me back together again-sort of. There's no way I expected him to use me to smuggle that gold. He knows I want no part of all these black market shenanigans. He accepted that, I thought. But," I paused to take a deep breath, "but why did he have the gold put in my suitcases instead of his?"

"A mistake, obviously. How many times do we have to go over this? His men made a balls-up. He and that boy Friday of his were hospitalized in Rome while those bludgers he's got working for him here handled the London ops. Foxy thought your suitcases wouldn't be scrutinized because you were with Walker."

"And he was right."

"Look, darlin', airport customs look for drugs and explosives mostly, and only spot-check for valuables. No customs bloke is likely to pull over a party accompanied by an Interpol agent and rifle through their stuff. He's looking for drugs, the explosives. Gold doesn't ring as many bells as you'd think. Foxy knows that."

And Max knew that, too. "I guess." Pivoting, I began pacing my lounge, around the oak table, past the loom, maneuvering by the baskets and baskets of yarn I had positioned on the floor.

I yearned to knit a few rows just to steady myself, but I had run out of time. "Rupert's going to want it all back. That has to be the next step. He used me as a conveyance and now needs to reclaim the goods, but I'm not giving it to him. He probably stole it from Nicolina in the first place. How could he do that? How could he steal from one friend and then turn around and hoodwink another? Am I really such a poor judge of character?"

"Foxy's a master trickster, Phoeb. Many a clever nut has fallen to his finagling."

"Like you."

"Like me," he agreed. "He'll want to wheedle you into accepting some of it. That way he assures your guilt will protect his."

"That's not going to happen because I am not keeping any of it, and I'm certainly not giving it to him, either."

"What then?"

I paused by the *Tide Weaver* tapestry hanging over the mantle, both pained and comforted by the piece my mother, brother and I had crafted nearly a decade earlier. Sometimes I thought it the best thing I'd ever done and that every single thing I'd touched since ended up in tangles. "I don't know," I said. "Somehow I've got to get it back to Italy. That's the only possible solution."

"Don't be daft, Phoebe. If you're caught with that stuff, they could put you away for a long time. They don't want to hear how you kept it here in London for weeks while you figured out what to do."

I should have alerted Interpol right away. I was tugging at my scraps of hair wondering why I hadn't. Why hadn't I just called up agent Sam Walker the moment I found that gold in my luggage and blown the whistle on Foxy? But I knew why: deep down, I still couldn't believe Rupert could have

done this to me, and couldn't figure out how
to finger him without sullying myself in the
process. Two good reasons. "Don't worry, I'm
not planning on hopping a plane with the
gold stuffed in my luggage. I'm trying to
contact Nicolina. It's her family treasure,
after all. The next time she comes to
London, I'll give it back to her. She was
interested in selling some of it anyway."

"Have you tried contacting her?"

"I've messaged her multiple times and
called twice, but no response. I hope she's
all right."

"Meanwhile, we need to get it off the
premises," Max sighed. "Got to find a safe
hiding place, at the very least. You know
Foxy's going to come after the stash. He
probably thought you'd just pass it over in
exchange for the yarn duffel boy brought
this morning. I could crack his jaw."

"No, you couldn't," I said turning to
him. "Stop saying stuff like that. You're
not some 25-year-old ruffian."

"Do you still have the pieces under
your mattress?" he said, changing the
subject.

"Of course not. They're under the
floorboards," I said, my eyes caught by the
Tide Weaver tapestry. I took comfort in
those luminous silk threads slipping in and
out of the woolly tapestry waves. That piece
had been such a tribute to McCabe family
harmony and artistic fervor before we became
undone. Time could be such an unraveler.

"The floorboards?" Max said.

"I know: Obvious Hiding Place 101."

"We should put them in the gallery
safe, at least."

"No way," I swung around. "That would be the first place Walker looks if he ever comes after us with a search warrant." I slapped a hand over my mouth. "Did I just say 'search warrant'? What am I thinking? We're a long way from that, surely?" I straightened. "Look, Max, I've got to get dressed for today's big sale. Isn't Mr. O arriving in ten minutes?" The "O" stood for oligarch.

"That's right. I'll head down and get those pieces out of the storeroom. End of conversation for today but think of how we're going to get that loot out of here. If Interpol gets wind of it, we could both end up in jail or worse."

"What's worse than jail?" I asked, halfway to my bedroom.

"Dead," Max said as he strode for the door. "It wasn't that long ago we had every two-bit crook in London after loot we didn't have. Think what they'd do if they ever get wind of this?"

2

Yagar Arkhangelsky would be my first
Russian oligarch, not that I expected to see
a bunch of Slavic billionaires queuing up in
my future. All I knew about this one was
that he was a wealthy industrialist with a
penchant for anything born on Russian soil.
Repatriating antiques originating in the
Baltic States was his modus operandus, and
textiles apparently qualified.
      I was excited to show him our fine
selection of flat-woven Bessarabians and the
rare Caucasian carpets that Max and I had
sourced weeks ago. I was even more thrilled
by how Baker & Mermaid's reputation was
growing internationally. I could only hope
that we'd caught the attention of Mr.
Arkhangelsky on our own merits rather than
through some criminal interest.
      "I think his name is pronounced
'archangel-less-ski', archangel as in
Gabriel," I said as I smoothed the carpet's
rich nap. "A man named for angels. That has
to be some kind of good omen, right?"

Serena, who was helping me prepare the carpets in the storeroom while Max and our part-time assistant, Jennifer, arranged things in the gallery beyond, glanced up. "It is 'archangel-less'," she pointed out. "Not so good, I think."

I laughed. "You mean as in the absence of archangels?"

"These rich Russians, they make me nervous," Rena said. "I do not see them as very angelic."

"Not every rich Russian is involved in the post-Soviet mafia," I pointed out. On the other hand, with my luck, this one probably was. Baker & Mermaid held an irresistible attraction to the criminal world due to Max's previous activities, my ex-friendship with Sir Rupert Fox, and my closest relatives, my brother included. It wasn't all that long ago that my brother, Toby, had helped pull off a major heist of pirate loot in Bermuda. Max and my romantic entanglement, Noel, were involved, too. As for me, I had always maintained a belief in my own innocence, though that was getting harder to defend.

"I like your hair today," Rena said, smiling.

I attempted to tug my front forelock straight, knowing it was probably doing a double-back flip. "Thanks but we both know it's a disaster." I'd had a dramatic cut and dye job done in Italy as an disguise attempt at Noel's prompting. For ten seconds I had actually looked punky-cool, but it didn't last. Soon my naturally kinky red roots pushed up against the blue-black dye to burn a ginger haze against my scalp. If head-on-fire was a look, I'd nailed it.

"We will fix tomorrow, yes?"

"Yes, yes." I had finally agreed to go to Serena's son, Marco's, hairstylist friend, some swanky guy who only went by his first name—Raoul or Giorgio, or some such thing. He apparently served as stylist to the theater crowd, and, according to Serena, didn't have a drop of Italian blood, despite the moniker.

After the carpets were smoothed and every fleck of lint picked off, Rena and I brought the pieces into the gallery. We had a row of hanging accordion racks positioned in one section so customers could flip through them as if leafing through the pages of a huge suspended book. As Max and Rena slipped the carpets into the slats, I dashed about the gallery doing a last-minute check.

Fifteen minutes left before Mr. Arkhangelsky arrived. Was everything bright, tidy, clean, and welcoming? Check, check, and double-check. I paused halfway to the door and gazed around looking for Jennifer. Missing in action again. I caught a glimpse of her sylph-like form in the storeroom, and launched toward the back. We had to set up the refreshment tray, unwrap the sandwiches, arrange the shortbreads. We'd ordered special delivery from Fortnum & Mason that morning and the exquisitely prepared trays needed to be retrieved from the fridge, all menial chores likely to bore our St Martin's fashion design student, who was probably mentally designing her next outfit that very moment.

Bursting into the storeroom seconds later, I ground to a halt. No trays in sight, only Jennifer bent over one of the rear packing tables. I crept closer. "Jennifer, what are you doing?"

She straightened as if spring-loaded. "Oh, hi ya, Phoebe. I was just, um, reassembling this … invitation."

My gaze landed on the paper shards she'd been carefully piecing together. "What's with you and my garbage?" This wasn't the first time she'd been drawn to my trash.

"Oh, I thought this can't be garbage. I saw the crest and the words 'ball' and like, I mean, really? I was gobsmacked to see it's an invitation to Sir Rupert Fox's famous Christmas costume ball. I mean, like we designers would give our eye teeth to go to an event like that. It's famous."

"We don't have time for this, Jennifer."

"But everybody who is somebody in London goes, in all Britain really. It gets written up in the social pages and everything. Celebrities fly in from New York and LA to attend."

"Jenn—"

"But you wouldn't destroy an invite like that on purpose, would you? You must have accidentally sliced it up with shears or something."

"Oh, sure. Max was trying to clip his nails with his Swiss Army knife and missed." So Foxy thought to lure me with an invitation to his renown fete.

"I knew it," she said, determined to ignore the sarcasm.

I pointed to the refrigerator. "Get the trays ready. Mr. Arkhangelsky will be here in minutes."

She cast one last look at the ragged invitation before heading for the fridge.

In seconds I had the pieces scraped off the table into the garbage bin. "Put the coffee on, please," I called. The costume ball. So that was it. I had mentioned the ball in passing to Rupert months ago, said how much I'd love to attend his celebrated fete, not that I had a clue what to wear—I mean, really, a costume? I had trouble dressing chic in regular wear, let alone in anything more elaborate. He had suggested I bring Max and the gallery staff, too. No doubt he saw that extending the invitation to everyone might bring him on better terms with Max. Foxy would love nothing more than to have us morph into one big occasionally happy family.

And he thought this would buy my forgiveness? Damn, damn, damn.

Yagar Arkhangelsky arrived at exactly 11:15 and, contrary to either my or Rena's imaginings, he looked neither particularly angelic nor murderous. A long-faced man in his late forties of moderate height with a receding hairline, pale skin, mud-brown eyes, and thinning gray-streaked hair, his appearance was so ordinary, he could have blended into any London street, at least at first glance—navy sports jacket over jeans, a brown turtleneck, and a long leather trench coat. And yet he carried himself with such tightly wound control, he emanated the quiet power of a loaded gun.

He simply walked through the door unaccompanied and began strolling around the gallery. Max was on the phone, Rena was entertaining a couple studying our carpets, and Jennifer was still in the back room

pretending to be useful, so it was I who
approached first.

"Hello, may I help you?" I asked.

"Yes," he said turning to fix me with
a dazzling smile. Very white teeth, the
result of the kind of dentistry designed to
embed headlights into human jaws,
temporarily blinded me. I smiled back. "You
are Phoebe," he said with a thick Russian
accent.

"And you must be Mr. Arkhangelsky."
What was I expecting, hark the herald
Arkhangelsky? If not fanfare, then at least
maybe a rich man's retinue, but the man
arrived solo. And why were we on a first
name basis already?

"I am Yagar Arkhangelsky, yes. I hear
much good things of Phoebe McCabe." He
continued to smile brightly.

"Really, from whom?" I held out my
hand to shake, which he took in his, and
wouldn't let go.

"Very good recommendations," he said,
the "very" pronounced as "welly." He
proceeded to turn my hand over in his to
massage the pad of my thumb. "You have star
in palm. This very good," he said, smiling
into my eyes.

"Let me show you the carpets we have
selected especially for you—all excellent
specimens." I attempted to retrieve my hand
but he only cushioned it deeper into his
own. "They are all … beautiful," I
continued. "I'm sure you'll be very …
pleased."

"I am pleased now. Your hand makes me
happy man."

"One in particular is a superb
Caucasian Star Kazak dating from the late

18th century in near perfect condition, but it's only one of many." This was crazy. I'd never been hit on by a client before.

"All you have, I take," he said.

"Pardon me?"

"No need to show. I buy. You come with me to lunch now."

"Lunch? No, I mean thank you for asking, but it's not even 11:30 yet, and I'm working."

"Not so busy here. You come. I have car outside."

Oh, hell. I scanned the gallery, saw Max hurrying forward, and tugged my hand away.

"Hello, you must be Yagar Arkhangelsky," Max said, sweeping down on us. He took Arkhangelsky's just-released hand and pumped it energetically. "Welcome to Baker & Mermaid. I see you've met my partner and goddaughter, Phoebe. Come, I'll show you our display of the carpets we've prepared. Did you fly over from Moscow today?"

"No, I stay in suite at Goring."

Max was not above placing his hand on the man's back and steering him along in a slipstream of bonhomie. Surprisingly, Arkhangelsky allowed himself to be led while trying to keep me in his sights.

I broke eye contact and slipped past, heading for the storeroom. I'd just assure myself that the refreshments were ready while trying to stay as much in the background as possible. Let Max handle Mr. O. I didn't need that complication.

When I burst through the storeroom door, I found the Jennifer putting finishing touches on the table arranged with napkins, glasses, and a bowl of white gardenias sprigged with pine and forest berries.

"Oh, that looks lovely!" I exclaimed with so much enthusiasm, Jennifer looked startled.

"You okay?" she asked while adjusting the napkins—Christmas napkins? I'd bought plain green ones—and moved the basket of cutlery slightly to the right. "It's called staging," she said. So, like, I'm hoping this will put Mr. Arkhangelsky in the mood."

"I think he's already in the mood," I said, "and not just for buying carpets."

"Excuse me?"

"The man's hitting on me."

"Seriously?"

"A little less incredulity would be appreciated, Jenn."

"Oh, I didn't mean it that way. I'm just saying like, wow, couldn't you nail him for sexual harassment or something?"

"No, I couldn't. I'm a business woman and he's a customer. The balance of power is defined differently in this instance. I'll leave him to Max and give him a wide berth."

"I can act as a distraction. You know, lead him off the scent."

"Are you offering to play decorative decoy?"

She beamed. "Sure, if it helps. I mean, I know how to flirt as well as anyone, and can just let him know I'm taken if he gets too, um, amorous."

She did bear a close resemblance to Gwyneth Paltrow, so if a man were smitten by long-legged gorgeous blonds, she'd do nicely. But when Max led Arkhangelsky to the back room for refreshments later, our client apparently only had eyes for scorched-earth redheads. Keeping away from him turned out to be more challenging than expected.

"And, as you know, Yagar, that particular carpet probably belonged to Czar Nicolas, later confiscated by the Bolsheviks. There's a small mark on the right-hand inside corner that hints of its royal provenance. Though I can't prove it absolutely, a carpet exactly like that is visible in a photograph taken of the royal family in the Alexandra Palace," Max said.

"If same one, carpet very prized," Yagar said while sipping his coffee, his gaze fixed on me. "What does Phoebe say?"

Phoebe, her mouth full of sandwich, swallowed quickly. "It's nearly impossible to claim that it's exactly the same carpet, but the probability is high."

As the coffee flowed and Max invited other customers in to share the yuletide treats, Yagar managed to shuffle his way around the crowded table to stand behind me. He pressed in so close, that when I pulled back after nabbing a prawn and avocado puff pastry, my elbow nudged his hand, slopping his coffee on the floor.

"Oh, I'm sorry," I staring at the puddle. "Here, I'll just get something to clean that up."

"No problem. I am happy we touch."

Dashing into the bathroom, I turned on the tap while glancing up into the mirror, startled to find him directly behind me.

"What are you doing?" I asked, turning to face him. He stood between me and the partially shut door.

"I wish to speak in private."

"No, sorry. Anything you want to say, you can tell both Max and me together. Step back."

"I like we are close, Phoebe. You come to dinner tonight."

"Tonight isn't good for me. I'll have to check with Max to see which night works for us both. Now step back."

Something flashed across Arkhangelsky face, something dark. "I talk to you alone."

I tried to laugh. "This is probably just a language problem, but that sounds like an order. You should say 'I want to' as in 'I want to talk to you alone', otherwise it sounds like you're trying to boss me around. Haha. Step back, I said. This is awkward."

But Arkhangelsky only placed his hands on my shoulders to draw me closer. I shoved him hard. He knocked the door closed with the weight of his body as I heaved him aside and squeezed out the door.

"I will talk with you, lovely Phoebe," he called after me as I bolted from the room.

3

Every Thursday at 6:00 p.m. for the last four weeks, I'd been taking self-defense lessons, a long overdue necessity that I refused to put off any longer. On the first night, each of the twenty-one women participants was asked to recount one incident where self-defense strategies would have come in handy. I had too many to mention. I finally settled on the gallery intruder I'd encountered months ago, though I got off lightly there. He wound up dead, I didn't, though his demise wasn't my doing.

"20,400 women were attacked in Britain alone last year and that's only the number reported. This class is about how not to become another victim," said our instructor, a retired police officer.

Despite this sobering statistic and my heightened need, self-defense apparently was not my forte. After two weeks of bumbling, I finally added private lessons with the instructor, Brenda Higgins, following the group sessions.

"You know what your problem is, Phoebe?" Brenda asked me one evening after class.

I could think of several. "What?" I asked picking myself up from the floor for the tenth time that night. Apparently I was an easy mark, often distracted and prone to daydreaming, but that was only the beginning.

"You are incapable of striking out defensively unless angry."

"Is that a bad thing?"

"It's a bad thing. Self-defense isn't an emotional response. You need cool precision in order to block an aggressor. Use your brain, not your emotions. Are you going to wait until the guy batters you to a pulp before you react?"

Technically, I had yet to be battered to a pulp but I'd received enough bruising to take this seriously, or try to. "I hope not."

"Forget hope, think maneuver. Work on preparation, act defensively, improve your response mechanisms. React swiftly to key triggers, like someone approaching you from behind. Get up, turn around and pretend to be walking down the street. Let's have another go."

Brenda came at me with a swift grab at my shoulders, and though expecting the attack, I still didn't protect myself adequately. I sort of flopped around like an ambivalent tuna. I attempted to shoot my elbow into her ribs and kick out the way I'd been taught. Or so I thought. She twisted my leg around and threw me face down on the mat in an instant. My body ached as if I'd been playing stand-in for pulverized meat—Phoebe scallopini.

"You put zero effort into that," she said in disgust. "You're the perfect mark, practically have 'attack me' engraved on your forehead."

"I'd rather not hurt people," I pointed out while still staring at the mat. Not that I hadn't harmed a few when angry enough. "I prefer attempting to talk them into a different way of thinking, or at least assessing their motivations before striking out." And right then I'd rather be knitting.

"Bollocks. Like talking them to death, you mean? You sound like an ex-lawyer."

"I said I was an ex almost-lawyer. I run a textile gallery now. Anyway, not everyone approaching from behind intends to ambush."

"The ones that grab you are. Get up and let's have another go."

But I didn't have it in me. Suddenly all I wanted to do was get home. I imagined the yarn beckoning me from soft heaps in my baskets with a glass of chilled chardonnay on hand to ease the flow. Peace and tranquility seemed preferable to pain and effort. "Shouldn't I make sure that person isn't planning to ask me for the time or something?"

"How many people even do that anymore? They use their phones. You're a smart woman. Start acting like one. Be on high alert at all times, especially when on the street by yourself. You need to protect yourself first, save the convo for your boyfriend."

What boyfriend? Oh, yes, the one thousands of miles away running from the police. Was he even my boyfriend? What was

the definition these days, anyway? I was
sure proximity had something to do with it,
and maybe a declaration of some kind. I'd
neglected to tell him how much I cared even
though he had tried.

Sighing, I flipped around to sitting
and looked up at this trim, fit woman in the
early years of retirement. Brenda, her hair
scraped back into a stubby blond ponytail,
looked as if she'd taken on the world for
the first half of her life and had no
intention of letting go of its throat for
the second. "What if I'm at home and I hear
an intruder?" I was just buying time.
Anything was better than being thrown on
that mat one more time.

Brenda stood over me hands on hips.
"Get away as quickly as possible and call
the police."

"What if someone starts shooting at me,
what am I supposed to do then? Self-defense
tactics might be useless when the attacker
is armed."

"True, but how many times have you been
shot at?"

I did a quick calculation. "Five, maybe
six times."

"What?" Brenda stared at me. "You said
you run a textile gallery."

"I do, but it's complicated." Then,
thinking that she'd probably keep drilling
me, I added: "It's a high-end gallery. We
get burglars."

"That often? For textiles?"

"We sell rare carpets and ethnographic
pieces."

"That many armed bastards break in to
steal a bloody rug?" Her denim blue eyes
nearly popped.

"They're carpets and, plenty sometimes." They were more likely after the fortune of gold we reportedly hid, or now maybe the Etruscan loot, providing they knew about it. Things like that rarely stay secret in the criminal circles. I kept my mouth shut, of course. Like I said, by then I just yearned to knit.

As it was, I left early, claiming a headache, which was no lie. Brenda's parting words jarred my nerves as I walked out the door: "If some bloke attacks you on the way home, tell him to back off 'cause you have a headache."

At 9:15 darkness had fallen heavily over the London streets, but this being late November with Christmas only a mere three weeks of shopping away, merry lights sparkled in the darkness. With its a festive flair, I loved London this time of year—any time of year, really—but Christmas always reminded me of the people I'd lost, mixing sadness into the revelry.

Though tired and bruised, I needed air so decided to walk along Oxford Street before hailing a cab. Forget the tube. I had yet to adapt to hurling underground in a metal cylinder. Besides, my wariness of enclosed spaces was simply a good strategy, given my track record.

I cut up to Regent Street to indulge my senses. The Liberty department store had a special window show designed in concert with the Royal Ballet that season, which apparently blended sight, sound, and scent. I longed to see it for myself but the damp air hinted of pending rain. People passed on the sidewalk burdened with packages. Coffee shops, pharmacies, and restaurants filled with weary shoppers were the only places still open. Suddenly, all I wanted was a hot bath and a little knitting time. The window show could wait.

I kept my eyes open for a cab. Though there were plenty on the streets this time of night, most were taken or heading elsewhere.

A black Mercedes veered from the traffic and slid up beside me. Instinctively, I stepped back, expecting someone to get out or step towards the car. No one did.

The car idled by the sidewalk as if waiting for someone. I had the uncanny sense it might be me. In seconds the smoked-glass windows on the rear passenger side began to lower, but I didn't stick around to find out more. I hefted my carpet bag over my shoulder and strode a few yards further down, navigating past the knots of shoppers also on the lookout.

Hailing a cab in central London required a delicate balance of respect for fellow hailers combined with polite aggression. Locating a spot near the corner with an excellent view of oncoming traffic in four directions, plus a place for a car to pull over for a microsecond, I settled in to watch and wave. Several cabs sailed by on the opposite side with their roof lights off. Others whizzed past with their Not for Hire signs glowing. Rainy Oxford street at closing time was not great for cab hunting.

After a few minutes, the Mercedes slid up beside me again. I stepped back as the passenger window lowered. "Phoebe, I offer you ride."

I leaned forward. "Mr. Arkhangelsky?" The accent was unmistakable.

"It is me, Yagar. It is to rain. I drive you home."

He looked up at me, smiling in that congenial way of his that communicated anything but. Every sinew in my body tensed. "That's very kind, but no thanks. What a coincidence that you should appear just now." I didn't believe in coincidences.

"I am lucky man. Please, you will get in. My car is warm and dry. I take you home." The driver appeared at my elbow to open the door.

The first rain drops splashed on my face as I backed away. "I just remembered an errand I need to run on the way home. I'll just take the tube." I swung away before he could protest and began hoofing it up the street without looking back.

Alarm jarred my nerves on every level. I couldn't define what I was afraid of, exactly. I didn't expect my client to murder me on the way home or anything so dramatic, and yet something was off, way off. It's like he'd been stalking me.

The closest underground station was Bond Street at least two blocks away. I'd be drenched by the time I arrived. All I wore over my yoga pants and hoodie was a trench coat adapted to style rather than function. I pulled a scarf from my bag to wrap around my head and pulled up the hood from under my coat. That would at least shield my face. My sneakers already squelched. Shoppers had popped open their black umbrellas and were dashing for cover like mushrooms on the run.

I risked looking back. Arkhangelsky's car still slid along behind me as if looking for a place to land. A cab cut in front of him leaning on his horn as a party of three pried themselves from a doorway and bolted for the cab.

I took that opportunity to scramble down Binney Street, thinking I'd take shelter in a favorite restaurant. Then I thought better of that. What would stop Yagar from joining me? No, I needed to get completely away. I figured I had maybe five minutes before his driver negotiated the traffic onto Binney and caught up with me.

Another black car, this one a Bentley, pulled up beside me. I paused as the back window slid down. This car I recognized.

"Phoebe, I insist we talk."

Arkhangelsky's car was just turning onto Binney street. I stepped towards the Bentley. "Fine. Let's get this over with," I told Sir Rupert Fox.

Sometimes a woman has to choose the greater of two evils.

* 4 *

I slid into the Bentley's leather seats without speaking. Rupert passed me a face towel and watched as I unwrapped my sodden headgear and dropped it to the floor.

"Rather a nasty night to be out, Phoebe," he said. "Would you like a spot of tea?"

"Why not?" Shivering, I leaned forward to warm my hands on the vents as Evan directed a heat blast to the back seat. I wasn't sure if my quaking was due to the cold or my fervent pursuer.

"Milk and sugar?"

"No sugar, just milk." Tea with Rupert always began with the ritual of him asking for information he already knew. I never took sugar and always requested milk.

A quick glance out the rear window confirmed that Arkhangelsky still tailed us. He must have seen me climb into the Bentley. Sitting back, I forced myself to regain my calm.

"Just who is following you this time?" Rupert asked mildly.

"You, obviously."

"Me of course. You mentioned your self-defense classes and I took pains to intercept you tonight. I am quite fixed on discovering what I have done to offend you, and would have resorted to a brief kidnapping had you refused to join me yet again."

"Kidnapping must be the least of your offenses."

"Let us not spar unnecessarily, Phoebe. I require answers. This situation has become quite intolerable, and I must say, most hurtful. How could you be so rude as to not even speak to me, to turn Evan away as if he were a mere ruffian? Truly, I am both dismayed and incensed."

"Stop trying to play me, Rupert. You know damn well what this is about."

"I most certainly do not."

"Oh, come on. Don't you ever get tired of playing me for a fool?"

"I beg your pardon?"

"Excuse me for interrupting," Evan said from the front, "but that car is sticking to us like jam to a blanket. Would you like me to shake him off, sir?"

"By all means shake away, dear boy. Who is he, Phoebe?"

I wrapped my hands around the mug Rupert offered while focusing on his amazing affinity for pouring hot liquid inside a moving vehicle. "That is Yagar Arkhangelsky. Do you know him?"

I counted two beats before he answered. "Of course—who in our business doesn't know of Yagar Arkhangelsky?—but why in the world is he following you?"

"He just purchased thousands of pounds worth of Caucasian carpets from the gallery and asked me out for dinner in the process. I think he thought I was a gift with purchase. He was very insistent and so was I in refusing him."

"Why ever would you refuse to have dinner with a client? That's part of our business, surely?"

"Easy for you to say, being a man with a bodyguard in tow, and don't put me in the same business category as you. I operate within the law, or try to."

The car suddenly took an abrupt right-hand turn onto the Ring Road encircling Hyde Park. I slurped tea on Rupert's sartorial thigh. "Sorry."

"Never mind the spillage and forget the Arkhangelsky. You are right to keep away from him, for he's dangerous and not all he seems."

"So, who is? And I am being careful. That's why I chose to get into a car with the devil I know."

"I beg your pardon? Oh, never mind. Back to the point at hand: Why have you refused to speak with me since Italy? And do refrain from insisting that I know the reason, for I assure you I do not."

"The gold, Rupert. How could you use me to smuggle Nicolina's Etruscan artifacts into Britain?"

Though the backseat was awash with street light chasing shadows, I felt his shock. "You know about the gold?" he said in a gasp. "But how? I haven't had the opportunity to explain."

"Did you think I wouldn't notice the false bottom of those two Vuitton roll-ons your man delivered to my door after I returned from Italy? I barely looked inside that gift wardrobe you gave me, and was attempting to ship those suitcases home along with your multiple trunks. For some reason, your agent delivered them back to me instead of sending them to your place along with all your other luggage as I expected.

"Well, I suppose he misunderstood, seeing as I put your name on the tags," he pointed out.

"It struck me as very deliberate and then Max investigated the contents. Imagine my surprise when I realized those roll-ons contained more than just pretty clothes?"

"I have false bottoms in all my luggage out of strategic necessity—one never knows when they will require extra storage space— but what's this about gold?"

"That's not the point."

"Phoebe, I didn't put Etruscan gold into that luggage. Why ever would I? I gave you a selection of chic outfits which you refused to wear, not gold. My word, as if I would ever give away ancient gold, let alone Etruscan gold. Why ever would I put gold into yours? The gold was in my trunks."

"Pardon me?"

"Nicolina and I arranged to have her Etruscan artifacts hidden in my luggage. I had fully intended to bring them to London myself before both Evan and I became indisposed. However, once I was hospitalized in Rome, I decided to request that you take my luggage with you—five trunks, three suitcases, and assorted smaller bags and boxes, as I recall—something I thought particularly fortuitous considering that you had agent Walker accompanying you. Really, where's the harm in that? I am most sorry for that little deceit, but I knew customs would never tear apart luggage accompanied as it was by an Interpol agent. You were perfectly safe. Evan stays on top of the latest screening technologies, and those cavities are shielded against current x-ray capabilities. I would have told you all this had you deigned to see me earlier."

"After the fact, you mean."

"Well, yes. Had I told you in advance, I'm quite certain you would have made a fuss."

"A fuss. You used me to smuggle artifacts into England and you assumed my reaction would have been 'a fuss.' Let's make something clear: I would have detonated on the spot."

"Precisely my point, knowing as I do both your temper and unwillingness to see the issue at hand. This way worked much better. Placing the items in my trunks was Nicolina's idea, in truth, though naturally I assisted with the details. The important point here is that the items were placed in my trunks, not in yours."

"Are you saying you didn't steal that gold from Nicolina?"

Rupert inhaled sharply. "How can you even suggest such a thing? Nicolina is my friend. She requested my assistance in obtaining and conveying her inheritance to Britain for sale, for which I was happy to oblige. Thanks to our help—and note how I include you in the accolades—Nicolina is once again a wealthy woman and a proper countess. To even think I would—"

"But in Italy Alexandra said the gold was gone," I interrupted.

"Phoebe, Alexandra suffers from dementia and clearly forgot the details. Meanwhile, Nicolina required my assistance to retrieve it from her grandmother's estate—well, your assistance, too, of course. Nicolina sent us all on a bit of a wild goose chase, I admit, but we have forgiven her, have we not? It was all by necessity."

I leaned back in the seat. "So you were in cahoots with Nicolina to smuggle the gold into Britain by using me?"

"'Cahoots' is such a distasteful colloquialism. I prefer to say we were in concert."

"Look, Rupert, couch your cahoots however you want, but you both deliberately set me up. I could have been imprisoned. I still might, if someone doesn't kill me first."

"You were safe, I assure you. I would never knowingly risk your safety or freedom. Had the authorities chanced to locate the items—which is highly unlikely given the aforementioned reasons—I would have taken full responsibility."

"Isn't that magnanimous of you, but just how does that help with the Etruscan gold I currently have in my flat?"

He hesitated. "You say you found it in the luggage I'd presented you in Amalfi?"

I gripped the armrest as the car took another abrupt turn, my other hand still clutching my tea. I had been unable to take a single sip. "That's what I said—the two roller bags contained more than clothes."

"Then there can be only one explanation: Nicolina is responsible."

"But why, if she already arranged for the treasure to be transported in your trunks?"

"Obviously it's a gift, Phoebe. Nicolina wishes to thank you for your services. How many pieces are there and of what nature?"

"Seventeen pieces of jewelry, mostly single earrings, plus one bracelet, and a gorgeous necklace."

"That's it then. Nicolina gave you a handful of lesser pieces, ones she thought may be more difficult to sell, but which you would still appreciate. If I could see them, I could assess them properly, but you should be honored, regardless. It is a gift, Phoebe. Do not be ungrateful. I, too, received gifts from Nicolina, notably a bronze chariot that I have no idea how to transport to Britain—one cannot exactly ride it across borders, can one?—but jewelry is much more manageable. I will certainly treasure the exquisite pieces she presented to me. You should be pleased, too. Why aren't you?"

"Because I don't want to be in possession of smuggled goods, obviously. Besides the trivial detail of illegally transporting them, they belong in an Italian museum."

"Nonsense. You and Noel do go on so about returning artifacts to their rightful owners. Who, pray tell, rightly possesses something after their owners have been gone for thousands of years?

"Their ancestors, the people."

"Nonsense. Pieces such as those you described would only languish in a vault somewhere. Italy has plenty of Etruscan artifacts on hand, so many, in fact, that single earrings would hardly make it to display. Besides, Nicolina will argue that those pieces are hers to do with as she wishes, having been found on her family estate. She is their true owner."

"And the Italian department of antiquities would vehemently disagree. I intend to return them."

"Give back a gift? How very rude. That won't do at all. Relinquish them to me, if you must."

"No way."

The car veered abruptly and my mug went flying.

"Evan, dear chap," Rupert called, "this centrifugal force is growing tiresome. I can barely drink my tea. What is happening with this Arkhangelsky fellow?"

"He is still tailing us, Sir."

"Will he not be shaken?"

"It appears not, Sir. Are we delivering Madam to her flat?"

"Of course," I said.

"Certainly not," Rupert said simultaneously. "We must get Phoebe away from this amorous Russian at once. Proceed to my house, Evan, dear boy, and deploy whatever maneuvers necessary to dislodge our tail. I will leave all in your capable hands." Then to me he added: "Sit back, Phoebe, and don't mourn the tea. I shall have a fresh brew waiting when we arrive at Belgrave."

I could have protested but to what end? Darting in and out of the London streets in the back seat of a car was as good as being held hostage. And there was the matter of the Russian, who I'd rather

dislodge before descending to my nest.
Besides, I admit to experiencing a thrill
watching Evan handle the car with such cool
precision, the way his eyes fixed on the
road, his gloved hands masterfully gripping
the wheel, tantalizing glimpses of which
were just visible in my line of sight.

I thought of Noel. Loving a man so
absolutely incommunicado hurt like hell.

"How well do you know Arkhangelsky?" I
asked Rupert, yanking my gaze from the
driver to the window. We were weaving in and
out of Kensington Borough now. Evan turned a
corner, shot past a bus, and gunned it down
Kensington Road, hotels and shops whizzing
by in a rainy blur.

"We had business dealings once, but no
longer remain on good terms. He is a trifle
unethical."

I almost snorted. "My mother would say
that's 'the pot calling the kettle black.'"

"Really, an old Irish homily, I
suppose? In any case, I choose to ignore the
inference that I am in any way in the same
category as Yagar Arkhangelsky. I refuse to
be cowed by such bullies. There was a
disagreement over an auction involving a few
rare icons a few months back. I won the bid,
a trivial matter, really, but it ended the
previously congenial nature of our
relationship."

"Who tried to cheat who?"

"It's 'whom', Phoebe, and, really, do
refrain from insulting me further. I won the
bid fairly by taking advantage of a
momentary lapse of attention on the part of
Arkhangelsky's hapless former employee, who
I understand has since met an untimely end.
Forget all that for the moment. I am quite

rankled by your suggestion that I attempted to steal from Nicolina while risking your freedom in the process. Really, what do you take me for?" I tried to respond but he carried on. "Still, it is a testament to my forbearance that I am willing to overlook these barbs in the name of friendship. I do miss our knitting sessions. Well, I confess, I simply miss you."

I stared out the window as we shot around a corner onto Grosvener Cresent. I missed him, too, but on no account would I tell him that. I needed to break off this friendship once and for all. It was too dangerous. He was too dangerous. If I was to ever achieve a peaceful, stress-free existence, certain disruptive forces had to be banished, and Rupert Fox remained at the top of the list. I swallowed hard. "Have you heard from Noel?"

"I did wonder when you would get around to asking me that. No, I have not. I had rather hoped you had."

"I've received a postcard from Toby but nothing from Noel." It was as if my heart was being sliced into multiple pieces.

"Never mind. I am sure he is fine. He is probably still in convalescence in that secret place Toby alluded to." He reached over and patted my hand. I snatched it away. "Try not to worry, my dear. The man adores you. Many of us do, for different reasons, of course."

I squeezed my eyes shut. I will not cry, will not cry. "Why is Arkhangelsky following me?" I asked, my throat a bit too hoarse. "I don't believe he's simply smitten by my person. He wants something."

"Dear Phoebe, you sell yourself far too short. As for why he chooses such an unsubtle method of pursuit, I can only say that he is a very insistent creature by nature, and tends not to stop until he achieves his desired end."

"How comforting."

"But, I hasten to add, I admit to having sung your praises to him back when we were on more congenial terms."

"Why?"

"That is obvious, is it not? I am fond of you. I was describing our capers in Turkey and Italy, all of which he found quite fascinating."

"Rupert, don't you get how spreading those stories only puts me at risk? Who knows what this guy is thinking now?"

"I rather believe he sees you as an interesting woman. He doesn't know about Noel, of course."

"I believe we've lost him at last, Sir," Evan said from the front.

A quick glance over my shoulder confirmed that we now wound through the residential streets unaccompanied. "So it's safe to take me home now," I suggested.

"I think not. Come for tea, after which Evan will deliver you home. We are quite close to my house."

I agreed or, at least, I didn't argue. This seemed as good a time as any for me to take the next step on the road to sanity.

***

I had never visited Rupert's Belgrave Square residence, or any of his properties other than the Knightsbridge shop and his vacation fortress in Orvieto. I expected something grand but not a corner mansion in one of the richest districts in the world.

A foyer the size of my apartment opened around me, all creamy marble floors with eggshell-white walls enlivened with splashes of color emanating from four majestic oil paintings suspended on the walls. A balcony circled over a grand staircase lit by a massive crystal chandelier, while subtle recess lighting cast a softer glow. Light, color, shadow, scent—Rupert's domain wrapped around me like a symphony to the senses.

Something fragrant teased my nose. I spun around to find the source overflowing from a vase on a pedestal table directly ahead—an abundant bouquet of blowzy flowers drooping ladened heads towards the polished surface. "Peonies and daffodils in December?"

"Yes, one must endeavor to bring a little spring into every month, Phoebe," Rupert said. "Anything jonquil plumped by rich fragrance is my preference. I liken it to inhaling spring in its purest form. Though we must soon change the arrangement to something more festive for the season, for the moment I cling to the more youthful spirit. I shall just ring for tea. Now, where is Sloane?" Rupert asked no one in particular, since Evan had since disappeared. "Oh, there you are, dear fellow. Tea for two in the library, please, and we shall have a tray of those lovely scones."

I looked up from where I'd been inhaling from a sweet-faced peony to see a small man in a suit rapidly descending the stairs.

"Phoebe, do disengage yourself from the flora to meet Sloane, my butler and house maestro. Sloane, this is my good friend, Phoebe McCabe."

Sloane. Rupert had an Evan and now a Sloane, and I was his "very good friend"? I straightened and smiled, suddenly excruciatingly aware of my appearance.

Sloane appeared not to notice, though I doubted that he missed a thing. I waved at him. "Hi Sloane. I got caught in the rain."

The little man, whom I guessed to be in his late forties, only smiled and bowed slightly before dashing off down the hall. My eyes followed his retreating back before focusing on the magnificent painting on my left. "Is that a Sargent?"

"John Singer Sargent, yes. Very good, Phoebe. You have not lost your art history studies."

"I've never seen that one before."

"No, you would not have, of course, since it has been privately owned by Mable's family for decades. Her great-great uncle had it commissioned in 1865. That is quite before the Paris Madame X scandal befell Sargent, you understand. Her great-great-grandfather, a stodgy old sod if there ever was one, would never have allowed such a besmirched artist to paint his beloved children. Those are his two little daughters playing by the river Cole, by the way, Judith and Lilly. Lilly was Mable's great grandmother."

"Oh, it's so lovely, children in white frocks playing amid a sea of daffodils."

"Jonquils, please. Yes, it is quite my favorite of all the artist's works. How lucky am I to possess such. Well, let us not dally further. Come along, Phoebe. We shall warm you by the fire."

But no sooner had I torn my eyes from Lilly and Judith by the Cole when my gaze landed across the foyer to yet another grand painting. This one consisted of five feet of regal portraiture bearing a seated long-haired man swathed in white satin and blue velvet with a scepter in hand. "Is that—?"

"Yes, King Charles the Second, another one of Mable's ancestors, but I fear her lineage follows the noble bloodline into an ignominious tributary. For you see, said ancestor was sired out of royal wedlock under the auspices of one of the naughty king's mistresses. Nevertheless, royal blood is royal blood, is it not? I brought the portrait up from the ancestral seat to display here only because this will be my subject for my costume ball. My tailors and seamstresses refer to it often as they prepare my costume."

"You're going as King Charles the Second?"

"Why ever not?" Rupert struck a kingly pose, his head half-turned towards the light. "Am I not a reasonable facsimile? Once I have the wig bestowed, the mustache expertly applied, and my scepter firmly in hand, not a member of the British empire will be able to tell us apart."

"Except maybe those still living."

"Humph. Allow me to show you how my costume progresses. You will appreciate this, your love for textiles being even more abundant than mine. I am quite excited to reveal this to you, for in truth, the pieces have been constructed as close to period detail as possible, a criterion for being admitted to my ball. I had so wanted to confer with you as my tailors worked on the layers comprising the royal couture, but you remained painfully incommunicado. Oh, how I have suffered in your absence. Never mind, you are here now. I trust you have decided which personage you will be modeled after for my ball? What fun we shall have! I hesitated from offering another such gala at first—so much effort—but then I thought of how you would enjoy it, and I just knew I must host another with you my honored guest. Rest assured, I will lend you whatever resources necessary for you to fashion your portrait of choice."

I hastened after him as he slipped down one of the corridors radiating from the circular foyer. "Tell me the scepter won't be the genuine article."

"Certainly not, Phoebe. The original is in the Tower of London. Here we are." We had arrived two doors down. Rupert switched on a light, and stepped back to usher me in. On a dais in the center of the room stood a mannequin in full regal attire, glistening with pearly satin against midnight blue velvet. "Though a court outfit suitable for royal portraiture, as you know this king was slightly less formal than many of his predecessors. To hire an embroiderer would take far more time than even I had at my disposal, so I decided upon this portrait."

"The details are exquisite." I stepped forward to finger the waterfall of snowy lace. "Brussels?"

"Flanders. Very similar, I should think."

Lifting a sleeve, I inspected the invisible seaming.

"Now, Phoebe, please do not keep me in suspense a moment longer. Who will be your portrait subject of choice, may I ask?" He clapped his hands together. "I have many suggestions and, indeed, have always envisioned you as a queenly personage. Perhaps Mary Queen of Scots?"

"Maybe I could have gone as the central woman in Vincent Van Gogh's the Potato Eaters. That would be more in keeping with my peasant stock."

"I beg your pardon? But that painting is not a portrait. The costume must be based on a portrait, Phoebe. My word. Oh, wait, you jest! Oh yes, quite amusing. Ha ha. What do you mean could have gone?" he added suddenly.

I swung around to face him. We looked at one another without speaking for a moment. I watched the amusement drain from his face.

"I'm not going to the ball, Rupert, as much as I would love to," I said finally, "I'm not going to attend your costume ball or continue our knitting sessions, or do anything further with you, either. I only accepted the ride tonight so I could tell you that I must break it off with you once and for all. It has to be final. It has to end."

"I beg your pardon?" His stricken expression was a mirror to my own despair. I struggled not to cry.

"I can't keep doing this, I just can't— the duplicity, the trouble you get me into, the life and death dashes across the world. It just can't go on. And there's no point in you telling me that you'll change, because you can't. You are who you are, and I'm just not cut out to live in your world." "But Phoebe, surely you don't mean this? Is this a result of the little smuggling matter?"

That almost made me laugh, the little smuggling matter. "Yes and no. The little smuggling matter was only my wake-up call. Really, it's the constant avoidance of full disclosure, the outright lies, the maneuvering me into dangerous, even illegal, situations where I'm continually compromising myself. I just can't do it anymore."

"But Phoebe, dear Phoebe, you have grown so much as a result, and have we not had great fun together? I know that I keep things from you. You did say, you did not, that you did not want to know the details of my little enterprises? But I did not deliberately force you into criminal activities. The smuggling was a minor exception but, really, I did not know about the gold in your suitcases, you do understand that, don't you? That was Nicolina, and I am quite certain she only wished to bestow thanks. I merely grow excited, too excited, I admit, by the wonders of the ancient world, and by how we together can rescue them from dark oblivion. Dear Phoebe, we must remain friends, we simply must!"

Now the tears were rolling down my cheeks. "No. We can't continue doing things together. I must stay as far away from you as possible, and try to put my life onto solid ground."

"But you are not born for solid ground. You adore the roll and wave of the sea. We are together in this. Phoebe, please!"

I shook my head. "I must go, in fact right now. Please, would you ask Evan to drive me home?"

It wasn't until I was walking out the door that he spoke again, quietly but tight with emotion. "I shall not let you go so easily, Phoebe. Good friends, regardless of how flawed we may be as humans, are always worth fighting for. You are indeed worth the effort, even if you believe that I am not."

*5 *

The next morning, a Wednesday, was my early opening day at 11:00 A.M. and usually one of my favorite times of the week. As the city burst into frenetic activity, the gallery's interior cushioned me in a calm, colorful oasis. Sometimes we didn't have customers before one o'clock, making those hours mine alone.

Only that morning, I felt physically and emotionally bruised. I'd spent a good hour knitting my Kelp Garden wrap upstairs, thinking it would help ease my wounds, and it had, but only temporarily. Soon enough, I had to lift myself from the chair, set aside my knitting, and force myself to plunge into the day. Ruminating on all my loose ends solved nothing but I couldn't stop. There was Noel taking center billing in my mind. Why hadn't I told him I loved him when I had the chance? Needing him and wanting him had created such a tense little knot in my chest, made tighter still by the knowledge we could probably never have a reasonable life together. And then there was Rupert—my friend, now excommunicated by me alone. My life was a mess.

Downstairs, I followed my morning ritual of strolling about the gallery, greeting the carpets by name, touching the weaves in reverence, and becoming acquainted

with each new addition. We had so many new
pieces that it took longer than usual to
make my daily rounds. Actually, I stood
transfixed before a recent piece Max had
hung yesterday to fill one of the post-
Arkhangelsky voids.

The door bell buzzed. I looked up.
Think of the devil. Yagar Arkhangelsky was
steaming toward me with an energetic
strength of purpose.

"Phoebe, good morning," he said,
striding forward. "I am happy to see you."

I stepped back. Serena wasn't due to
arrive until another hour, Max not until
much later. The alarm bell was across the
room under the main table, too far for easy
access, and I'd left my cell phone on the
back desk. "Mr. Arkhangelsky, what a
surprise."

"Last night you did not let me drive
you home." More accusation than statement.

"You made me uncomfortable," I said.
"And you still do. Are you stalking me?"

"What is this word 'stalking'? I
follow, yes. I want to be friends." He was
beaming, flashing those overbright teeth in
my direction, eyes sharp and intense.

I took a deep breath. "This doesn't
feel friendly to me."

"But last night you have other
follower, you take ride with him," he said
in that accusatory tone.

Oh, crud. "With a friend, yes." I
caught myself. Not a friend anymore. Either
way, damned if I'd explain myself to him,
and yet somehow I was.

"That car followed, too. Like stalker."

"Are you saying you were concerned for
my safety?"

"Young woman alone on city street. Yes, very concerned."

I didn't believe him, couldn't quite fathom what he was getting at. "What do you really want, Mr. Arkhangelsky?"

He spread his hands. "To be friends, to talk, please. I see good things in our future, special things."

I stared at him. "You mean like what you saw in my palm, the star? Look Mr. Arkhangelsky, Baker & Mermaid really appreciates your business and would be delighted to keep sourcing rare carpets that suit your interests, but anything else, anything personal between you and me, is out of the question." I held up my palm. "Read my hand now. It says back off."

He smiled the tiniest smile, not mocking exactly but close. "You have boyfriend?"

"What difference does it make whether I have a boyfriend or not? Don't you understand that 'no' means 'no'? I'm not interested, I said. I'd appreciate it if you'd leave right now." I turned and strode towards the display table, stopping only when my finger rested on the alarm button.

"Wait, I apologize." He shook his head as if he couldn't believe his blunder and followed me over, one hand slapped over his heart. "I am very rough man, I know this—like jewel still in rock—but my heart beats strong, and I feel deep. I see beautiful young woman who loves what I love—treasures from long ago, the signature of the ancestors, all history, all art, and I think, we are meant to be together. I am single man, you are single woman. I wish to make an offer, please. My English is not good but I try. Come with me to dinner tonight."

"No. Thank you, but no. Absolutely not."

"You do not know what I offer."

"I can guess."

"Just one dinner. Where is harm?"

I squeezed my eyes shut and counted to ten. Brenda claimed that I could only defend myself when angry, and she was right, but what she didn't realize was that I was capable of almost anything when on the boil, random outbursts and undignified spasms of shouting included. I wouldn't increase this man's bad behavior by heaping on my own.

I took a deep breath. "Mr. Arkhangelsky, if you don't leave right now I will sound the alarm. I find your presence threatening. Please leave."

He stepped back. "We will talk soon." He did an about-face and left the gallery as quickly as he had entered. I stood staring at the door, my body trembling. He would be back, I knew that, and then what? Was I supposed to jab him in the elbow or shoot a knee to the groin? Women needed far more self-defense strategies than just the physical to navigate this world.

My shoulders began to loosen as I continued to breathe. Maybe I needed to take up my Pilates instruction along with self-defense to balance things out? Yes, I'd definitely add that to my weekly to-do list, even if it meant even less knitting. In the meantime, and in the absence of an immediate dose of fiber, I required tea with a side of vitamin C.

By the time Rena arrived, my body, if not my heart, had been restored. I decided

to wait until she settled in before sharing
all my recent events.

"Good morning!" Rena swept past me,
darting through the gallery towards her back
desk, arms full of parcels. The air behind
her trailed a lemony jasmine fragrance,
indicating that something either white or
yellow lay beneath her black winter coat.
"Today I shop," she said over her shoulder.
"The doors open in Camden and Serena is
there. I buy lovely gifts for everyone. You
will love what I buy you, but no peeking
until Christmas. I will show you what I get
Max." She shrugged off her coat, hung it up
in the back room, and returned seconds later
in a black, white, and yellow paisley dress
over her tall black boots.

"I was waiting for you," I said.

"Look what I find in Camden. They hold
it for me until today. What do you think? He
will like it, yes?"

She held up a striped green silk
vintage waistcoat. Just Max's size, too. "It
will go perfectly with the green Harris
tweed jacket he wears with his crocodile
boots." My godfather had a jaunty and
eclectic style.

Serena smiled, holding the vest out as
if the man himself stood within. "Yes, he
looks so handsome in that. This will bring
out the green in his eyes."

"The green in his eyes?" I caught
Serena's gaze over top of the vest. My
breath expelled slowly. "Oh, Rena. When a
woman mentions a man's eye color, she has
more than just a casual interest." I asked.

She sighed, lowering the vest.

"How long have you felt this way?"

"Oh, months. I did not want to tell you. I hoped it would go away. I try to stamp it out like fire." She stomped the floor with one booted foot. "I think, I am too old for this, but it does not stop. First I think he is too loud, too rough. Then one day, I find I like these things. I find I like everything about him—his good heart under the bad temper, the way he smiles when a beautiful carpet hangs in the gallery, the delight at a good sale. He smiles and the heart sings, yes?" She dropped her gaze and began folding the vest back into the bag. "It is silly. He feels nothing in return, does not see me."

"Maggie kicked the heart out of him, remember? It will take a while before he can recognize the good woman under his nose. I—" But before I could continue, the door opened and in walked a couple, the young woman exclaiming her delight over the Zulu beaded cuff we kept in the window.

"I take care of them," Rena offered. "It will help me think of other things." She quickly placed the package under her desk and dashed towards the front,

After that, the day whizzed by in an endless troop of customers. The pace never waned, so I had no time to talk to Rena further about either Max or my own troubles. Even lunch was a quick forage amid the Arkhangelsky leftovers, with both of us eating on the run. Only when Max arrived for the late afternoon/evening shift, did the gallery finally empty.

"G'day, lovely ladies," Max greeted, sailing in wearing his Akubra hat. Sometimes he overplayed the Australian thing. "How are my girls today?" he asked, sweeping past us on his way to the back room. "Is the coffee on? I could use a brew right now."

"I will put it on for you," Rena offered, jumping up from her desk. I shook my head, indicating for her to sit. "Max knows how to make coffee," I told her. "He just needs practice."

I followed him into the storeroom, watching as he stared at the empty coffee pot. "The coffee's in the jar to the left, the paper baskets are on the right, and you know where the tap is," I pointed out.

He grinned. "All right, all right. A man can take a hint. So," he said while launching the coffee-making machinations, "what's new, darlin'?"

"Our most recent best customer, Mr O, has been harassing me, for a start."

"What?" He swung around, coffee pot in hand.

I filled him on the recent events.

"Bloody hell. What did you do?"

"I told him 'no', like I've been telling him all along. He's insistent."

"I meant last night?"

"I ended up taking an offer from another man, also on my tail. How lucky can a woman get—two wildly unsuitable men chasing her at once?" While the one she loved remains a million miles away.

"Who's the second?" Max stood frozen, one hand still clutching the pot.

"Rupert—better the devil you know."

"You got into the car with that slimy little weasel?" he said, his head on a tilt, face flushing. "I thought you were done with him?"

"I chose between two evils, okay? Even Rupert seemed preferable to Arkhangelsky, but the latter still tailed us until Evan shook him loose."

"What's his bloody game? I should knock his lights out."

"Not good for customer relations, I would guess. Look, maybe you need your blood pressure checked? You're turning a funny shade of pomegranate."

"Continue your story, Nurse Phoebe. Save the health check for another time."

"Doctor Phoebe, please. Not everyone has the guts to be a nurse. So, like I said, first thing this morning, he shows up again to press his suit, or whatever. It felt more like an order to me, and you know how I detest bossy men," I added pointedly. "He practically demanded that I go out with him. He says he has a proposition for me."

Max plucked the paper basket from the counter. "Bloody Russian viper. Just because he drops twenty-five thousand quid on us doesn't mean my goddaughter is part of the deal. I'll tell him to back off."

"He's my problem. I'll take care of it. If I need help, I'll let you know."

Rena appeared at the door holding what looked to be a shoe box. "This just came for you, Phoebe. No return address. The mail woman brought it in. She said a tall good-looking man with a bandage passed it to her at the door."

"Evan. It's from Rupert, then. What is it this time?" I took the blue satin-wrapped package and untied the ribbon securing the lid. Inside nestled a small exquisitely embroidered satin shoe. Turning it in my hands, I marveled at the workmanship, at the delicate violets blooming across the stained

silk toe. "Late eighteenth century," I
marveled. "This is the real thing."

Rena gasped. "Oh, a court shoe!"

"Who else but Rupert would send me an
authentic eighteenth century shoe?" I
plucked the thick note from inside the shoe
and read "Dear Phoebe, please agree to dance
the night away in the company of your
devoted friend. Sir Rupert Fox, Esquire."

"What tripe," Max sneered. "Is this
some Foxified notion of Cinderella?"

I carefully tucked the shoe back into
its box. "It's just another ploy to lure me
to the ball. He said he'd never give up on
our friendship, told me that a good friend
is worth fighting for."

"What bollocks is that?" Max said,
flipping up the coffee maker lid.

"The truth," said Rena. "Sir Rupert, he
adores Phoebe, and wants to be forgiven. A
good friend is worth fighting for, Max,"
Rena said.

"Phoebe's always worth fighting for,
any fool knows that, but hearing that coming
from some rodent who uses my goddaughter for
his smuggling operation is bloody
infuriating. I'd like to wring his neck."

"Stop saying things like that, and keep
your voice down," I cautioned.

Max switched off the tap and slammed
the pot under the coffee apparatus. "No one
can hear us back here," he said, lowering
his tone. "I'm just trying to figure you
out, darlin'. You get your knickers all in a
twist over that gold escapade—and for good
reason—and then you go off on a drive with
the same bastard who put you in this mess."

"I told you, I was trying to get away
from Arkhangelsky." Catching Serena's look

of alarm, I quickly filled her in on last night's events, finishing with, "so I let Rupert drive me home eventually, but not before telling him our friendship was over and why. Did you catch that, Max? I said I ended it with him."

Max swung around. "It's about time! What did the bludger say?"

"He had his own explanation for how the gold ended up in my luggage."

"I just bet."

"He said Nicolina must have put it there as a gift, that she must have been thanking me for helping her in Amalfi."

Rena caught her breath. "May that be true?"

"Possibly," I said. "That makes sense. I mean, the countess has no compunction about smuggling her antiquities out of the country, and Rupert was in hospital at the time. She was grateful for my help, so maybe it is true. I still can't get in touch with her. Anyway, that doesn't change my need to pull the plug with Rupert. It's just that I didn't expect it to hurt so much."

"Of course, it hurts," Serena exclaimed, throwing her hands in the air. "You two, you have so much in common, have so many good times together—bad ones, too, maybe, but that makes the bonds tighter, yes?"

"No!" Max interrupted. "He's risked her neck too many times."

"Much like my entire extended family has risked my neck, you included, Max," I pointed out.

"I'm reformed now," Max said.

"And a bit self-righteous about it, too, aren't you?" I countered. "Anyway, the point is, I'm hurting. Foxy may be a crooked, conniving liar but he is—was—my friend and I miss him. He had really good qualities, too. Describes the human race, when you think about it."

I caught Serena's gaze and in seconds she had enveloped me in a lemon-scented hug. "Do you think this is so good?" she asked while still squeezing me tight. "Rupert, he adores you, and you him."

"Yes and no," I said, her hair tickling my cheek. "I had to do it, didn't I?" I pulled back to meet her eyes. "He's dangerous."

"You love danger," Rena pointed out.

"I do not."

"You do. I see it. You get bored," Serena said.

Noel had said the same thing.

"Rena, whose side are you on?" Max asked, towering over us.

She smiled up at him. "I am on hers, I am on yours, I am on everyone's."

"Hi ya."

Together we turned to see Jennifer standing at the door, a fashion statement calling out loud and clear in some kind of pink posy-applique shift and boots. Her studies at Central St. Martins conjured some very innovated get-ups. "Are you ready for the big event, Phoebe?"

"What big event?" I asked. "My day seems big enough already."

"The appointment with Lorenzo, the Lorenzo, remember? Marco's coming over in like ten minutes to give you a personal escort to the salon."

I slapped my hand onto my fuzzy black and red fringe. "I forgot."

"How could you forget that? This is important. I'd die to have Lorenzo do my hair."

"Considering that your long golden mane might require a microscopic trim at most, I think you'll survive," I said.

"That's so not the point," she told me sternly. "The point is you need help and Lorenzo is going to rescue you."

Apparently I needed rescuing by half the male population that day. "Right," I said while weaving my way out of the now crowded back room. "Is anybody looking out for customers out here?"

But the gallery lay empty, caught in a brief presupper lull.

"You should maybe comb your hair or something before we go," Jennifer said, following me out.

I laughed. "There's nothing left to comb. Besides, isn't it a bit ironic to do one's hair before seeing a hairdresser?"

"Stylist, Lorenzo's a *stylist*. He works magic. He does all the theater stars," and she rattled off a few famous names in case I missed that part. "I could come with you," she suggested. "The three of us could go together. Wouldn't that be fun?"

"You're not budging a corpuscle, Jenn," Max said, sailing out of the storeroom. "All hands on deck tonight until closing. This is our busiest time, girl. You can help Rena hoist the Christmas decorations for now. Go upstairs and bring down the tree. I have it tucked against the wall by my office."

Jennifer hesitated, shooting a quick glance towards the door, but soon trounced up the stairs. As her footsteps receded, the door flung open and in swept Marco Fogarty,

Serena's son and Jennifer's boyfriend for an entire year, which I understand is a lifetime when you're 23.

Marco made an entrance without trying. His Italian and Irish genes conspired to form what had to be one of the most beautiful men on the planet. All curly black hair, agate green eyes, and elevated cheekbones, he launched a million hormones wherever he went. As his acclaim on stage and screen grew, so did female attention, and the current stage production of *Pride and Prejudice* didn't lessen his appeal. At least today Darcy had swapped breeches for jeans.

"All ready for the big event, Miss Phoebe?" And then there was that musky booming bass teased by honeyed decibels. Even I was not immune.

"Ready," I said grinning despite myself.

"If you don't mind terribly, I shall just make the introductions and beat a hasty retreat. I have a rehearsal with my stand-in this afternoon."

"No problem. I'll just grab my coat."

Later, Marco introduced me to Lorenzo as if I were a star myself, leaving me in the stylist's artful hands. The result of his wizardry wasn't quite what I expected. When I left the salon hours later, I sported hot orange hair, more like me but not even close. Now I had a kind of Annie-Lennox-during-the-Eurythmics thing going on with a spiky buzz cut. Apparently, I hadn't left Lorenzo much to work with. I just sighed, thanked him, and prayed my follicles would undergo a growth spurt over the festive season.

By then, it was late afternoon and the shoppers were diving into the cafes and pubs along King's Road. I was near Sloane Square, the sun wouldn't drop for another hour, and I was down the street from a few marvelous shops.

Sloane Square during Christmas was an urban fairy fire with lights stringing like stars high in the trees. Even the department store, Peter Jones, had strung a waterfall of blue lights down the full length of its front, the total effect seeming to splash the world with merriment. I strolled into the high-end deli, Partridge's, to stock up on edible stocking-stuffers, temporarily relaxed and happy.

An hour later, I left Partridge's with a bag full of goodies and spent a moment gazing at the lights embedded into the concrete plaza. Even the rain couldn't spoil the effect. Yet, once it began pelting down in earnest, I stuffed my packages deeper into my carpet bag and bolted towards the taxi stand opposite the Sloane Square Hotel.

Perhaps because I was half-expecting him, I didn't react when I saw the Mercedes parked by the curb across from the fountain. Though thousands of black Mercedes sail the London streets every day, I just knew Arkhangelsky awaited me in this one. And it wasn't rain that drove me to his door, it was anger.

6

I leaned over as the window lowered. "Leave me alone, Arkhangelsky. I don't want to be followed; I don't want you to drop by my shop. In fact, if you have gallery business, deal with Max." I scanned my brain for Russian words, came up empty, and continued my tirade in the same vein. I was oblivious to the fact that the driver now stood directly behind me.

Arkhangelsky only smiled and looked up at me as if I was describing a favorite vacation destination. "You get in and we talk more," he said.

"No!" I yelled, "I don't want to talk! Why don't you get that?"

"We must discuss important things. You will want to hear what I say."

"Why would I want to listen to somebody who refuses to hear even my simplest message. I—"

"We talk smuggling," he interrupted. "Your smuggling."

"What?" I straightened. Surely to God I didn't hear right?

"Your smuggling," he repeated. "Ancient gold, yes? Very bad business, if police discover. I have proof. You get in and we talk."

The driver opened the door and nudged me inside as Arkhangelsky shifted over to make room. I got in, numb, my thoughts roiling, while clutching my carpet bag to my chest. "What are you talking about?" I asked, my mouth suddenly dry. The door slammed shut as the driver returned to his seat.

Arkhangelsky smiled at me from the other side of the plush leather interior. "You smuggle Etruscan gold from Italy. I know this. Very bad business. Though prison here much better than in Russia, you will not like it."

I caught my breath, staring straight ahead as the car lurched away from the curb. "I don't know what you're talking about."

"Yes, you do," he said pleasantly. "It is simple: you smuggle Etruscan gold into England and I have proof. I show." He passed over a laptop opened to a stream of pictures, pictures of me holding up the precious Etruscan earring, pictures of me hiding the gold under the floorboards, pictures of me wearing the gorgeous necklace, pictures of me standing naked in my bedroom!

I swore vehemently, my hands shaking as the laptop slipped to my knees.

"My man make slide show. Good pictures," he said, his hand brushing my knee as he returned the computer to his own lap. "I enjoy looking. We have audio, too: you talking to Max. 'Where do we hide gold? In the safe where police don't look. Oh, no, not there, Max. Agent Walker, he look there first.' See, very incriminating."

I leaned over, wanting to retch. "You bugged my flat," I managed to say. "How, why?"

"Always on Wednesdays you alone in shop. Last week, young couple comes. While she buys, man goes up to flat and installs devices. You never notice."

"That would be on our security tapes," I said.

"Not now. You leave the door unlocked to office and flat. Easy for man to erase tapes and install devices. Be more careful in future, Phoebe. You need man to take care of you."

Shit! "I need a man to bug my flat and photograph my private life? Are you serious?"

"Serious, yes. I need your help. If you will not give freely, I will insist."

"Blackmail." I spat out the word.

"I did not want this. I thought you would like me as I like you. We date, perhaps marry. I would make good offer, very lucrative. Your godfather and friends taken care of, you taken care of. Max runs London operation, I handle Russia. You travel with me, wear nice things. So beautiful. But now time runs away. You leave no choice. I must go less pleasant route, but offer still stands. I would still marry you."

I struggled to muster a coherent thought. I took a deep breath. "What exactly do you want?" I asked, not looking at him.

"You pretend to be my girlfriend just for little while. Until Christmas."

I swallowed. "Why?"

"I need your assistance and also from Max. Very easy for you both. Just do as I ask and no one is hurt."

"And if I refuse, if we refuse?"

"Do not refuse, Phoebe," he said, his tone woven with steely sinew.

"And if I say I don't care what you do, that I'll take my chances with the law, since the acquisition of the gold was not my fault, which must also be on your audio tracks?"

"I have other options. Think of Max, your brother. Think of your friends. I know everything about your family. It is so easy for bad things to happen. Do not refuse or people will suffer. I persuade very hard."

"Stop the car and let me out right now."

"You have not heard details."

"Let me out now!" I was screaming by then.

Arkhangelsky signaled the driver to pull over, which he did right there somewhere along King's Road. "I let you go, but no police or I must do something unpleasant."

"Like what? This is so ridiculous, as if I would ever date you."

"Do not make me demonstrate. You talk to Max now," he said. "Tell him what I say. He is smart man. He knows the dangers. You beautiful, foolish girl. When you and Max are ready to talk, call me. You have number. Don't wait long, lovely Phoebe." He reached for my hand but I slapped him off, turning away to grip the door handle. Those seconds bore into my skull like hours: me staring out at a rainy, car-slick road waiting for the lock to pop.

Once the lock released, I sprung out the door, splashing through the puddles in a blind run. Soon, I turned the corner onto a narrow side street and plunged on, not looking back, not caring where I was heading. Just get away, that's all that mattered. Drenched in rain, misery, and fear, adrenalin was my only fuel.

Where could I go? Not home to my flat with its camcorder view into my private life, not to Max who'd erupt into some kind of bullrage and try to barrel down Arkhangelsky with steam-roller finesse, not Noel or my brother, both of whom were too far to help me anyway, and certainly not to my friend whom I had just excommunicated for my own protection. I snorted into the streaming rain. Now there's a joke: Rupert, my fiendish friend, also happened to be my greatest protector. If I were to go to his house right then, he'd know exactly what to do with Arkhangelsky.

I splashed to a stop, turning slowly to look behind me. The street lay utterly deserted. A taxi whizzed by on the pavement, but no Bentley. Nobody would rescue me from either rain or bad guys that night. I had only me, Phoebe McCabe, a woman who had acted too blindly and too foolishly for too long. I had to be my own rescuer. I had to learn how to be dangerous.

Half an hour later, a cab dropped me off at Serena's place. She arrived at the door in a mumu writhing in giant vine print straight out of some Art Nouveau dreamscape. There she stood, staring at me in shocked silence before erupting into reams of Italian, firing short sentences like a battery of flaming exclamation marks.

"You are soaked! I cannot believe this! Mother of saints! What happened?" she said, finally calming enough to speak English. She steered me upstairs into her lovely nest with its second-hand glory of mismatched furniture and swathes of silk scarves draped over every available surface.

I saw no reason to hide the details. I told her everything, while she ran me a bath amid more exclamations and poured something strong down my throat. "Vermouth," she said. "Good for crises. Drink more, yes?"

An hour later, I sat curled up in a vintage pink Chinese silk robe by her propane heater, holding my glass out for a refill.

"You will stay the night. I have extra toothbrush."

"I remember." This wasn't the first time we'd had a boozy sleepover, but usually we drank wine while streaming movies. "I don't suppose you have an emergency yarn kit somewhere, too? My fingers are itching to knit."

"Next time, I promise. Now we must decide what to do. This man, he wants to blackmail you," she said emptying the bottle into my glass. "You must tell police."

"No, I must absolutely not. I do have stolen goods in my possession, remember? Or I think I do. I suppose his henchman could have stolen them while he penetrated my flat, but that would defeat the purpose, wouldn't it? Yes, yes, of course I still have them." I dug my fingers into one temple. "This vermouth is pickling my brain. I fondled the gold just this morning."

And then I recalled how I'd climbed out of the shower and straight into the living room with a towel half-draped over my naked body that morning, too. I even stood mid-room, removed the towel, and ran it over my

fuzzy scalp. Shit, shit, shit. What a
spectacle we make in the privacy of our
homes. But that was the point, our homes
should be private, not open to spies and
peepers. "Oh, God, Rena, maybe Arkhangelsky
and his boys are entertaining themselves
with those cam pictures and videos at this
very minute?"

Rena jumped up and shook the last drop
of vermouth into my glass. "I knew I did not
like this man, this fallen Arkhangelsky. So
no police, but what about Sir Rupert?"

"No Rupert, either. I can't go running
to him just because I'm in trouble, even
though he's partially responsible for
putting me there."

"But he did not put the gold in your
luggage."

"No, but he arranged for me to
accompany stolen goods into the country and
he's been babbling about our joint escapades
to any of who will listen. Rupert doesn't do
innocent, remember? He goes as far as being
slightly less guilty than you may originally
expect, and then only on good days. I refuse
to use the user."

"But he is your friend and would want
to help."

"No."

Rena sighed. Standing over me gazing at
the empty bottle, I wasn't certain whether
the gusty exhale was directed at the drained
vermouth or the absent Rupert. "You must
tell Max, in any case," she announced
finally, setting down the bottle.

"I intend to, first thing in the
morning. He is, after all, part of
Arkhangelsky's plan, whatever it is. He
wants me to be his girlfriend until

Christmas? Shit, I can't even stand having him as a customer." I got to my feet.

"But why does he want this?"

"I don't know. I didn't stick around long enough to find out."

"But Max will help. I think you do not always give him credit. Trust him to be the person you need him to be."

I gazed at her and smiled. "Good advice, thanks. Maybe if I work with him instead of around him, he'll rise to the challenge. But first I need to make a call." I checked my phone. It was 10:00—not too late. I scrolled through my contacts until I found the number and pressed TALK.

"Brenda Higgins," the voice announced.

"Phoebe McCabe."

"My star student."

"The same."

"Did you get attacked on the way home?"

"I did in a way, but look, Brenda, I'll get right to the point: can I hire you full-time for a month or two? You can still teach the class, of course, but I'd like to accelerate my one-on-one instruction. I'll pay well."

"Are you bloody kidding me?"

"I bloody well am not."

"Didn't you say you work full-time at a fabric shop?"

"It's not a fabric shop, and I do work full time, but when I'm working, you can be our security guard. I'm guessing a woman like you doesn't consider retirement the end of work so much as an opportunity to do something more interesting. This could get very interesting. I'm talking full-time employment with good pay. You see, there was a break-in and some perve sneaked into my flat and wired my space with surveillance equipment." I heard her sharp intake of breath. "I need to enact a little serious defensive living. Can you help or not?"

"Let's talk. Supposing I come around to this rug shop of yours tomorrow?"

"Make it 1:00. Since the whole place may be bugged, don't mention your reason for being there until I know it's clean. I'll have my security company at Diamond & Dew sweep the place as soon as possible. Oh, and please do the plainclothes thing. I don't know if you have a uniform lying around or not but don't wear it. I want this to be strictly undercover."

"I'm strictly a plainclothes kind of woman. I'm retired, remember? Unless you want me to wear me bulletproof vest. I still have one of those."

"You won't need one yet."

"What do you mean 'yet'? I was only joking."

"I wasn't."

7

Max's topiary hedges seemed to bristle in the fog like irritable gnomes as I stared through his kitchen windows. "I'm amazed at how calmly you're taking this, at least on the surface." I sat across from him at the table, my hands cupping a mug while his appeared ready to crush his own into shards. I gently pried his fingers off the handle, just in case.

"If you only knew how much I'd like to throw something right now, maybe drive over to the Goring and wring that little Cossack's neck."

"Only he has big, burly driver to protect him and you do not," I said in my best approximation of a Russian accent.

He grimaced. "I still know a few moves, darlin'."

"I bet you do, but let's save them until absolutely necessary. We've got to use our brains to maneuver our way around this one—just you and me, with maybe a few of our friends. First we'll find out what he wants, and then we'll make damn sure he doesn't get it."

Max crossed his arms and glared down at the table. "I can't believe that snaky dropkick actually wired your flat, bloody well took pictures of you, threatened you, my own goddaughter."

"Yeah, yeah. How dare he mess with your little girl?" I flicked my hand as if all that was just so much surface noise. "It drove me nuts, too, until I pulled myself together."

"I did some checking around on him," he said, eyeing the butter dish, which I shoved out of reach. "Seems this guy has a reputation as a big philanthropist in Russia—the wealthy industrialist using his money for worthy causes, like feeding the poor and repatriating Russian artifacts. Buys up the relics and returns them to the Motherland, half the goods ending up in the Hermitage, or some other noteworthy museum—all a front—while the rest disappears. I'd bet my last quid he keeps the good stuff for himself. Probably poaches his breakfast in Faberge eggs. You can find his name online associated with cement refractories in Siberia, steel mills and the like, but some say he also owns a sizable chunk of the dark web. Have no idea what that means, but it's got to be bad."

"Technology. The dark web is the Internet gone wild, beyond the reach of cyber policing or government regulations."

"I know what the dark web is, Phoeb, I just don't know specifically what kind of businesses he runs there."

"Probably the same sort of thing those kingpins run topside—prostitution, drugs, porn…" that last bit trailed away in vivid images of my cam shots being sold somewhere on the midnight frontier. No wonder he could wire up the necessary equipment in record time. I groaned.

"Look, Phoebe," Max said grabbing my hand. "I know people who could get rid of him. He'd be dropped into the English Channel in a matter of days."

I pulled back my hand. "That's crazy. His kind has associates, too. It would all come back at us, big time. Besides, we're not going to stoop that low or act like crime lords just because that's his thing. We're just trying to play it clean in a dirty world, remember? Anyway, that's no way to talk about a potential father-in-law, or whatever he'd be if I accepted his marriage proposal." I was trying to lighten the mood. "I think he's angling for some kind of legal front in the UK, and sees Baker & Mermaid as a prime acquisition. Marrying might be a way to tidy up the deal—like a contract with benefits. I'd receive lots of money in exchange for my servitude—an old story."

I could have kicked myself as soon as I'd spoken, especially after Max erupted into explosive swearing more vicious than I'd ever heard before.

"Calm down. I'm only joking, Max. Loosen up. It's never going to happen. You know we're never going to let this go that far." I wanted to vent, launch my own angry spew about how my skin crawled just thinking Arkhangelsky's offer, but if I didn't stay calm, Max never would.

"So, look," I said with a shrug, "he wants to talk to you because you're the big man, and I'm just the arm candy or something—can I even play arm candy looking like a razor-cut Raggedy Anne? Anyway, let's find out what he's up to, so we can work out our plan. Ready to make that call? It's 10:30 already."

"Pass me the phone."

I whipped the phone from its stand on the counter and handed it over. "Careful now. Play eager to please."

"Don't worry, Phoeb. This used to be my playing field. If I act too eager to please, he'll get suspicious. He's done his homework. He probably thinks I'm a money-grubber willing to do anything for the right price. That's got to be my role in this scene."

"And mine?"

"Be whatever he thinks you are. He wants you to be decorative, so do decorative. I'll just tell him I'll keep you in line, as if that's possible."

"I'd rather be myself."

"Bad idea. Then he'll clue in how you're nothing but trouble." He winked.

I watched as he dialed the hotel and asked for Arkhangelsky's room. In seconds, he was through. "Yagar? Max Baker here. What the hell is this about you propositioning my Phoebe?"

I inhaled sharply. Max silenced me with his hand.

"Yeah, but I expected you to talk to me first, man to man, none of this going behind my back. And that surveillance shit just burns my gut. My girl doesn't even want to sleep in her own bed now. Is that any way to treat a lady?" Max sat back in his chair, crossed one leg over his knee, and smiled while listening intently. Suddenly, I was excluded from an exclusive club where half the world's population were automatic members and the other half left out in the cold. "Of course I'm interested. Leave Phoebe to me," Max continued. "I'll bring her round. She's a good girl. She'll see reason. Right, right. When?"

Max caught my eye. "Tonight? What time? Right. Pick us up outside the gallery." He clicked off and tossed the phone on the table.

I stared at him. "I think I'm going to puke."

"Pull it together, darlin'. The game's afoot."

* * *

At 1:00, the former Sergeant Higgins appeared at the gallery door. "Posh place," she said as she strolled through the space. "People really drop this kind of money on rugs?" she asked, inspecting a discreet price tag tucked behind the Khotan carpet.

"On carpets, and, yes, the more discerning clients really do."

"What's the difference between a carpet and a rug?"

"Nothing, really, but I designate the word 'carpet' to denote an elevated sense of respect. These beauties deserve it after what they've been through. If not dragged through wars, they've been transported thousands of miles by foot or on the back of a donkey. 'Rug' just sounds like something you walk all over."

She grinned broadly. "So, if it's called a carpet, you get to charge more for it?"

"Something like that."

"But if some nob drops a couple of thousand quid on a carpet, they can still walk all over it, can't they?"

"Most don't. Collectors tend to use these rare textiles as wall art."

"No offense, but I'd rather have a nice painting."

"No offense taken. Diamond & Dew are up in my flat combing for surveillance equipment. They've already found one camera in my bedroom, another in my lounge, and," I took a deep breath, "one over my tub."

"This some ex of yours?"

"Hell, no."

"Don't look so shocked. Sex tapes are a thing right now, and most parties are mutually agreeable."

"Well, I'm not, and these aren't sex tapes, anyway. They're spy cams, put in place without my knowledge."

"Nasty piece of business, either way," Brenda remarked.

"Agreed." I shot a quick glance to the door as a man strode in, assuming an air of studied fascination over everything and anything. Max, catching my eye, strolled over to greet him. "Let's just continue our conversation upstairs," I said to my companion.

"Sure thing." Brenda followed me up the stairs. "So, you know the bloke that installed this stuff?"

"Kind of."

"What kind of answer is that? Going to press charges or not?"

"Not. It's complicated. Look, I need discretion. I need you to teach me how to protect myself, think strategically, keep this kind of thing from happening again. And while we're at it, I want you to watch my back and teach me self-defense strategies. I need to get seriously kick-ass. There's stuff going on around here that can't be disclosed because others are involved. Are you all right with that?"

"Dunno," she said, gazing at me. "I'll have to think about it. There's lots about you that I can't fathom, Phoebe McCabe. Is any of this stuff illegal?"

"There are some criminal types trying to push us into the fold because they see us as well-positioned to serve their needs. Here's my flat."

The door stood wide open with a uniformed man standing directly in our path aiming what looked to be a walkie-talkie at the ceiling.

"Have you found anything else?" I asked him.

"Not since the bathroom. We've assured ourselves that you're now clean."

So why did I feel so dirty? I wondered if I'd ever feel quite the same in my own nest again.

Stepping past the security guy, I stood in the center of my lounge, wincing at site of my yarn evicted from their baskets and cubbyholes, a colorful homeless disarray. Though care had been taken not to unravel my three work-in-progress items, it still felt like a travesty. I picked up my kelp wrap, gently pushing the stitches further along the needle.

"I apologize for the mess," the man I knew as Brian said. "We couldn't risk not checking everywhere in case a device might be planted inside the balls and …"

"Skeins," I offered.

"Right. We couldn't take the chance. Those things make perfect hiding spots."

"I get it."

"The guy planted three cameras, one each in your bathroom, bedroom, and lounge. I understand you've seen the footage?"

"Some of it."

"Ms. McCabe, I don't want to push, but if this guy's been stalking you, spying on you, Metro should know about it."

"Sorry, but no. I'm handling this internally. No police. I expect Diamond & Dew to give me the discretion I pay for. Just make sure this can't happen again."

"We'll send you a thorough report with recommendations as soon as we return to the office. Have you met Martin, my colleague?"

I turned to see Martin, an older man I judged to be in his fifties, emerging from my kitchen carrying a briefcase with an iPad tucked under one arm. "Afternoon, Miss McCabe. Martin McCormick. We're attempting to trace the signal source but—"

"No, stop that, please. I expect everything here to be kept in strict confidence. Sorry, but that's what we pay you for."

Martin smiled. "Sure, whatever you wish."

"Good."

"We've checked the office and programmed it to post text alerts should the equipment be tampered with. That means that you and Mr. Baker will have to key in your security code even for a routine task. We noted that you've overridden that feature in the past."

"We won't bypass any security features from now on. As for the upgrade, just do it."

"I was going to add that to our report, plus anticipated pricing options. I—"

"Excellent."

"Ah, um, may we be of assistance elsewhere?"

"Not for the moment, thanks." I led the men to the door. "He sooner you can install that upgrade, the better."

"That's a good company," Brenda remarked once the men left, "but, if you're not willing to bring the police into an obvious break-in, you're hiding something. They know it and I know it. How'd this guy break into your flat?"

"He didn't break in, he walked in," I said, beginning the delicate process of returning the yarn to their respective homes. "The door was open and I was distracted downstairs. I'll be much more vigilant in the future. Will you help me learn how to defend myself or not?"

Brenda gazed around at the yarn scattered all over the floor. "You need help, all right, but I don't want to enlist in something without full disclosure."

I climbed to my feet, holding a hank of green silk. "I just can't tell you everything yet, Brenda. Sorry."

"Stop that."

"Stop what?"

"Stop saying you're sorry to everything. You're not sorry."

I took a deep breath. "I'm Canadian. We apologize for everything."

"So stop. Don't be sorry for what you have to do just because the person you're doing it to doesn't like it. That's their problem. Only apologize when you make a mistake, nothing more, and then only when you know it's your mistake. Now, I'll agree to teaching you self-defense, but I'll hold off on the bodyguard thing until I get the lay of the land. Deal?"

"Deal."

We shook hands, Brenda nearly crushing the bones in my fingers. "Here's another thing. Your handshake says *I'm pliable.* Don't be pliable, Phoebe McCabe. Be firm. Let your handshake say: *I'm friendly, but don't mess with me.*"

Remembering my handshake with Arkhangelsky, I withdrew my hand. "Right. Can we start tomorrow afternoon? I get off at 4:00."

"See you tomorrow. I'll let you get back to reorganizing your hobby."

"It's not a 'hobby', it's a necessity like breathing," I called after her, but I doubted she understood, let alone heard.

8

Arkhangelsky's car arrived at precisely 7:00, but not with the man himself in attendance. Max and I slipped into the back seat, Max looking dapper in a Saville Row suit, me in my Ottoman Silk tunic over velvet pants. I refused to do sexy, despite Max's prompting. I would go as myself and try to keep my mouth shut where necessary.

"Mr. Arkhangelsky welcomes you to suite at Goring," the driver said while keeping his eyes fixed on the ground. Anything Max asked him after that was answered by way of a grunt, so we sat in the back seat without speaking while the car wove through the streets.

We weren't planning on talking anyway. The whole world could be bugged for all we knew. I'd even had the Diamond & Dew boys scan my carpet bag which, sadly, I'd left behind in lieu of a nineteenth century petit point evening purse, a birthday present from Serena. The silk pouch felt so small and delicate in my lap, I could have been holding a silky kitten. Only I knew it contained a minute ball of yarn and tiny needles, my emergency Prozac of choice.

I might have relaxed slightly had we been heading to a public restaurant. The thought of being holed up in a suite with Mr. O turned my stomach

"Let me do the talking," Max whispered once we put distance between us and the driver leading us through the lobby.

"What if I don't like what you say?" I asked.

"You won't like what I'm going to say, I guarantee it, but you've got to zip the lips. I know how bludgers like Arkhangelsky think, Phoeb."

"I can't just keep quiet and let the big men talk."

"Just try for once. This guy is old-school Russian. It's the way the world has worked for thousands of years, and Arkhangelsky has enough money to keep it that way, at least for himself."

"There are plenty of strong women in Russia, too. I hope some of them kick his butt the way I intend to."

"And live long enough to kick another day. He's dangerous, Phoebe, don't forget that. Just remember that the objective here is to find out what he wants, and then make damn sure he doesn't get it—your words, not mine. Act like you'll cooperate."

"Depends on what he wants."

My voyage through the hotel flew by in a mix of impressions. The polished marble, the silk wallpaper that I swore must be hand-painted, the smiling staff in pristine uniforms, all passed in a blur. When we reached the penthouse, the door opened on more of the same, only enhanced. A sumptuous suite furnished in the epitome of English luxury gleamed around me, all glossy surfaces and plush gold velvet. My eyes fixed on the man standing directly ahead, the man whose presence seemed to suck the light from the room. Arkhangelsky, dressed in an exquisitely tailored suit, beamed at me as if he'd fastened on his smile along with a pair of cuff-links.

"Max, good to see you and, dear Phoebe, so beautiful!" he exclaimed, stepping forward with hands outstretched.

I grabbed one and squeezed hard. Surprise flashed across Arkhangelsky's face before Max slipped between us. While Max pumped Yagar's hand, a servant removed my coat. I gazed around at the four servants waiting nearby. How many of these men—and they were all men—had seen me naked? Were they covertly staring at me right now, peeling my clothes away with their eyes?

We were ushered into a lounge where I took a seat on a couch where an array of hors d'oeuvres awaited on a coffee table—caviar on toast with little buns stuffed with cabbage.

"You drink vodka? Tonight I give you Russian feast," Arkhangelsky announced, snapping his fingers at the two servants waiting nearby.

"I'll take Perrier, please," I said.

"Vodka good drink," Arkhangelsky said.

"I'm sure it is, but I prefer to keep a clear mind," I said.

"And Perrier's fine for me, too," Max said.

"What kind of drink is frizzy French water for man, Max? Ah, you have drinking problem. I understand. Many men do not hold their liquor. Perhaps a small glass? Vodka best for conversation between colleagues.

Water for lady but bring my friend vodka,"
Arkhangelsky told the waiter.

Max left the drink untouched while
Arkhangelsky's eyes sparked at him from
across the coffee table, a gauntlet already
thrown between the men. No doubt admitting
alcoholism was a kind of weakness to this
man's thinking.

"Nice spread you have here. I've never
been to the Goring. I'm a Ritz man myself."
Max swept a hand around the well-appointed
room.

Arkhangelsky shifted in his seat. "This
best hotel in London, maybe world. Princess
Kate stayed in room before wedding."

"Really, the royal wedding?" I asked.
"If it's good enough for a princess, it's
good enough for you, right?" My attempt at
smalltalk effectively stymied the
conversation long enough for our host to
down a shot of vodka before speaking. "It is
good enough for me."

The men bandied about a volley of
conversation, mostly discussing sports while
shooting subtle barbs. Once politics hit the
airwaves. Yagar, a Trump supporter, enthused
over the need for big business to assume its
proper role in American politics, and why
was Britain so far behind? Max countered
with just the right balance of opinion and
concession, the goal being to imply he was
no pushover. I admired his ability to keep
the conversation rolling, but kept quiet,
since I was unable to modify my fiercest
opinions. How had centuries of women
survived by playing decorative mutes? In
order to bite my proverbial tongue, I had to
focus on other things, specifically the silk

wallpaper, the fine finishing on the furniture.

Once Arkhangelsky prompted me with: "And what does Phoebe think?"

"Actually, Phoebe thinks too much. Where do I begin?" I said.

Max flashed me a warning.

"Men's talk does not bore you?" Arkhangelsky asked.

I smiled. "It's not too far over my little head, if that's what you mean."

Arkhangelsky boomed out a laugh. "Phoebe, you are very funny."

Good. Maybe he'd die laughing.

Once or twice I caught my host's eye across the coffee table, the same eye I suspected had been eye-peeling my clothes off seconds earlier. I smiled and he grinned back. Oh, crud.

Finally, I excused myself and allowed a servant to show me to the bathroom. Once inside, I leaned against the locked door with my eyes closed. This evening was dragging on and on. How would I survive the hours ahead? I tried perching on the mahogany chair, pulling out my yarn, and indulging in a knitting fix, but it was no use. Restlessness itched. I needed to move. I tucked my dose of fiber into the pouch, investigated the bathroom's fine detailing, including the little rubber ducks on the tub edge, and slowly opened the door.

The hall was empty, all the minions no doubt busy doing their master's bidding. It was a short corridor—three closed doors. The first opened onto an empty-looking room, richly furnished but clearly unoccupied. The next was much smaller with multiple pairs of shiny shoes lined up on the dresser with the heavy scent of shoe polish weighing down the air. The valet's room, perhaps? The final door opened up onto something else again. A muffled squeal followed by rustling and the sound of a door clicking closed on the opposite wall. I stood stunned, taking in the tangled bedclothes of an enormous master suite, the silk bathrobe draped over a chair, the fashion magazines strewn across the bed. The potent floral perfume poked my sinuses. I pressed my hand against my nose. Yagar Arkhangelsky had a lover? And said lover did not want to be seen, either that or she'd been ordered to stay hidden.

I backed away, softly shut the door, and headed back to the lounge.

Arkhangelsky arose the moment I appeared. "Phoebe, dear, you are well, yes?"

"I'm fine," I said, realizing I must have been gone for nearly 20 minutes.

"Supper is served. I escort you," he insisted.

The man's flesh felt inert beneath my fingers as he steered me into the dining room. Borscht soup followed by dish after dish, which I chewed without tasting, eyes downcast, my mind roiling.

Once the servants cleared the table and the scent of coffee rode the air, Max leaned back in his chair. "Delicious. The most excellent coulibiac I've ever tasted, better even than what I had at the Hermitage museum's fete back in 2013."

"I am happy dinner pleases. We have lymonnyk for desert. I had recipe faxed to kitchen to make perfect," said our host.

"Why don't we talk specifics, now. Tell us why we're here, Mr. Arkhangelsky," I said, unable to suppress myself a moment longer. "What do you want from us?"

Arkhangelsky beamed. "Phoebe, dear, we have coffee first. We continue being friendly."

"We can talk and sip, too," I suggested. *And I'm never getting friendly with you.*

"Yes, let's get down to business, Yagar," Max added, throwing down his napkin. "It's time. Why do you want Phoebe to pretend to be your girlfriend?"

Our host gazed at me steadily. "Phoebe is friends with Sir Rupert Fox."

Former friends.

Max leaned forward. "What does Phoebe's friendship with Rupert have to do with this?"

"Phoebe gets information for me."

I stared at him. "Are you suggesting I spy on Rupert?"

"Spy, I do not like this word." Arkhangelsky said with a shrug. "I prefer we say *study*. You will *study* Rupert Fox and help me find what I need. If you are girlfriend, he will not resist if I go with you."

Max caught my eye. *Careful.*

But I have trouble heeding warnings. "Rupert would never believe you were my boyfriend," I said. "He knows I am in love with another."

Yagar made a show of looking over his shoulder, lifting up the damask tablecloth to peer under the table. "Where is this other? I do not see this man."

"He's not in London," I said, sensing Max eye-boring me from across the table. "It's a long-distance relationship with

somebody Rupert knows. The point is that
Rupert would never believe that I'd suddenly
throw him over for you. Or anybody," I
added, realizing that the Russian's spy
network had only gone so far. He didn't know
about Noel.

Yagar shrugged. "What kind of man
leaves woman for so long? He cannot be such
a man. I would not treat you this way. I
would take you with me everywhere." He
smacked his hand over his heart.

"And lock me up in your bedroom like an
inconvenient pet?"

Arkhangelsky stared hard at me and let
out a bark of laughter. "Very funny! I like
woman with humor. Not like pet, no," he
added, suddenly serious, "like precious
diamond man keeps close."

"And what kind of man spies on his
precious diamond while trying to blackmail
her?" I asked. Max kicked me under the
table.

"Yagar, Phoebe has a point," Max said.
"If you're trying to win her heart, you have
a damn poor way of doing it. Those cams you
had installed are invasive and infuriating.
We got rid of the equipment, as you probably
know, but the damage is done. Trying to
blackmail her, are you?"

"Blackmail gets her attention. She
would not talk, so I encourage her." Another
shrug, "I spy. Phoebe and the Etruscan gold,
all very interesting, and everything else, a
bonus I enjoy very much."

Max's face reddened but not half as
much as mine. If he tried to break
Arkhangelsky's jaw right then, I wouldn't
stop him. I yearned to try out Brenda's knee
jab instruction.

"We want those videos. Erase every damn thing you've recorded about my goddaughter before we can discuss what you want of us," Max said.

Yagar shook his head. "No, I keep for incentive. I do not want to put Phoebe's pictures on Internet or harm her, but must if you do not help." He pulled back from the table to relax in his chair. "Let us stop this unpleasantry. I am fond of Phoebe. I offer her marriage. I have good proposition for you, too, so I will not need to post videos, or tell police about smuggling."

"I didn't smuggle," I said between my teeth.

Yagar smiled. "You are friends with smuggler. You are partner with former smuggler. Your brother is thief. Who will believe? Forget that. Back to Rupert. You will tell him that I am new boyfriend."

I took a deep breath. "No."

"Yes."

"What do you want from Rupert?" I asked.

"Rupert has things I want, many things. You will help me get these."

"I told you, he won't believe you're my boyfriend."

"Then you convince. Say you have not been with other man for long time and are lonely. Say you have needs and Yagar Arkhangelsky fills them. Tell him Yagar great lover. Tell him how much I offer—fine jewels, big houses, beautiful clothes. Make him believe."

"But—" I began.

He held up his hand. "Convince him."

"But why is my pretending to be your girlfriend so important?"

"Because I will be your date to Christmas ball." He was leaning forward over the table now, all amiable host solidified into something menacing, intractable. "I must attend ball."

"Foxy's bloody annual clown party? Are you pulling my leg?" Max erupted. "Why do you want to dress up like a twat and prance around a big room? Oh, wait," Max snapped his fingers. "You want to infiltrate Having Castle. You're after his loot."

Yagar smiled. "We men understand one another, Max. Good. Yes, I will attend ball as Phoebe's date. You will go, also. Both of you will help."

"Help steal from Rupert? Never." I shoved myself to my feet. "It's not happening." My body trembled so badly, I thought I'd quake to death.

"Sit down, Phoebe," Max ordered. The message he fired beneath the words sent me struggling to rein myself in. *Remember our plan.*

"But I ... "

"Sit down," he repeated.

I sat down, clutching my clammy hands together.

"Are you proposing a heist?" Max asked, sounding coolly interested, his own temper in check.

"A heist, yes. For this, I reward Phoebe well and you, also, Max. Head of London operation. Unlimited wealth, opportunity, and more if Phoebe marries me. We join together in arts and antiquities trade. We corner world market."

My nails dug into the brocaded chair tops. I nearly spat out my words. "What exactly is it that you want to steal from Rupert?"

Yagar spread his hands. "Everything," he smiled. "On December 17th, I steal it all. You will help."

9

"I can't do it," I told Max the moment we were safely inside the gallery doors. I paused the security system and headed towards the stairs. "I can't help Arkhangelsky steal from Rupert."

"Phoebe, listen for a minute."

But I wasn't in the listening mood, I was in the exploding mood. Dashing up the stairs, I unalarmed my flat, and burst in to the lounge, Max close behind.

"The man makes my skin crawl. It's ludicrous. Rupert would see through that in a second."

Max stood in the center of my lounge, holding up his hands. "Calm down. Take a deep breath, knit a few rows, do whatever is bloody necessary to get your brain back in control. You'll ruin everything, and I mean everything."

"Rupert's my friend!" I wailed.

In two strides he had me by the shoulders. "Ex-friend, remember—the weasel who tricks and uses you at every opportunity? Besides, we're not actually going to steal from the bastard—not that he doesn't deserve it—we'll pretend to, go along with bludger's the game."

I began breathing deeply. "That's what I said, wasn't it, that we'd play along?" I

94

said in a small voice. "But that was before I knew what Arkhangelsky had in mind. We'll just refuse, simple as that."

"That's not simple, that's deadly." He released me and turned away, running his fingers through his silver mane.

My legs gave out beneath me and I sank onto the couch. Pulling one of my yarn baskets forward, I plucked out my kelpy wrap and began knitting with trembling fingers. "I can't pretend this, that's all."

"You can pretend. You did it in Bermuda, you can do it now."

I jabbed my needle into the wool, tightening the tension. "That was different. That was with people who didn't know me. Rupert knows me, he knows me too well."

"If we don't agree to do this thing—at least look as though we're going through with it—there will be consequences, and they won't be pretty."

"Like what?" I looked over at him. "What can he do? So what if he posts those pictures on the Internet? Millions of women deliberately post more demeaning photos of themselves on the Web all the time. I'll just ride it through. And so what if he goes to Interpol with those other shots? I'm not in possession of stolen goods, but items somebody gave me, and I was unaware I was transporting them. I'll battle that in court, if I have to. I'm not afraid of that, either."

"There are worse things, Phoebe, and this bastard will likely use every one of them until we relent. It's better we pretend to go along with it before someone gets hurt."

"Rupert will know."

"Convince him otherwise, like Yagar says. Rupert trusts you."

I threw down my project. "You mean, use his trust against him?"

"Foxy does it to you all the time."

"He does it without rancor. It's all a game to him."

"So? Play the game yourself."

I took another deep breath. "Max, you can't seriously consider going through with this."

"Listen to me: I'm saying that we have to convince that Cossack bastard that we're going through with it any way we can, do whatever it takes to make it look real. Then, once we're into it, I mean deep into it and understand his plan, we make damn certain it doesn't happen."

Still breathing deeply, I exhaled slowly and picked up my knitting. "Outmaneuver him, you mean."

"Your suggestion, I believe."

"If I thought I had a hope in hell of convincing Rupert that I would throw Noel over for this megalomaniac pig, let alone outmaneuver the bastard, I might consider it, but I know Rupert won't believe me. He's no fool. The game will be up before it starts."

"You can convince him, Phoebe. I know the weasel, too. He can be surprisingly innocent, in a bizarre way. Start up your knitting sessions again. Tell him you want to attend the ball, say that you want to bring the whole gallery staff as a Christmas treat, and we'll go from there. Think about it overnight but don't take too long. He wants the answer by tomorrow."

And he left me to a long, dark night of grim, twisting thoughts.

* * *

The gallery looked far too cheery the next morning. By then, the tree was blinking merrily in the window, each bell bearing an ethnic motif, the ribbons streaming down in an equally festive spirit. Serena had hung a sign wishing the world Peace on Earth in several languages, but every twinkling light and merry symbol struck me as a travesty. I'd settle for a little peace in my heart that morning.

"I can't do it, Rena," I said as I labored over the bookkeeping in my gallery office while Rena leaned against the railing. Since my office was nothing more than an open glass landing suspended over the gallery floor, she could still keep an eye on things from that perch.

"You could tell Rupert what the Russian does so he could pretend, too," she suggested.

"I thought of that, but part of me, by far the largest part, refuses to play this game. Why give him the satisfaction for even a millisecond?"

Rena shook her head. "Because maybe that is sometimes best. Pride is not always a good thing."

"I'm not being proud, I'm being kick-ass." But even I didn't believe that. For me, kick-assedness was a learned, rather than an innate behavior and I was still only at the first stages. "Besides, can you imagine me pretending to be his girlfriend? Every time I see the man, I want to retch."

"You must decide in your heart what to do," she said as the doorbell announced a customer's entrance and she clattered down the steps.

I returned to staring at the numbers on the screen, good numbers, all of them—no red lines, only healthy profit margins—and yet nothing positive registered. Hours passed before I successfully finished a task that usually took less than an hour. By the time I shoved away from the desk, it was noon and Max was just entering the gallery. He looked up at me as I leaned over the balcony, reading my decision in my eyes. He swore under his breath and headed for the back room.

In seconds I was coming in behind him. "We'll get through this. Look, I've asked that ex-police person I told you about, Brenda Higgins, to teach me self-defense, and maybe even be my bodyguard. As soon as Arkhangelsky realizes I'm no pushover, maybe he'll find another way."

"Do you think that Russkie works that way?" Max asked, pouring himself a mug of coffee. "He didn't get to be a czar of his empire by giving up at the first resistance, and that lady ex-copper of yours is no match for him. Hell, a whole police force wouldn't take him on easily. You're making a huge mistake, Phoebe, huge. Why can't you take my advice for once?"

"Max, this isn't about you and me. I told you that I can't lie to Rupert. Anyway, that's my decision."

Up in my flat later, I made myself a smoothie for lunch and sat in my little oasis of solitude knitting, trying to weave in threads of resolution with every stitch. I was doing the right thing. I was doing the only thing I could. Do what you believe to be right, follow your heart, and all that.

Back in the gallery later, Max went silent on me while Rena compensated by darting around the gallery like an over-caffeinated Jack Russell terrier. Up went the volume on our usually subdued symphonic background music, everything hyper-cheerful.

Arkhangelsky's call hit my cell phone around 3:45 while I was holding the door for an exiting customer. I plucked the phone from my pocket wondering who was calling, since I gave my number out to only be closest friends. "Hello."

"Yagar here. How is lovely Phoebe this day?"

My stomach clenched. "Just peachy."

"You have made right decision?"

"I've made only decision I can live with and here it is: go to hell, Arkhangelsky." And pressed END.

When I turned around, Serena and Max stood side by side looking at me, Rena clutching her hands to her chest, Max apparently suppressing some kind of volcanic eruption.

"You couldn't have made it any more of a declaration of war had you sent him a hand grenade," Max said through his teeth.

"I wanted to make sure he got the message. That man doesn't do subtle," I said, trying to sound jaunty.

He turned on his heels and stormed towards the back room, leaving me with Serena.

"I have a feeling he's going to chip a mug back there," I said, thumbing over my shoulder. She did not return my grin. "Rena, stop looking at me that way. It'll be fine."

"I have a very bad feeling," Serena said as I followed her away from the security camera to the blind spot behind her desk. This, besides the backroom, remained disconnected from Diamond & Dew's system while the gallery was open, our privacy safe zones.

"I had a bad feeling, too," I said, "but I knew it had to be due to trying to force myself to cheat a friend, or former friend, on behalf of Yagar Arkhangelsky. I won't do it. End of story."

"What if he hurts you, posts videos on the net, calls police?" she whispered.

"So what if I end up as a queen of dark web for maybe a millisecond, and so what if Agent Walker drops in to follow up on yet another shady lead? All survivable. It wouldn't be the first time Walker received a tip. He's used to them."

"But the pictures..." Rena said, eyes wide, hands holding up an invisible gold earring.

"So what? Yes, I admit the thought of being charged for smuggling is pretty grueling but, on the other hand, what would Arkangelesky gain from trying to finger me, or even Rupert?" I tapped my skull, recoiling slightly at the fuzz my digit encountered. "Look," I lowered my voice to a whisper, "he's after Rupert's collection, most of which is smuggled. How will it help

him if those items end up in the hands of
Interpol?"

Rena eye's widened. "You are right. Why
would he do this?"

"Yes, why would he? So relax. I'm not
going to be intimidated that easily. I had a
taste of pretense with Arkhangelsky last
night and I don't have the stomach for it.
Now, I'm going to get changed for my self-
defense lessons. Are you working tonight?"

"Yes. Max is off but Jenn will join me
after supper."

"Good. I'll be upstairs all night, if
it gets too busy."

So, Serena returned to the gallery
floor while I went upstairs to my flat. It
may only have been my imagination, but I
swore Handle's Hallelujah shot up a few
decibels.

Brenda arrived promptly at 4:00,
bringing along a couple of padded mats for
flinging me on to. We moved the loom to one
side, shoved the yarn baskets against the
bookcases, and centered the mats. I hadn't
even finished the furniture rearranging
before she attacked me from behind. I shot a
leg at her shin, which she swiftly used as a
lever to flip me onto the mat.

"The least you could do is wait until
I'm ready," I complained as I pushed myself
to my knees.

"Think an attacker's going to send you
an invite? And this isn't judo where you bow
to your opponent before beginning. This is
real. Get up, Phoebe. We'll have another
go."

So Phoebe got up and had another go,
specifically another flop, another toss,
another fling. All my shots went wide, my

kicks missing their target by feet, then
inches. I always ended up on the mat,
sometimes face-first, sometimes on my back.
Once, frustrated by the constant trouncing,
I surprised Brenda with a sharp jab in her
stomach with my elbow, followed by a swift
kick to her shins.

"Great!" she exclaimed. "Bring it on!"

But once my burst of fury abated, so
did I. Later, over supper of take-out India
cuisine, she reviewed a number of what-if
scenarios she'd encountered on the force. If
I needed to break down a door to tackle a
bunch of suspected drug dealers living in a
housing flat, at least now I had a few
strategies.

"This is all very interesting but I
need a gun," I said over a carton of butter
chicken.

"You don't," she said, helping herself
to the jasmine rice.

"I do. How do I get one?"

"Britain has one of the tightest gun
laws in the world. You have to apply to the
police, and you'd never qualify. Saying that
you want to protect yourself against rug
burglars won't cut it. Self-defense isn't
even a good enough reason. You need two
high-quality references here in Britain—
respectable types who've known you for two
years—for a start. Your Max wouldn't qualify
and neither would your other friends."

I paused, a spoonful of chicken en
route to my mouth. "What do you mean?"

"I looked into you and Max Baker—a few
priors, a couple of red flags on his part,
and suspicious activity on yours. No way
they'll give you a gun."

I lowered my spoon. "Me, suspicious activity?"

"Oh give over, Phoebe. I know you're into something. I might be retired from Metro but I keep my ear to the ground. You've got a brother on the international most wanted list and hang around with criminal sorts. Why not tell me what's really going on here so I can figure out if I'll help you or not?"

I passed her a carton. "Help yourself to the samosas. Stuff yourself."

An hour later, over tea and cookies and a discourse on more self-defense scenarios, the phone rang on the kitchen table. "It's Rena calling from downstairs. Excuse me for a sec." Taking the phone, I hauled my aching body up from the chair and strode into the lounge.

"Phoebe. It is Rena."

"I know. Hi, Rena."

"It is Jennifer, she is 20 minutes late. I am worried."

I froze halfway across the floor, the darkened windows in my line of sight. "Maybe she just got held up. Maybe she's with Marco?"

"Marco is at the theater and Jenn always calls if she is to be late. She is never late."

And that was true. Jennifer was not only welded to her phone, but usually punctual. "Don't panic. I'm sure there's a reasonable explanation."

But after another hour with multiple phone calls to Jennifer's mother, her best girlfriend, and finally in desperation, to Marco, we had run through all of them.

10

"Maybe she had an accident?" I said while watching Rena stare through the door into the street. Though only minutes from closing, we still had browsers.

"We should phone the police," she said.

"Wait at least 24 hours first," Brenda suggested, standing with her arms crossed nearby. "She's young. Maybe she took off with her friends."

"Not Jennifer," I said. "Her life is all about Marco, studying fashion, Marco, and showing up here in between, in that order."

"And Marco," Serena added. "I am so worried. Marco, he says he will phone again at intermission. Maybe he hears by then."

But when that call came, an anxious Marco informed his mother that instead of the battery of text messages usually received from his girlfriend, nothing came.

By the time we locked the gallery doors at 9:00, we were officially frantic. I called Max.

"Where was she last?" he asked.

"At St Martin's. She was supposed to leave straight from class to work, and pick up take-out along the way. She gets the tube at King's Cross, stops off at an EAT, and heads here."

"I'll take my car and drive around. It's a long shot but worth trying."

I dropped my phone back into my pocket. "Max is going to drive the route."

Brenda had her own phone to her ear and was strolling towards the back. "Checking with my mates at the station," she said over her shoulder. "See if there's been any pedestrian mash-ups."

Rena's eyes widened. "Mash-ups?"

"Accidents," I said.

"Oh, no!" Serena spun around and began darting around the gallery, dimming the lights, straightening the hanging rugs, over-watering the plants. "We sold the seventeenth century Cairene today. Jake will deliver tomorrow."

"Nice," I said staring through the glass door. "I watered everything this morning."

"We will have another space to fill."

My gaze dropped to the floor. What if Jennifer was hit by a bus? That had nearly happened to me once or twice, but only because I'd been looking in the wrong direction. No, Jenn was a Londoner. "We'll bring out the wild Shekarlu when it goes," I said. "I've been wanting to display that for months."

"The wild one is lovely," Rena commented, pausing by our sound system to up the volume of the Nutcracker Suite.

Brenda returned from her stroll. "Good news: one middle-aged pedestrian hit on Oxford Street, multiple fender benders, and one t-bone between a cab and an Audi in Trafalgar Square. It's been a quiet few hours in London, traffic-wise," she called over the ripping symphony. "Can we turn that down?"

I turned it down.

Several minutes passed before Serena's cell phone rang a few bars of *Bohemian Rhapsody* from her pocket. We watched as she pulled it out. "It's Jennifer!" We waited expectantly as she stared at the screen without speaking. "She hung up."

"Hung up?" I strode towards her. "Redial."

"I am, but she does not pick up."

Serena pressed the TALK button again and again. "Wait, a text."

I was looking over her shoulder when she read the text message labeled *For you*. A photo enlarged on the screen. Neither of us could believe what were seeing, a photo of a swollen-faced Jennifer holding up a bloody wrist. Rena dropped the phone. I picked it up, staring at the photo in disbelief. "What's happening?"

"Hostage, kidnapping, maybe." Brenda snatched the phone from my hands. "This just amped up a few degrees. I'll call the station."

The police hadn't yet arrived before Jennifer's mother called saying that Jennifer was at the St. Pancras hospital. We all hopped into a cab and headed down, but once we'd found the right floor, we weren't allowed into Jenn's room. "The police are interviewing her," her mother, Susan, told us. "Somebody hurt my girl! He cut her!" She collapsed into Rena's arms.

Rena patted her back. "It is okay. She is alive, that is most important thing."

"Who did this?" I asked Susan over Rena's shoulder. "Is Jenn all right?"

"She doesn't know who," Susan sobbed. "There were two of them. They wore masks and didn't speak a word. They grabbed her off York Way. Took her into a car and slapped her around. Cut her wrists—not deep enough to sever an artery, thank God, but close. Who would do this?"

"Did they … ?"

"No, God, no, but they slapped her a few times, terrorized her. Who would do such a thing to my baby? Who would hurt my Jennifer?"

"I don't know but we'll find out, I promise you that." And I meant it.

When I turned to ask Brenda's opinion, she'd disappeared, and why not? This wasn't her worry. Soon Susan returned to her daughter's room. Once Max arrived, it was only the three of us alternating from sitting to pacing the waiting room.

"Why would somebody do this? Why cut her up and drop her onto a street?" I said, staring into my hands. For once, I didn't think those fingers could even knit.

"It's a warning," Max said, his face grim.

"From whom?" I asked, turning to him, but I knew. "You don't really think he'd do this, do you?"

"Yes, I bloody well do."

"If that's true, he'll pay," I said.

"How are you planning to do that when you won't even play the game?" Max said staring at the wall.

I twisted my hands together but said nothing.

Marco strode into the room at 11:45, fresh from the last show, still wearing breeches and a riding jacket. "Where is she?" he boomed.

"With her mother," Rena said. "Keep down your stage voice. This is a hospital."

"My apologies, Mum. Where is Jennifer?"

"You must wait. Only one at a time, the doctor says." But Marco took off for her room, hospital staff parting to let him pass.

Brenda reappeared moments later. "Darcy's just charmed his way into Jennifer's room."

"You disappeared," I remarked as she entered the waiting area.

"I was chatting up the officers working the case. They say this is a one-off, not part of a series of similar cases. Odd, that. The girl was snatched, roughed up, but not seriously hurt, other than a spot of trauma. Does she have enemies that you know of, anyone who might want to give her a fright?"

"No," Rena told her. "Jennifer is very well-liked."

Brenda stared at me.

"I don't know who did this," I said. And I didn't, not for sure.

"No ideas?" Brenda pressed.

"No."

"Right, so I'm clocking off now. Got to get home and catch my beauty sleep," Brenda said, heading for the hall. "See you tomorrow."

"Wait, I'll walk you out." I fell into pace beside her. "I want you to be Jennifer's bodyguard, once she's up and back at it again, I mean. Will you do it?"

"I'm not agreeing to be anybody's bodyguard until you tell me exactly what's going on, Phoebe McCabe." And with that she strode out the front doors.

By the time I returned to the fourteenth floor, we were finally permitted see Jennifer, though only briefly. Marco sat on one side of the bed holding Jenn's hand, Susan on the other.

"She's been sedated," her mother said. "She was frantic thinking she might not be able to finish her design in time for Christmas hols. It's due this week, but the doc says she'll be released tomorrow. She'll be fine. For now, the poor darling needs to rest."

"We won't stay long," I said, leaning over to squeeze Jennifer's hand. I couldn't bear to see her poor, swollen face. Her eyes blinked open and she smiled. "Not going to … let them beat me," she said.

"Who, Jenn?" I whispered.

"Lulu and Fritz … they're … so *competitive.*"

"Lulu and Fritz?" I asked, bewildered.

I turned to Marco, who widened his large green eyes. "You think those two knobs did this to you, love?"

But Jennifer had already drifted off.

"Lulu and Fritz are one of the pairs she's competing against at school," Susan explained. "The instructor has the class divvied up into partners, with each pair working on a design for the catwalk show on Friday. Guess it's pretty heated, but I can't imagine them going that far. I'll ask the police to question them just in case."

* * *

"I want you to stay at my place for the night," Max said after dropping off Marco and Rena at their respective flats.

"No. Look, Max, my flat is probably more secure than the Tower of London now that Diamond & Dew have enhanced everything. I'm not letting anyone chase me from my own home." I watched the deserted streets slide past. London streets, unlike many big cities, hibernated in the wee hours, all the night owls heading for the clubs.

We drove in silence for a few minutes, each of us tucked deep into our own thoughts.

"You have to call that cabbage-loving bastard and tell him that we're in. Do it first thing in the morning, Phoebe, before anyone else gets hurt. They chose the most innocent and vulnerable for a reason. It's a show of strength. It will only accelerate from here on in," Max said, sliding the car to the curb outside the gallery.

"We're not even sure Arkhangelsky is responsible for this. It could be that pair at school."

"I don't believe that for a moment, and neither do you. I'm just going to park here for a minute and see you safely up to your flat."

"Thanks, Max, but that's not necessary. I'm fine."

But he had already jumped out of the car and loped around to open my door. Max insisted upon being the gentleman, at least half the time. Sighing, I let him escort me into the gallery. "You might get another ticket. How many so far this month?"

"Just two. That's a bit of a disappointment, that. I was considering starting a collection."

"Oh, cool: parking tickets and inkwells—the collector extraordinaire."

He waited while I keyed in the new code, using the new fob-sized remote to activate the "stay alarm," which signaled that two authorized bodies were crossing the gallery floor.

"How complicated is that thing?" he asked as we headed for my flat.

"Very. I haven't even figured it all out yet. You need to be careful that you don't turn on the oven by mistake. Just kidding, Max. It's easy."

"I'm not good at that tech mumbo-jumbo. I'll probably set off the alarm multiple times before I get the hang of it. I mastered the smart phone, though."

We entered my flat, where I disengaged another system and pointed to the new monitor installed in one corner of my lounge. "I hate having to check a surveillance system just to get a good night's sleep," I said. "But it's better than the alternative."

Max studied the screen, currently tuned into a deserted gallery floor. "Impressive," he said. "You could watch the telly on this. Got any good films? We could watch one together and then I'd just flake out on your couch."

I gave him a hug. "Thanks, but I'll be fine. If anyone tries to break through these defenses, Scotland Yard drops down from the ceiling."

He gave me a bear-hug squeeze back. "Seriously?"

"No," I said laughing. "I'm still joking. Let me go." But he held me tighter.

"Phoebe, call Arkhangelsky," he said overhead.

I struggled from his embrace. "'Night, Max."

He ran one hand through his thick gray hair and strode for the door without another word.

After he'd gone, I refortified my sanctuary, which felt less and less like the haven I'd so tried to create. Where once I'd return home to a cozy nest designed to restore body and spirit after a long day, or week, or month, now the same space felt like one more place requiring vigilance. I strolled around the flat checking the monitor, testing the bug detector, and reactivating the multiple alarms.

Exhaustion hit like a truck by the time I finally fell into bed. I tossed and turned for at least an a hour before falling asleep. When I awoke in what seemed only moments later, I was locked into a vivid nightmare. I couldn't talk, couldn't move. The dark world heaved with shadows and shapes. I fought like crazy to force myself awake.

"Phoebe, do not struggle. The more struggle, the harder Slavko holds," said a voice from the darkness. I knew that voice, hated that voice.

I could just make out a shape before me, but whatever pinned my arms and clamped my mouth, pressed so hard I thought my bones would crack. My heart thumped in my chest. I couldn't breathe, couldn't scream. *This is no dream!* I was not alone in my bed.

A light flicked on. There stood Yagar Arkangelesky pulling a chair over to my bed with one of the oranges from my kitchen in his other hand. "Now Phoebe, I am nice to you. I offer marriage. What do you do? You say *go to hell*." He shrugged and sat down. "What kind of woman tells man to go to hell at Christmas?"

I kicked out, or tried to, before I realized that I sat wedged between a man's legs with my own limbs snarled in the bed covers. The arms tightened their vise grip on my shoulders as something sharp nicked my throat.I realized that a man sat behind me on the bed, wedging me between his legs while holding a knife to my jugular.

"Now," Arkhangelsky began while studying the orange. "I will not be kind next time to pretty Jennifer. Next time my man cuts deep." He jabbed the knife into the orange flesh, twisting the blade until the juice oozed to the floor. Then he removed the knife and licked it long and lovingly, smacking his lips along the way.

My attempts to speak ended in a smashed gurgle. Again I kicked and strained.

"Do not fight, Phoebe. You will not escape Yagar. I will find. And this security is joke," he poked his knife towards my bedside alarm unit. "We beat such things. Stop struggle and I have Slavko release you."

He brought his face so close to mine, I could smell the orange on his breath and something sour. "You stop now, Phoebe?" The gloved hand dropped from my mouth as Arkhangelsky's lips landed on mine, plunging his tongue deep into my mouth, while his man pried open my jaw. I gagged.

Arkhangelsky pulled away, wiped his mouth on the back of his hand, and nodded to his man. The grip released but I remained vised between Slavko's legs.

"Tell Yagar how good you behave now," Arkhangelsky said. "Tell him you will play girlfriend and fool Sir Rupert."

I fought to find my voice. "Promise you won't hurt anyone else if I do it, promise me," I sobbed.

"Do as I say," said Arkhangelsky. "No bargain until I know you are good girl." He got to his feet. "Tomorrow you call Rupert. Say you will knit on Wednesday. Yes, I know you knit with Rupert. Such silly thing. Say new boyfriend drop you off."

"His driver … " I took a deep breath, " … usually picks me up."

"Say boyfriend drive you."

I nodded.

"Say what you will do when you knit with Rupert."

"I'll say that we are dating, that I want … that I want you to be my escort at the ball."

"You convince him."

"Yes."

"You do this or Jennifer is hurt badly and other friends meet bad end."

"Yes," I whispered, staring at my bedroom wall where daybreak washed a pale light across my Serapi carpet.

"We go now. At all times we watch. I know what you say and where you go. You cannot escape Yagar Arkhangelsky. Do not make more mistakes, Phoebe. Do not tell police. I listen. I will know."

Once I was alone in my apartment, all I could do was sit on the edge of my bed and shiver uncontrollably.

11

"Rupert, it's Phoebe." I stood by my kitchen window, staring at the back of a brick building through my puffy eyes. It had been a long night on top of an even longer morning, with every inch of me wrung out like a squeegee at a car wash. I needed that wall view to bolster me up.

"Phoebe? What a surprise." Rupert's voice held a note of hesitancy.

"I wanted to call to say I'm sorry for trying to break us up—listen to me, I sound like we're a couple or something." Pressing a hand over my mouth, I stifled a laugh that teetered dangerously towards a cry.

Rupert cleared his throat. "Phoebe, I must admit to being most pained by your words the other day, quite disturbed, if truth be told."

What did they say about lying? *Always try to weave in something true to add emotional authenticity.* This part was easy. "Remember when you said that a good friend is worth fighting for?"

"Yes, of course."

"Well, you're right. A good friend is worth fighting for, worth doing anything it takes, no matter how insurmountable." My gaze fixed on the brick wall. "I'm going to fight for you, Rupert—for our friendship, I mean." Arkhangelsky was probably listening. "Forget what I said the other day. I'll deal with it."

I heard a gusty sigh from the other end. "Well, I am most gladdened to hear this," Rupert said. I could imagine his smile, pictured him standing somewhere at home wearing a silk paisley bath robe, a cup of tea cooling on a table. "This day has turned out rather promising, I must say."

"And it's our knitting day."

"Yes, indeed. I have not forgotten, only I hasten to add that I have gone forward with other plans, as I did not expect to be keeping our regular appointment. My seamstress is due to arrive at two o'clock to finish the lining on my ceremonial robe."

"I can come to your house rather than to the shop."

"Yes, indeed you could. Why don't you? What a splendid idea. I could continue your tutelage on the linen stitch. I rather fancy a scarf featuring a fine linen/silk blend I sourced from Canada. Oh, do come. The more I think of it, the more perfect it sounds. Wait, does this mean you will attend my grand fete, perchance?"

"It does. I would love to come to your ball, and so would Max and Rena. Could you spare a couple more invitations for Jennifer and Marco? Jennifer needs something to cheer her up. I may request an invitation for one

more, but I'll tell you all about that when
we meet."

"Yes, of course. Isn't Jennifer dating
that splendid young actor, Marco? Bring them
along. Invitations will be issued forthwith.
I shall await eagerly to see what portrait
everyone chooses. Oh, how delightful! I'll
have Evan pick you up at out appointed
time."

"I'll get my own way there. I'll
explain everything when I arrive."

"Very well. Until then."

I hung up, still holding the phone
while staring at that brick wall. The
building was just visible around the edges
of the framed rectangle of Victorian stained
glass I'd suspended to block the view. Now
I'd rather stare at that impenetrable mass
than anything frivolous or ornamental. The
world had descended into something bleak.

I set the phone back into its cradle.
Ordinarily, I would have used my Foxy phone,
the secure phone Rupert had given me last
year, but it had disappeared, no doubt
stolen by Arkhangelsky. That meant the
bastard planned to listen in on all my
conversations, especially those I had with
Rupert. What else had he taken?

I scanned every room, including the
place where I currently hid the Etruscan
gold. Everything remained. While on my knees
before that not-so-secret-crevice, I lifted
out the little velvet pouch containing the
necklace, the most fabulous piece of all the
treasures Nicolina had stashed in my
luggage. This single artifact must be worth
at least hundreds of thousands of dollars
and yet Arkhangelsky left it. What he wanted
from Rupert must be worth far, far more. I

tucked everything back into the hidey-hole and replaced the board.

From there, I wandered into the bathroom to wash up. He could be watching me now, could see every single thing I did, even in the bathroom, and yet oddly, that seemed the least of my worries. Arkhangelsky might read my actions and hear my words, but my thoughts, at least, were sacred. I was doing a lot of thinking.

By the time I'd showered and dressed, shielding myself behind a towel as much as possible, my cell phone was ringing.

"Good Phoebe," Arkhangelsky said. "Very convincing. This pleases. I come to gallery at 11:30."

I swallowed. "That's early. I mean, I'm not supposed to be at Rupert's until 1:00 and it's already 10:45."

"I am boyfriend. You want to see me." He hung up.

He is monster. I hate sight of him.

I forced down a protein smoothie and went through the motions of tidying my bed, the flat. Bundling up the bedclothes, I tossed them into the wash and wiped down every surface, trying to scrub the taint from my sanctuary. It was no use. The stink of Arkhangelsky's presence, the sticky sense of being watched, gummed the atmosphere.

How did they get in? There were no signs of forced entry at either the doors or the windows. Down the hall in Max's office, I replayed the security footage, finding the critical hours when I was being accosted tuned in to a seemingly empty apartment with me safely tucked into bed. How could that be?

I stared at the screen, reviewing everything Arkhangelsky had said. He told me not to tell the police, yet said nothing about contacting Diamond & Dew. An oversight, or didn't he name them because they were in on the deal? I thought back to the two guys who had scanned the flat after the first violation, the same two who had returned the next day to install the upgrades. One, if not both, had to be in on this. I had been under surveillance the whole time.

I slammed the door on Max's office and stormed back to my apartment, catching myself seconds before bursting into my flat. *Play the game, Phoebe, and play it cool.* I would not let on concerning my suspicions. I sailed into my lounge, gathered up my knitting bag, and exited the flat, locking the door behind me, as if locks still meant anything.

Downstairs in the gallery, Serena had just arrived, her hand still on the door when she turned to greet me. We had 15 minutes left before opening.

"Phoebe, you look—" Rena dropped her hand, gazing overhead as if the right word might be caught flying around up there.

"Exhausted? Like hell? Like I'd been crying all night?" I suggested.

"Yes, yes." She enveloped me in a lavender-scented embrace, signaling that purple was the color of the day. "All of that. Maybe not the hell part. For me, you are always beautiful."

I smiled into her shoulder and hugged her in return.

It is all right, Phoebe," she patted my back. "Jennifer, she will be released today.

Marco, he says she is doing very well, better than you, perhaps?"

I gently tugged myself away. "If she's doing better than me, good."

"You have been crying," my friend said, studying my face.

"Nerves, no doubt, but here's the exciting part: we're going to a ball."

"We are?" Emotions flew across her face. "You have spoken to Rupert?"

"I have. I'm joining him today for our knitting session. My boyfriend is picking me up at 11:30."

She could have been slapped. "Yagar?"

"Who else? He dropped by to see me last night, and offered me a lift to Rupert's today."

"Last night?"

"Yes, late last night. You know Yagar," I flipped my hand. "He just drops in any time since I gave him the key. Can't leave me alone. Anyway, you can fill Max in when he comes in later. For now, I have to get ready. Yagar wants to take me out to lunch. Isn't that sweet?"

"Yes," she said slowly. "Sweet."

"Think I look all right?" I did something like a pirouette, stumbled once, caught the edge of the display table and force-grinned. "I just can't twirl like you. So, what do you think? Black pantsuit, intarsia knit cowl?"

"Orange, it looks very fine on you," Rena nodded, indicating the cowl. "Good to wear to lunch, I think."

"But Rupert hates me in black pantsuits. He always complains when I wear this."

Rena steered me into the safe zone
behind her desk. "Phoebe, what is
happening?"

"We're being watched all the time, even
now, for all I know. Arkhangelsky can get
into my flat whenever he wants, apparently.
So," I took a deep breath, "I am Yagar's
girlfriend until further notice, and we're
going to the ball, in that order. I can't
risk any more people getting hurt, including
me. Oh, it's almost 11:00 and I've got to do
a few more things before I go. Better start
planning your outfit. Max has a big book of
portraits from the National Portrait Gallery
somewhere."

The black Mercedes pulled up outside
the gallery at exactly 11:30. I climbed into
the back seat beside Arkhangelsky, placed my
carpet bag between us, and avoided his eyes.

"Phoebe, you are ready?" Yagar asked.

"I'm ready," I said.

"You say I am boyfriend."

"Not yet," I said, turning to him.
"First, I have to get Rupert used to the
idea, and that won't be easy."

He hesitated. "You must make him
believe."

"I will," I said. "In time."

"No time," Arkhangelsky said, slicing
the air with his hand. "Ball in two weeks.
You meet Rupert only on Wednesdays."

"I'll arrange it so that I'll see him
more often. I'll figure something out. In
the meantime, give me back my phones. Rupert
will get suspicious if I don't use it to
contact him."

"I will give back later."

"What are you doing with them? I need
something to communicate with." My phone was

my lifeline. Most of the important numbers
in my life were stored there, not in my
head. I'd even hidden passwords there, if a
person knew where to look.

He said something in Russian to the
driver.

I gripped my bag as the car turned onto
Clerkenwell Road heading away from city
center towards Islington. "Where are we
going? I thought you were taking me to
lunch?"

Arkhangelsky laughed. "First work."

Work? What did that mean? After several
minutes, we turned towards Bunhill Row. The
only place I knew of in this area was
Bunhill Fields, where John Bunyan and other
notable nonconformists were buried. "We're
going to a cemetery?" I had visions of being
tossed into an unmarked grave, the only
consolation being plunged into eternal
repose in the company of freethinkers.

"Not cemetery." Yagar spoke Russian
into his cell phone as we pulled into a
driveway of a nondescript building. A garage
door began to raise as we cruised into a
dimly lit garage.

I turned in panic to see the door
lowering behind us. "What's going on?"

"You see," Yagar said, still on his
phone. "You get ready."

"Ready for what?"

The driver opened the door and waited
for me to get out, which I did with
reluctance. Yagar remained in the car with
the door open, still talking on his phone,
holding my carpet bag. *Hell.*

We were in an area large enough to fit
three, maybe four cars, but the Mercedes was
the only vehicle. Mounds of tarp-covered

objects lined the walls. Two men stepped out
from somewhere, one short and stocky with a
brush cut, and the other tall and string-
bean thin wearing a parka. The parka wearer
pointed at me. "Take off coat."

"No," I said.

"Take off coat or I remove." The
shorter guy lunged towards me as I stepped
back into the driver.

Yagar poked his head out of the car.
"Take off coat, Phoebe."

I took off my coat, which the driver
held. Then one of the two men grabbed my
arms while the other patted down my body,
obviously enjoying the process. I tried
kicking out at him but he swiftly threw me
against the hood of the car and made me
splay my legs while he searched. Brenda
hadn't covered the part where a woman's
accosted by two, maybe three men. I needed
to rectify that, if I ever got the chance.

"Do you think I have a gun or
something?" I cried.

They released me. I turned to find them
emptying out my carpet bag on the floor,
pawing through my stuff. "Don't mess up my
knitting!"

The buzz cut guy got to his feet and
smiled.

"Shit," I said.

"Take off jacket, woolly thing, and
shirt," Parka Guy said.

"That woolly thing is called a cowl," I
said, "and no way."

"Who cares? Take off."

I hesitated, but knowing they'd
forcibly undress me, I removed the cowl,
taking fleeting comfort in the feel of those

fibers in my hands, passed it to the driver, and then took off my jacket.

"Take off shirt," Buzz Boy demanded.

I began unbuttoning my shirt, sending a part of myself down deep where I'd survive while unpleasant things were going on externally. So what if I was supposed to strip for these morons? They'd probably already seen much more of me in multiple positions inside my flat. Maybe half the Russian underground had watched the crime time reality special of Phoebe McCabe in the flesh going about her life, lucky bastards.

Moments later, I stood shivering in my bra, awaiting the next humiliation. The men could barely suppress their smirks, kept shooting comments back and forth in Russian while Arkhangelsky remained in the car plastered to his phone. Buzz Guy stepped towards me holding a black wire with some small device dangling at one end.

I backed away. "What are you doing?"

"You wear device," Parka Boy said.

Oh, God, was that a wire? There went my plan to tell Rupert what was afoot. Now they'd hear everything. I cringed when Buzz Boy's cold stubby fingers shoved something down my bra, taking seconds longer than necessary, while Parka Boy leaned over me, breathing coffee and cigarettes in my direction. "Done," Buzz Boy said, stepping back.

"Give clothes back," Arkhangelsky ordered, now out of the car, standing hands in pockets. Four men watched me re-dress while I attempted my best rendition of nonchalance. Now how could I communicate to Rupert? I'd just lost my one chance. My fingers fumbled with the buttons as I scanned my brain for an alternative plan, finding none. Every word I said to Rupert would be monitored.

I was about to don the cowl when Arkhangelsky stopped me. "No. Put thing away. I have present for girlfriend," he said while pulling a box from his pocket. Out came a gold chain with a beautiful amber enameled triangular locket set with diamonds encircling around a large ruby. "Once belonged to Romanov princess."

"One of the ones who were shot?" I held still while he fastened the piece around my neck, catching my breath as the cold metal fell into place above my breasts.

"Lovely! You look more like Yagar's girlfriend," he said.

Though exquisite, it wasn't my style. "It has a camera inside, doesn't it?"

Arkhangelsky slapped on hand on his thigh. "Bright girl! Yes, necklace has small camera. No one will know. You tell Sir Rupert gift from Yagar. We go now." He jerked his head towards the car and in moments we were cruising back towards central London, me staring out the window without registering a thing. I desperately needed a new plan.

"You will get blueprint of Wilshire estate," Arkhangelsky said.

My head shot around. "Pardon me?"

"You will get map of Having Castle where ball is held."

"How? Why would Rupert give me such a thing?"

"You will get."

"I will try."

"Better than try."

"Give me time. I can't go in there today and suddenly ask him for a blueprint of his frigging estate. Do you want him to know something's up?"

"You have three days. Then, I expect map, or—"

"Or what, you'll slice my head off, or terrorize more innocent people, and otherwise act like the monster you are? I get it."

We were turning into Chester Street. Arkhangelsky grabbed my hand and twisted it until tears sprang to my eyes. "Do not make me angry, Phoebe. Remember, I am boyfriend now." The Belgravia terrace slipped by the windows, the window boxes and topiaries' twinkling lights blurring before my eyes. "Tell Rupert you like me."

I gasped as he released my wrist. "Bastard."

We parked outside Rupert's house now, just in time for my 1:00 appointment.

"We kiss now."

"What?"

"We kiss, Phoebe. Rupert may watch."

It was like holding my breath under water, a necessary struggle against a natural impulse. Only here, I wanted to bolt, maybe lash out at this beast. Instead, I leaned forward and pressed my lips to his as if—like kissing a lamprey eel. I gagged.

And Yagar enjoying my discomfort, grabbed my head and dug his tongue deeper into my throat before pulling away. "Do better next time," he said with a smile. "More passion. I am Russian. Russians passionate people."

I clutched my carpet bag and sprang for the door, moaning in frustration when the handle refused to budge. The driver slowly made his way around to open the door.

"Be good in there. I watch," Yagar said once I finally climbed from the car and bolted for the gate, my face composed into something I hoped looked happy.

12

I was still trying to identify the doorbell's complicated chime when Sloane opened the door. "Ms. Phoebe, good afternoon."

"Good afternoon, Sloane. What's that tune?"

"At the moment it is still a strain from *Carmen* but will change today to *the Holly and the Ivy*."

"Nice."

"Indeed. Sir Rupert awaits you in the library. May I take your coat?"

After removing my outerwear, I followed the butler through the marble hall, passed another exuberant bouquet—this one composed of pine boughs, holly, and red roses—into a library larger than our entire gallery. For a moment I stood transfixed, soaking in three levels of books rising overhead to a high, domed ceiling where a painted skyscape of clouds danced in soft glowing light. "Oh," I gasped. "It reminds me of the ceilings in Nicolina's villa, minus the neutered cupids."

"A bit of an indulgence that," Rupert said standing nearby. "I designed it so that

the lighting, now set on daylight, dims to
silver moonlight and twinkling stars at
night. It was a birthday gift to my Mable a
decade ago. She so loved it."

"Magical."

"Yes, that was the effect I strove to
emulate. One must impart a touch of magic to
our lives wherever possible and, I must say,
you have added a touch to mine."

Swallowing, I turned to him. "Most of
the time I feel the same about you, though I
admit the magic is often mixed with mayhem
with doses of terror."

He smiled. "What is magic without a
little mayhem?" Today he wore a deep blue
velvet smoking jacket over gray trousers.
"In any case, I am most glad you are back in
my life, and will strive to avoid driving
you away in future." He studied me closely
for a moment. "You seem a bit flushed, my
dear, and why no color? Black does not suit
you without a dash of exuberance."

"The exuberance is in my satchel by way
of my orange cowl, which I forgot to put
back on after lunch."

"Phoebe, are you well? It rather seems
as if you've been crying."

"Crying? No, just allergies. Oh, and
I'm a bit excited, perhaps. So much has
happened since I saw you last."

Rupert clapped his hands together. "You
must come sit by the fire and tell me all.
Tea, Phoebe?"

"Yes, please, Rupert."

And so I nestled deep into the leather
armchair, taking pleasure in the warmth, the
atmosphere, the whole fantastic luxury of
Rupert's world, knowing that what money and
prestige didn't buy him, his black market

dealings had. Yet I didn't care. He was my friend. He cared about me and only now did I realize how much that meant. No way would I let Yagar Arkhangelsky steal Rupert's ill-gotten gain. The only question remaining was how in hell I could prevent it.

"I am embarking on a linen stitch scarf," he said, setting his cup aside long enough to lift four inches of multicolored texture from the basket by his feet. "What do you think?"

I leaned forward, brutish Russians temporarily forgotten. "Oh, it looks woven." I fingered the piece, admiring the way the multiple colors slipped in and out from a tightly woven surface.

"It is very much like weaving. I dare say you could add a little linen stitch to your piece, too. Whatever are you working on now? Do show me."

I pulled back, lifting my wrap on its needles from my carpet bag to hold before his eyes while shaking it slightly to release the silk tendrils.

After a second or two of awaiting a response, I lowered the wrap and met his eyes. "Well?"

"Well," he said, clearing his throat. "How … extraordinary."

"You don't like it?" I asked.

"I refer to your necklace. It looks like genuine Faberge."

"Faberge? Oh, I didn't ask for details, I was that overcome when he fastened it around my neck this morning."

"Max presented you with this delicious gift?"

"No, it's from my boyfriend. That's the exciting news I wanted to share with you today."

Rupert jolted upright. "Boyfriend? You mean—?"

"No, not him, Yagar."

"Yagar … Yagar Arkhangelsky? Surely you jest?" He looked as though he'd swallowed sewage.

My gaze dropped to my wrap. "No, I'm not joking. As you know, he's been following me around London and I finally let him catch up with me. I thought I'd give him a chance. He's so ardent, and it's such a nice change to have someone here for once, instead of … well, elsewhere. Anyway, we're dating."

"You're dating Yagar Arkhangelsky?"

"Yes, I'm dating Yagar Arkhangelsky. There's a whole other side to him you probably don't know. He's very, um, attentive."

"So are wasps if you fall into their nests. What about Noel?"

"Where is he, Rupert? He's never here. He can't be, can he? I need someone in the here and now, someone who gives me jewelry, and takes me to supper, and dances with me." I never cared for expensive gifts, didn't care whether I went out or stayed in, and since when had I been dancing? "His ardent pursuit is a pleasant change." I risked looking over at him. "I enjoy being the center of a man's attention."

"You are always the center of Noel's attention, even if he can't be here to lavish it all over you," Rupert said with asperity.

"So, maybe I want to be lavished over."

"Since when?"

"Since I realized I was hitting my mid-thirties with not a prospect in sight."

"How very Jane Austen of you. Are you now some nineteenth century spinster languishing away on a chaise lounge?"

"No, I'm a modern woman who doesn't want to spend her life flying solo. I'm tired of being alone. Can't a woman change? I want something different in my life now." This wasn't going well at all, and to make it worse my stomach emitted a ferocious growl as if passing commentary.

"This all rather sudden, isn't it? Not that long ago you were telling me how you wanted Noel. You said you loved him," he said, ignoring my bodily complaint.

"What's love got to do with it? Sorry, Tina Turner," I whispered. I did love Noel, and love had everything to do with it, I was just a little late coming to the party. "Look, Rupert, just accept it, please. I'm dating Yagar Arkhangelsky. I'm trying a new way of life on for a change. Can't you just support me as my friend?"

Rupert looked away, both hands now flat on his thighs. "You are asking me, as your friend and most stalwart supporter, to accept that you are no longer hankering after a handsome, intelligent, basically kind and decent human being, in lieu of a middle-aged, rough-edged, bully of a man who achieves his desires by violence? I know his methods."

"But do you know how he behaves as a boyfriend?"

"A man on his best behavior during courtship may show quite another side after he's caught his prize."

I doubted his behavior could get much worse. "Rupert, I am not about to be 'caught', as you put it, and I'm certainly not a prize."

"Any man with half a brain would recognize you as such. Break off with him at once, Phoebe. He is a liar and a thief, not to mention an arms dealer."

"An arms dealer?" I said without tempering my tone.

"Most certainly—one of the most active operating between Russia and Europe. He also deals in importing Russian girls as sex slaves all over Europe."

"Oh," I said, struggling to recover, thinking of the girl in the bedroom. "Oh, nobody's perfect." I took a deep breath. "Rupert, do I tell you what to do, and whom to play with? I don't know what went on between you and Yagar, business-wise. I don't have to. Aside from the arms dealing and the other thing, both of you are more or less in the same business, so it's not surprising you've crossed swords. I have no doubt that Yagar can be quite cut-throat when he's been thwarted, but so can you. Can't you just accept this new direction in my life?"

Rupert removed a hankie from his pocket and dabbed his forehead. "I would find that much easier if I were not convinced that this relationship could have serious repercussions, that you will become utterly miserable should it progress. I fear for you, Phoebe. Please end this dalliance at once."

"Yagar has asked me to marry him."

"What?" He dropped his knitting to the floor and jumped to his feet. "I trust you refused?"

"I haven't said yes and I haven't said no, but he's persistent."

"A union between you two would be disastrous! You two are so horribly ill-suited."

"Actually, we have lots in common. We both love art and artifacts, and beautiful objects of all descriptions." How I hated this. The lies seemed to stick in my throat.

"He's a brute, Phoebe."

My stomach growled again. "Really, Rupert, don't throw stones." Did I really say that?

"The thought of the two of you together is simply unbearable."

"Oh, come on, Rupert. You're not the first person to dislike a friend's boyfriend, and won't be the last. Why not do as others do and wish your friend the best while accommodating her beau? I could use the support."

"You always have my support, you must know that," he said gazing down at me, "but I cannot with any conscience support a friend who is engaging in the most glaring error of judgment."

I looked away. "And some would say that my friendship with you is a glaring error in judgment."

"Do you intend to be unkind?"

"Certainly not. I'm being truthful. There are some who do say that," I said. "Max, for instance."

"Ah, yes, Max. What does Max say about Arkhangelsky?"

"That as long as I'm happy, he's happy."

"Then he's not the man I thought him to be. Perhaps I don't know either of you as well as I believed. And I suppose you wish your 'new beau', as you call him, to accompany you to my ball?"

"Well, yes, I had hoped that." I tried to sound as though the idea filled me with delight.

"You do realize that Arkhangelsky and I are not on the best of terms?"

"So, bury the hatchet. Shake hands and leave it in the past. Max is willing to do that with you, why not you with Yagar?"

"You have no idea what of what you ask," he said.

Keeping this lie in place was exhausting. "I only ask that you provide Yagar with an invitation to escort me to the ball. That seems simple enough."

"Au contraire, it abhorrently complex. And what portrait would be come as, pray tell, Ivan the Terrible?"

I almost laughed. How fitting. "I will ask him what costume he wants."

"Not yet, for first I must give this matter serious consideration. It has all rather come as a blow, and I have yet to decide how I will manage it. Allow me to ruminate on the development. In the meantime, let us change the subject. Do tell me what personage you have chosen for your own costume." He sat down beside me and awaited my reply.

At that moment, the library door opened and in walked an silver-haired lady in a stunning argyle sweater in vivid golds and blues.

"Phoebe, meet Mrs. Montgomery, my secretary."

I wrenched my gaze away from the sweater to the woman's face. Blue eyes smiled down at me from over a pair of wire-rimmed glasses. She had to be in her early seventies with a quick, energetic step.

"Ms. McCabe, what a pleasure it is to meet you at last. I have heard so many wonderful things about you."

"That's lovely work you're wearing. Did you knit it?" I remarked.

"Why, of course" She turned to Rupert. "Forgive me for interrupting, Sir Rupert, but Lady Ashton's secretary phoned to say that the lady has chosen the *Girl with the Pearl Earring* as her choice."

"Yet another one-earring girl. And how many is that now, Mrs. Montgomery?"

"Twelve, as of today."

"Wonderful. We shall have many girls roaming around bearing single pearl earrings. I wonder if we should forewarn them that they will being seeing multiples of themselves?"

"I suggest we leave it, Sir Rupert," Mrs. Montgomery said. "The choice may have been driven by the need for simplicity, the costume being relatively easy to create. No one truly knows how the rest of the dress may appear."

"Indeed, head portraits are most easy to invent. Very well. Are there others?"

"Mr. and Mrs. Langston Scott are coming as Napoleon and Josephine, the coronation portrait."

"How splendid. I knew Langston would wish to capitalize on his diminutive stature. Any others?"

Jane Thornley

"Those are the latest, Sir."

"Thank you, Mrs. Montgomery. Please do inform Sloane that a round of tea sandwiches is in order for this chilly afternoon."

Once she'd exited, Rupert turned to me. "I hired Mrs. Montgomery only a few weeks ago. Isn't she marvelous? It truly was quite unfair to expect Sloane to handle the ball details along with all his other duties."

"She seems very efficient. And she knits."

"Yes, how fortuitous. Now, on to the matter at hand. It is most important that you decide upon your costume forthwith. I have stringent security features established requiring each individual to submit a photo of the portrait at least one week in advance."

"Of course," I said. Yagar had to be catching all this.

"Also, I assure you there will be no tedious gatecrashers permitted. Oh, the trouble we have had in the past! I once had two sets of Beatles evicted at the start of my Rock Star ball, along with four sets of Mick Jaggers. I had seen quite enough of tight leather pants by the time that evening was over, I can tell you. Regardless, these costumes require considerable forethought. I cannot stress enough the importance of executing your own costume in advance. Therefore, it is imperative that you, Max, Serena, and that dashing young actor and his girlfriend—"

"Jennifer and Marco."

"Jennifer and Marco choose your outfits within the week and inform me of your choices accordingly. No more dawdling."

"You neglected to mention Yagar."

138

"Quite deliberately. Moving along, do assure me that you are not still pondering coming as one of Van Gogh's Potato Eaters?"

"That was a joke, but—" and in walked Sloane to whisper something into Rupert's ear.

"One moment, please, Phoebe," Rupert left the room and returned moments later looking distraught.

"Is everything all right?" I asked.

"Yes, of course," he waved away the notion and resumed his seat. "You were discussing your portrait choice."

"I had been considering one of Renoir's portraits, such as the portrait of Jeanne Samary—you know, crimson lipstick, maybe a gown with a corsage, all very doable. I prefer not to choose anyone too grand, and I think I could pull off that outfit."

But Rupert was gazing up at the cloud-scudded ceiling, apparently preoccupied.

"On the other hand, I could come as Nemo, maybe Moby Dick," I continued. "You know how I love fish. There would be the little matter of the tail, but a hydraulic lift might help there."

"Yes, yes, very good," he said absently.

"Rupert, what's wrong?"

He turned to me, peering at me with intense scrutiny. "My apologies, Phoebe. What were you saying?"

"I'm considering Renoir's Jeanne Samary as my portrait."

"Very good. Yes, yes. That would be acceptable. I always imagined you a queen, but it is, of course, your choice. Remember that I've offered my resources to assist with your costumes, an offer which extends

to your immediate circle, but does not
include Arkhangelsky, should I permit him to
accompany you. Forgive my rudeness, but I
really must ask you to leave."

"Leave? But I only just arrived. What
about our knitting session?"

"I do apologize. I am most involved
with my fete—so much to organize, so many
minute details to consider. Of course, I
have staff but someone must oversee the
operations."

"Can we get together soon—tomorrow
maybe?" I was being steered from the library
into the hall where Sloane awaited with my
coat. "It's just that we have a few sessions
to catch up on, and it would be really
special if I could get together with you as
soon as possible."

"We will see. Pardon me if I leave you
with Sloane and return to the issues at
hand. Lovely to see you again, Phoebe," and
with that he took off down the hall. I
stared after him, puzzled. Never in all my
countless knitting sessions had I been so
speedily dismissed.

Moments later I was on the sidewalk,
head down, carpet bag flung over my
shoulder, hunkered against a chill wind. I
was just rounding the corner when the
Mercedes slid to the curb. Resigned to my
fate, I climbed into the back seat beside
Arkhangelsky.

"Who is this Noel?" he asked.

"The guy I'd been seeing, my real
boyfriend."

Yagar snorted. "He comes near, I kill.
Tell him that."

"Don't worry, he's nowhere near here,
and that won't change any time soon."

"Good. I am not happy with today."

"I tried, you must have seen that, or heard it."

"Not try enough," Arkhangelsky said. "Do better. I must go to ball. This happens."

I turned to him. "I can't force him to let you come. You heard me try to convince him. Now we have to give him time to think about it."

"No time, I said. You convince."

"What am I supposed to do, force him at gun-point?" I hastened to rectify that. "He'll get suspicious if I push too hard. He's having a hard enough time swallowing you as my—stop it! Let me go!"

He'd grabbed my wrist again, twisting viciously while glaring at me. "You take seriously."

"I am taking this seriously! You heard me in there, telling how much I liked you, asking him to give you a chance, the whole time hating you with every inch of my being!"

And then he yanked me forward long enough to slap me full across the face with his gloved palm. I held my cheek, stunned.

"I am Yagar Arkhangelsky. I am boyfriend. You respect." He released me, snapped an order in Russian, and the car swerved to the side of the road. "Get out," he said. "Think of other way with Rupert Fox. I give until tomorrow."

I climbed out of the car and ran down the street, one hand on my burning cheek. As crazy as it seemed, and no matter how many times I'd been shot at or attacked, that single act of casual brutality affected me like no other. I felt so defenseless, so utterly inept and, at the same time, strangely worthless, which was so damn wrong.

I was on Wilton Street, part residential, part busy thoroughfare, and suddenly became aware of how I must look—a woman running down the street in tears. Passersby stared. This wasn't New York where the population fortifies themselves against minor human suffering. In London, a woman crying still attracts attention and, in my case, that was attention I didn't want.

I dashed into the Prince of Wales Pub, plowed through the four o'clock social crowd to the ladies room, found an empty stall, and locked myself in. Ripping off the wire, I stuffed it into my carpet bag before bawling as silently as I could, slobbering into lengths of toilet tissue until I'd calmed down enough to function. Once the washroom was empty of patrons, I splashed water onto my face at the sink.

One glance at my hand-burned cheek stopped me cold. "No," I whispered, touching my reddened flesh. *No, no, no! This was not happening to me!*

A few minutes later, I was back on the street, striding across several blocks toward the gallery as the sun sank lower and lower into the sky.

13

Brenda Higgins was waiting for me by the door when I arrived at the gallery. "Phoebe McCabe, you're an hour and 20 late. I don't appreciate hanging around your rug shop."

"Sorry, Higgins," I said stepping past her, "Something came up. And it's a carpet and rare ethnographic textile gallery."

"Yeah, yeah. I call a rug a rug. Are you standing me up to go knitting with this Sir Rupert Fox?" she asked, falling into step behind me as I headed for the back room. "I've heard about him."

I nodded at Rena who was busy selling our Animal Tree Engsi to a fur-clad woman.

"It's a regular appointment every Wednesday," I told her. "I just wasn't expecting to keep it today

"You miss your self-defense training to knit?"

Max stepped out of the storeroom, caught sight of me and froze.

"Yes, to knit. Brenda, do you mind giving me a moment with Max? I'll be right out, I promise." I didn't give her a chance to protest but led Max back into the storeroom and shut the door behind me.

"What the hell happened, Phoebe? I've been worried sick. You wouldn't answer your phone. I—" Max began.

I put my finger to my lips while fishing the necklace out from under my coat with my other hand. Aiming the pendant towards him, I said: "Say hello to Yagar, Max. He's got a device tucked away in this lovely Faberge necklace, along with more surveillance stuff throughout my flat. I now star in my very own reality show."

"In your bloody flat?"

"Yes, apparently. He's watching me 24/24 and can get in any time he wants, as in last night. He's the one who had Jennifer traumatized to make a point, as you suspected. I'm pretty sure he'll come up with lots of other ways to hurt us if we don't play along."

"I knew it. What did the bastard do to you?" He lifted my chin, his eyes sparking fiercely.

I said nothing at first, letting him figure it out. The struggle to stay calm tensed all his facial muscles. "He told me that if I didn't get Rupert to agree to let him come to the ball by tomorrow, there'd be more consequences," I said finally. "I believe him."

He stepped back as if he'd been struck. "I'll—"

"Do as he says, like we said we would," I said quickly. "Can't afford not to, can we? On a brighter note, Rupert said we can all go to the ball, all except Yagar, that is—for now, anyway. He's still making his mind up there. I'll help him along somehow." I scanned my brain for some way to communicate that didn't involve the visible

144

or audible, but came up empty. "Mind unclasping this thing?"

He unfastened the necklace and dropped it onto the table. I snatched it up before he could smash it with the tape dispenser. "This is real Faberge. Let's put it in the safe along with this." And I pulled out the wire from my carpet bag.

"Put it back on the table. I'll put them away later—intact."

Then he steered me by the arm to our walk-in safe at the back of the room. Tapping in the combination, he swung open the door, and crammed us both inside beside our most expensive carpets, leaving the door ajar an inch.

I filled him in with all the things I couldn't say earlier.

"He wants the blueprint of Having? He keeps the plans in his London house," he whispered, all hunched over inside that steel closet, "but you'll never get past that guard dog of his. Evan's got that place wired with more high-tech devices than anything Diamond & Dew can dream up."

"Somebody at Diamond & Dew is in on this. Arkhangelsky got to one of the guys who upgraded our system, maybe both. Nothing's secure anymore."

Max swore. "I know a guy who might be able to help there. Leave it to me."

"What's the point? He'll only get someone else to do the same thing all over again. We've got to hit the source somehow, put Arkhangelsky away."

"We'll nail the bastard, don't you worry. In the meantime, how are you going to get Foxy to let Arkhangelsky go to the ball?

If there's bad blood between them, that won't be easy."

"Still working on that," I said, banging my elbow on the steel wall. "He hates Yagar and thinks a whole lot less of me for supposedly dating him. Max, you should have heard the garbage I fed him. It was disgusting. And then Yagar still hit me."

"I'm going to kill the bastard!"

"No, you're not. We're going to outsmart him, let him rot in jail. If anybody gets to kill him, it will be me."

"He's ruthless. If I knew even a quarter of what I do now, I would have never let him in the shop."

"The arms dealing?"

"And the sex trade and a whole pile more."

"I have to get out of here—can't breathe, and Brenda's waiting."

We climbed out and I left Max opening up a smaller safe to store the surveillance devices, still cursing under his breath. When I flung open the door, Brenda stood with her arms crossed.

"You're wasting my time, Phoebe McCabe."

"Right, let's go." I dashed for the stairs. Halfway up, I stopped, dropping my carpet bag. I couldn't go back up into my fishbowl world and engage in self-defense training, let alone scream and throw things the way I wanted to. Turning around, I said, "Let's go back to the hall for our practice."

"Thought you wanted to be close to work?" she asked, looking up at me.

"I've changed my mind."

"Tell me what's really going on." She took two more steps up until we stood eye to eye, her straw-blond hair packed away into a tight ponytail, the blue eyes boring into my skull. "Who is he?"

"Who's who?" I leaned against the railing, hoping no one on the floor would notice the strange interaction taking place above.

"Serena said you were picked up by your boyfriend. First time I ever heard about a boyfriend. You been dating for long?"

"Not really. Why do you ask?" I was vaguely aware of Rena laughing with her customer below.

"Strange that you wouldn't mention a boyfriend."

"I didn't ask if you were dating or not. That's none of my business," I said.

"The difference is that you asked me to be your bodyguard. That makes it my business. A boyfriend complicates everything, especially if he knocks you around."

I caught my breath. "What are you talking about?"

"I'm talking about that red welt across your cheek, Phoebe McCabe, and … " she lifted my arm to shove back my sleeve, "and this."

I winced at the sight of the blue-black bruises rising over my lower arm, some shaped like finger impressions. I tugged my arm away and pulled down my sleeve.

"Think I can't see that he's an abusive bastard for myself? Some men know how to rough up a woman without showing any marks. Looks like this one didn't want to permanently damage your face. What's next, cigarette burns?"

"So he knocks me around, okay?" I never thought I'd ever hear those words escape my lips.

"It's not okay. Break off with him."

"I can't."

"Why not?"

"Because he's threatening to kill me. Are you going to help me or not?"

14

By the time I arrived home after a day of more physical and emotional abuse than I'd endured in a long time, all I wanted was a hot bath and bed. I'd already figured out that I'd do everything in the dark in the off-chance my watchers hadn't installed night vision cameras. Was a little privacy too much to ask?

Though the gallery was closed for the night, the light was still on at the top of the stairs. I unlocked the front door and slipped in, thinking I'd call out and, if no one answered, bolt down the street. "Max?"

"Up here."

I leaned against the doorjamb in relief. "Are you waiting up for me?" I asked, turning to relocked the door. "I was afraid Arkhangelsky and gang were planning a welcoming party. It's been a whole five hours and I haven't seen or heard from him, not even so much as an offer to drive me home."

"Where's your phone?" he asked, dashing down the stairs.

"Yagar took it." I pressed a hand to my temple, caught sight of his face and dropped my hand. "What's wrong?"

"After you left, I minded the shop while Rena went out to get us take-out supper. She never returned. I called her cell multiple times but no one answered. It's been three hours."

"No," I said, swallowing hard. "He wouldn't," but that was crazy because I knew he would, could, and probably did. "I can't stand this. If he harms even a hair on her head—oh, Rena! She'll be terrified. Why's he doing this?"

Max started pacing the floor, digging his fingers into his hair. "You know why."

And then the gallery phone rang. I looked over at Max. "That's him."

"Answer it, Phoeb."

I scrambled to Rena's desk and plucked up the phone. "If you do anything to harm her, I swear I'll make you pay, honest to God I will!" The laughter in my ear infuriated me. "What do you want, you brutal bastard? I'm doing everything I can to accommodate your demands."

"I go to ball, yes?"

"I said he needed time."

"No time. I get invitation by tomorrow or friend dies."

"Dies?" I couldn't believe I'd heard right. He was threatening to kill Serena now? "Put her on the line," I said, suddenly trembling. "Let me speak to her. Don't hurt her, please don't hurt her. I'll get what you want."

"Serena is not here," he said. "My boys keep her safe. You do what I say. Get invitation now."

"Why do you need it now? I can't phone him tonight. It's almost ten o'clock."

"Now." He hung up.

At least I knew Rupert's number by heart. I tapped in the digits and waited, heart pounding, but it was Sloane who answered. "I am most sorry, Ms. McCabe, but Sir Rupert is dining out tonight. May I take a message?"

"Please tell him that I must talk to him as soon as possible."

"Of course. Have a very good evening."

When he hung up, I sent the phone clattering across the table. "If I had my Foxy phone, Rupert would have answered. That was our code. This is going nowhere."

And then the phone rang again. Max whipped it up from the desk and passed it over.

"He's not home," I said.

There was a ten second delay before he answered. "You have until tomorrow. If no invitation by twelve noon, I kill Rena piece by piece." And he hung up.

I hastily re-dialed but the call spun into some kind of loop before clicking off. When I tried again, the same thing happened.

I held the phone out to Max. "Is this really happening?"

"It's all right, Phoebe, darlin', we'll beat this bastard. I'll pulverize him to a pulp."

I was too upset to chastise him for the macho talk. Hell, I wanted macho talk, craved it, even. I'd love it even more if he threatened to bring in the cavalry and half of the world's armed forces while whipping out a machine gun from his back pocket. But this was one battle where I wanted to be on the front lines.

Reinforcements were nowhere to be found. Not this time. "How can we beat him?

We can't call the police, can't call anybody," I cried. "My usual backup is Rupert and Evan, but now they're our targets. Who knows how many brutes he has in his employ?" I looked up. "Max, how can this bastard even think he can get away with this? I mean, it's now kidnapping and extortion. There are witnesses like you and me. Does he believe he's above the law?" And then a horrid thought struck so hard I nearly reeled backward. "Oh, my God. He's not planning to leave witnesses."

15

"Let's find that garage in Islington and see if they've got her hidden there," Max said, stopping mid-stride across the gallery floor.

"Worth a shot." I jumped to my feet. I couldn't just sit around. I had to do something.

Neither of us mentioned how crazy this was. These were hardened criminals, while we were just terrified friends, or so I thought.

"I have a gun," Max remarked, as we took the Islington exit.

"Since when?"

"Since I found one of Maggie's tucked into her lingerie drawer. Actually, I found three. Maggie loved her guns."

"I remember. Don't tell Higgins. Anyway, these guys are armed, too. I mean, I haven't seen a gun on any of them, but if Arkhangelsky is an arms dealer … " I let the sentence trail away.

"My thoughts, exactly."

"So, what are we going to do—walk up to the garage door and knock?"

"Don't be foolish. We'll use subterfuge: I'll kick the bloody door down," he muttered.

"Very funny."

The street stood lifeless compared to my first sighting the day before. The cars were gone, the shops were closed, and the wall of garage doors hung lifeless in the dark. There were seven garages, all identical, all attached to narrow office buildings rising three stories overhead.

"Okay, so I think it was the one in the middle." I pointed.

Max peered out the window. "You think?"

"Nothing looks the same at night, but I'm sure that's it. Let's check it out."

We left the Bentley parked down the street and padded up to the building. Though there were no lights on in the offices above, and no cars to indicate anybody might be working late, it still felt like we were being watched. "They'd have surveillance cameras," I whispered.

"Everybody does." Max strode up to the garage and pressed his ear against the door. "Can't hear a thing."

"I'll check around back," I said. Only, technically there wasn't a back. I jogged to the corner, only to discover that the front of the office block was actually on the parallel street. Each building had a glass door opening onto a small reception area. After checking each, I realized that half the offices were empty, including the one fronting ours. Pressing my nose against the window, I could just see paper on the floor, a dropped smartphone charger, a broken printer. Somebody had left in a hurry.

I bounded back around to the garage where Max was fiddling with the latch. "Looks like they left. There's no sign of life in there. What are you doing?"

"Electronic door," he said, and then he stepped back and kicked the latch, the sound reverberating through the metal and down the street.

"I thought you were joking!"

But he kept on kicking, followed by poking at the handle with what looked to be a steel toothpick. In seconds, the latch hung limp as Max lifted up the accordion-style door.

As we stared into the deserted garage—the same one I'd been taken to—an alarm ripped into the night. Max swore and let the door crash to the pavement.

"Run!" he called.

We bounded down the street and back into the Bentley, which Max pealed from the curb before I even had my seatbelt fastened.

"You could have used stealthier methods," I said.

"Just wanted to confirm what I suspected: that they weren't keeping her anywhere that you could identify. Still, we had to try."

"But we're no closer to finding Rena." Something made me check the rear-view mirror, studying the dark blue Mercedes tailgating us. I didn't need to see the driver to know we were being tailed. "Someone's following us."

"Figures. He's been on our tail off an on since we left the shop."

"Yet you said nothing?"

"Look, Phoebe, somebody's always following me, so I didn't think it mattered."

Seconds later, the Mercedes rammed our bumper as we paused at a stop sign.

"Guess it mattered," I remarked.

"Shit! It costs me a fortune to source parts for this model!" Max growled.

Though not the former Formula One driver that Evan was, Max still had a few vehicular moves of his own. We darted down a side street and up a hill, taking an abrupt right turn through a lane onto a back street. "If it is one of those Russki bastards following us, he won't know these streets the way I do."

I checked behind us. "He's sticking to us."

"Not for bloody long," Max said. At a roundabout, we went the opposite direction, up over the curb, and down another road, probably giving at least one motorist a heart attack. We were now weaving in and out of the outer boroughs of London, and the only thing on our tail was a National bus.

I sunk back into the seat. "Nice driving," I said, "but it's not like these bastards don't know where we live."

Max was grumbling by the time he parked the Bentley near the gallery, this time in a legal parking spot. "Don't worry, they won't follow us. That was just intimidation tactics."

"What if somebody checks the cameras? Each garage had one over the door."

"Arkhangelsky already knows what we did, and he's not going to be notifying the police, I can guarantee you."

We remained silent all the way back inside the gallery, where we re-alarmed the security system as if it still mattered. The phone was ringing by the time we shrugged off our coats.

"That's him," I said.

"Answer it, Phoeb."

I scrambled to Rena's desk and plucked up the phone, putting it on speaker mode. "You tried to find Rena. You will not find Rena. I have her in safe place," said that horrid voice.

"What do you want?" I yelled into the phone.

"You know what I want."

"Foxy said he needed time," Max interjected.

"I get invitation by tomorrow." And he hung up.

I turned to Max. "Well, that's it then. I need to put the pressure on Rupert somehow."

"Use blackmail," Max suggested.

"Like threatening to go to the police about what I know about his business practices?" I asked in disbelief.

"There is more than one kind of blackmail, Phoebe."

16

The call came by 10:00 o'clock the next morning. "Good morning, Phoebe, Rupert Fox here. I initially tried our private line but you did not answer. Where, may I ask, is the secure phone I provided?"

"I misplaced it," I said. "I've been so preoccupied lately."

Silence stretched by seconds on the other line. "Anyway," I continued much too brightly, "Thanks for calling back. Have you had a chance to consider the invitation to Yagar? I'm so eager to start planning his costume and, as you said, time is of the essence." I had no idea whether he'd said that or I'd dreamed it. "I just need to know soon. It's the matter of the costume." This time the silence on the end of the line stretched on much too long. "Rupert?" I prompted.

"Yes, Phoebe, I am still here, though I admit to being immensely puzzled. After all, I did express my utter abhorrence of the man, yet still you insist."

"Why do you even hesitate after all you've put me through? Have you forgotten the last few months—the outright lies, the maneuvering me into deadly situations, the conniving, and half-truths? Leading me into situations where I could get killed or arrested? And now I ask one thing, one little thing, and you hesitate. Are you kidding me? Letting Yagar attend the ball with me is a minor compensation for all you've put me through." Talk about manipulation.

"Phoebe," he said, "If you asked anything else of me, I would comply, but not this."

Thoughts banged around in my head, each painful and frightening. I had to get a message to him without alerting Arkhangelsky. Then one hit me between the eyes. "Teach me to knit socks."

"I beg your pardon?"

"Socks, Rupert. You know how I've always wanted to knit socks, lovely plain socks on teeny-tiny needles the size of toothpicks? I will make Yaggie a pair for Christmas. Teach me how."

I counted fifteen seconds before he answered, his voice tight. "Very well."

I caught my breath. "Very well to which?"

"Very well to both. Yes, Yagar Arkhangelsky may attend the ball and, yes, I will teach you how to knit socks. I realize I have deprived you far too long and that, indeed, I do owe you compensation for all the excitement I've subjected you to."

I exhaled. "Thank you, Rupert. May I come over today for my first session? Less than two weeks left until Christmas, so I'd better get started."

"Yes, indeed. Our usual time will suit, I presume, and your boyfriend will arrange for your transportation once again?"

"Yes and yes. I'll be there."

It took a mere ten minutes before Yagar called. "This good," he said, "this very good. Idea to knit socks brilliant. Many women knit boyfriends gifts. I look for my gift at Christmas."

"So glad you approve. Now release Serena."

"I keep until you have blueprints of Having Castle."

"No!" I yelled into the phone.

"No? What is no? You do not say no to Yagar Arkhangelsky. You do what I say or I cut Serena bit by bit."

"You said that you'd let her go if I got you that invitation."

"I lie. Wear necklace today. I come at 11:30, and tell the son and girlfriend no police, or I send first ear to him personally."

"Wait, no! I—" but he hung up.

Downstairs in the storeroom moments later, I found Max pacing the gallery. Though we didn't open until 11:00, he had arrived early. "Well?" he asked as I came clattering down the stairs.

I nodded towards the back room and led him back to our safe house. We crammed ourselves into our secure conversation zone as I filled him in on the latest. "Now he says he's not releasing Serena until I bring him the blueprints of Having Castle," I said. "I'm sure that once I deliver those, there'll be something else."

Max slammed the steel wall with his fist. "I knew he wouldn't let her go, I just bloody knew it! He's going to use her for collateral."

"Max," I said grabbing his arm, "we have to think, think!"

"Look, Phoebe, darlin', you know there's no way he's going to let her go, but we can't let that bastard hurt her."

I took a deep breath. "No, we won't. We need a plan." The doorbell jingled. "Who would that be this time of day?" I asked.

"Marco. I was on the phone to the lad all last night. I tried to keep him calm— like that was easy with me jumping out of my own damn skin. He wants to call the police. We need to tell him what's going on before this place is crawling with cops."

I dashed from the safe and let Marco in. One look at the beautiful green eyes smudged with dark circles told me how much he suffered.

"What the hell is going on?" he bellowed. "What have you done to find my mother?"

I put my fingers to my lips and dragged him to our safe zone behind Rena's desk. "Max and I went looking for her last night, but he's moved her someplace 'safe', as he calls us. We're making a plan. We will get Rena home safely, I promised."

"Tell me why we're not bringing in the Yard?" he said between his teeth.

"Because if he gets so much as a whiff that we've called the police, Rena is dead, understand?"

Max leaned over the desk. "Listen, Marco, this guy is bad news. He means business—no messing around—but we'll beat this bastard. Just hold tight."

It took almost an hour for both of us
to convince him that we could win this
battle on our own. By 11:25, Marco had gone
and I was waiting outside the gallery
wearing my Faberge necklace, my stomach in
knots. Now that the game was afoot and I was
too deeply mired to extricate myself, I was
finally getting a grip. Something like a
plan was actually taking shape. Maybe it was
only a filament of an idea to support a
notion, but it was something. And it was
risky, it was crazy, and just maybe my hunch
was way off-base, but it was the only damn
thing I could think of.

The moment I saw Yagar's face, his long
face and mud-brown eyes had taken on an
expression both benign and menacing. I
almost lost my breakfast.

"You have done well, Phoebe. Yagar is
pleased," Arkhangelsky said as I slid into
the seat beside him. "Today you bring me
plans for Having Castle."

I reached deep inside myself for a
measure of calm. "I will request that, of
course. You understand that Sir Rupert will
likely photocopy it rather than just hand
over the original?"

"I am patient man, but must have them
by tomorrow afternoon."

"You call that patient?" I asked as the
car slid down the street. "Anyway, let's
forget that for a moment and discuss your
costume. This ball is of major importance to
Rupert, and the details are critical. People
just can't show up dressed in something they
invented at the last minute. Each guest must
submit a photo of the portrait they're
basing their costume on."

"This I know. Rupert will be what?"

"King Charles the Second, his ancestor by marriage."

"Ah, a king, then. This does not surprise."

"Have you decided which portrait you will emulate?"

"I have thought, yes. Must wear long robe and must be king. I first thought Peter the Great, for he is great Russian, but I remember breeches. No breeches. My portrait must have long robes."

"How about Rasputin? He was big into robes."

"Rasputin! Haha." He slapped his thighs heartily. "Not Rasputin, though he mystic like me, but no king. Must be king. No, I will go as Ivan IV Vasilevich as joke. Rupert likes jokes, but this 'Ivan the Terrible' was great diplomat, art patron, and founded Russia's first printing house—not so terrible."

"He also killed people for fun, tortured animals, murdered most of his wives, and wasn't above slaughtering children. Sounds like your kind of guy. Do you have a photo?" I asked.

"I choose this portrait, artist unknown." He handed me a glossy photograph of a somber man garbed in elaborate brocade robes richly embroidered in pearls, gems, and gold. Possibly the dead animal trimming the collar and hat was mink. With the heavy gold pectoral cross, the scepter, and the jewel-encrusted orb, the combined worth probably exceeded Charles the Second's finery. If not for the beard, Yagar and Ivan looked strikingly similar.

"I will give this to Sir Rupert today," I said, tucking the photo into its sleeve.

"You go as Ivan's wife."

I almost spat out an emphatic *no*, but pulled myself together. "Of course, but which one? Didn't he have eight?"

"The first, his Anastasia. You go as Anastasia Romanova."

"The one he poisoned?"

"Ivan did not do this. He loved Anatasia very much, and her death made him angry man. I arrange costume. No official portrait but we use this."

I took the photo of a woman, possibly fashioned in wax, wearing a long ermine-trimmed robe, carrying a bejeweled muff, and wearing what looked to be a pearl-encrusted lampshade on her head. Maybe I only imagined long suffering in her pale face, but I felt for her as I slid the photo into my bag with the other. "Fine. I'll give them both to Sir Rupert."

"Good."

"Look, he's suspicious because I don't have either of my phones and keep calling him other lines. I need my phones back to keep up appearances."

Arkhangelsky pulled both my iPhone and the Foxy phone from a briefcase at his feet, and passed them over. "Today I give them to you for good behavior."

Good behavior? This bastard had no idea how bad my behavior was about to become. I took the phones gratefully, even knowing that both had likely been tampered with. "How is Serena?" I asked. "I need to know she's okay."

"Yes, yes," Arkhangelsky said while flipping open his laptop. "When you are good, Yagar is good. Today your friend is treated very good because today you please me."

I leaned towards the screen, so hungry for the sight of her, I almost cried out. She was gagged, tied to a chair in a bare room, her feet and hands bound, shivering as though she'd been doused in ice water. No visible signs of blood or bruising, at least.

She stared out at the camera as if she knew I was watching, and communicated to me beyond words. *Don't let these bastards win.*

I pulled back. "Untie her immediately. Let her move." The area didn't look like the garage, but it was still bare and definitely cold. "Give her a blanket or a coat or something."

Arkhangelsky spoke into a phone in Russian. "She will be untied and warm things given."

"What about a cup of hot tea and food?"

"You think this the Goring? No tea," he said with a smile.

"You said that when I was good, she'd be treated well. All I asked for was tea to warm her up."

"If you please me today, more treats for Serena tonight. Enough now. You wear necklace?"

I fished the out the pendant from beneath my coat.

"Good. This time you walk around house so I see more."

"I thought you were interested in the castle's contents?"

"Everything interests Yagar. Bring pictures. Now put on wire."

I fished the contraption from my bag and held it out, but quickly withdrew it

before he tried to fasten it on me himself.
Clipping the microphone on top of my bra, I
was careful to ensure nothing showed. He
wanted to listen in on everything I said and
was said to me, but didn't insist on ear
buds for communicating instructions live.
Probably he worried Rupert would detect
that.

"I will return to collect you at 4:00
promptly. Ready?" he asked.

"Ready."

We slid up to the curb beside Rupert's
Belgrave mansion, but before I could exit
the car, Arkhangelsky beckoned me closer.
"We kiss," he said.

Oh, hell. I closed my eyes and thought
of Noel. Now that man knew how to kiss.
Arkhangelsky's slippery lips descended on
mine like a giant clam sucking the life from
an urchin. It took everything I had not to
retch, especially when his tongue plunged
down my throat. Even memories of Noel's
passionate lovemaking couldn't erase my
disgust. Once out of the car, I resisted
wiping my mouth on my sleeve, at least until
my back was turned.

Halfway to the front door, I stopped.
How could I not notice the snow? I loved the
first snowfall of the season. Soft white
flakes sifted down around the street,
muffling traffic, enhancing the fairy lights
on tree and bough. Christmas was only weeks
away. The season of love. Suddenly
heartsick, all I yearned for was safety for
everybody I cared about. I craved to be
tucked safely away in some place where bad
guys never penetrated, wars never happened,
and the world truly was a peaceful place.

But I did not live in that world. Taking a deep breath, I continued walking.

Moments later, I stood on the steps before Rupert's door, admiring his giant holly wreath decorated with balls of gleaming, snow-dusted yarn. I could hear the doorbell playing *The Holly and the Ivy* as I fought back tears. The door opened and there was Rupert stepping forward to embrace me. The strength of his affection took my breath away, literally. I gazed over his shoulder bewildered as Sloane and Evan waited inside the door.

"I am most delighted that we are friends again," Rupert said, squeezing hard. "Friends are far too precious to waste on mere differences of opinion."

"I agree," I said, my voice cracking.

As he released me, my carpet bag slid from my shoulder onto the damp step. I turned to pick it up.

"Oh, my," Rupert said. "How terribly careless of me. Do pass it over, Phoebe, and I shall have Sloane clean it for you."

"It's fine, Rupert. This bag has taken so much abuse, how's a little damp going to hurt?"

"Nevertheless, we will take care of it." Rupert whipped the bag from my hand and passed it to Sloane, who darted off down the hall as if holding a skunk-infested mongrel.

That left Evan standing quietly studying me. In his brown turtleneck sweater—I suspected it was cashmere on principal—he looked as handsome as ever. He returned my smile.

"Sorry about the other day," I said. "I shouldn't have chased you away like that. I was angry."

"I understand, Madam. No need to apologize. I only wanted to know that you and Rupert are once again on good terms."

"Yes, that's a relief for me, too."

Rupert caught Evan's eye and something was communicated that I couldn't understand.

"Allow me to take your coat, Madam," Evan said. I shrugged off my pea jacket into his care and stood in my green tunic top.

"I brought my green and brown feather-and-fan wrap but it's in my bag," I told Rupert.

"Have no fear, Phoebe, for you are in no danger of hypothermia for the moment. Come along," Rupert said, clapping his hands together as Evan slipped into another room. "Shall we have tea?"

"Yes, please."

I followed him into the library, my hand touching the hidden microphone through the crepe fabric. Why couldn't this be an uncomplicated knit date between friends instead of a covert mission with me playing spy? Then again, I reasoned, as I stepped into the magnificent library, with Rupert, something covert was usually afoot, just not by me.

Tea was waiting by the fire. Rupert, dressed today in a maroon velvet smoking jacket over gray flannel trousers, waited while I sat down before joining me on the other side of the tea tray.

"Sugar, Phoebe?"

"Yes, please. Two spoonfuls with just a dash of milk."

He didn't hesitate but filled my order with careful precision, passing me the cup. The teaspoon rattled in its saucer as I lowered the delicate monogrammed china to the table. I shoved my clasped hands deep into my lap, willing them to settle. If Rupert noticed the trembling, he didn't comment.

"Have you given thought to the style of your sock present, perhaps something with an apt motif such as skull and crossbone?"

"Tempting, but no, he'll prefer plain. I thought I'd make him a pair to go with his costume, so if they could be as authentic to the period as possible?"

"Of course," he sighed, studying me carefully from over the top of his cup. "And which personage did he choose?"

"Yaggie wants to go as Ivan IV Vasilevich in your honor—he thought you'd enjoy the joke—and I will go as his first wife, Anastasia Romanova."

"Such a charming pair: Ivan the Terrible and Anastasia the Insipid."

"Now, Rupert, don't be unkind. I understand Ivan was smitten by her sweet, pliant nature."

"Before he poisoned her."

"There's speculation that he may not have murdered his first wife, but merely knocked off the others. Anyway, with a wig, I'm sure I'll be a dead ringer." I slightly emphasized the *dead*. "As long as she dresses well—I'm hoping for pearl-encrusted everything—I'm good. Yaggie will take care of having the costumes made. I'm looking forward to the lampshade hat. The portrait photos are in my bag. As soon as it is returned, I'll pass them over."

"Very well. Let us begin working your socks. I have selected a few yarns for you to consider."

My eyes met his over our respective cups. "That's just so generous of you."

"I am nothing if not exceedingly generous."

He pulled out three little baskets from beside his chair, each with its own set of needles, and set them on the table between us. I studied the mounds of black, white, and gray yarns in various weights and fibers. "If you truly want them to be authentic to his Ivan the Terrible costume, I suggest the thicker options. The wool, perhaps."

"Wouldn't Ivan the Terrible wear silk hose as a king?"

"Phoebe, do think. Ivan the Terrible was a Russian living several centuries prior to central heating, tromping about in a frigid castle where a stray draft might easily freeze a man's thoughts from his brain, that is, if said brain was not overheated by pondering which hapless minion to impale or which wife to poison. Wool, Phoebe, wool, was a Russian's silk, that and fur. If you study that painting of Ivan the Terrible, you will note that he is dressed for drafty conditions."

"I get your point. In that case, I choose this." I fondled a pile of black skeins. "Merino and cashmere?"

"Just so. I retrieved them from my yarn repository just this morning."

"You have a yarn repository here? Oh, of course you do. Shall we begin?"

And begin we did, but with little of the chatter that usually warms the air between us. Rupert remained all business, presumably intent on teaching me the art of knitting socks. After a few minutes fumbling with the toe, I remarked, "You know, I've never had a tour of your house. Think you might indulge me in a bit of a stroll about the property?"

"It is not the best time for such things, seeing as the household is in a bit of an upset as we pack for Having Castle for the holidays," he said without looking up.

"You'll be going to Having for the festive period?"

"Why yes. We leave just before the ball and do not return until the new year."

"Oh."

He looked up and caught my eye. "But, indeed, a brief stroll might be good for the knees. Come along."

We placed the emerging sock on the ottoman and exited the library, while I ensured the Faberge necklace hung unobstructed over my tunic. I could only hope that Arkhangelsky, wherever or however he listened in, was suitably impressed by the ease in which his plans were falling into place. Here was I infiltrating Sir Rupert Fox's private domain as a trusted guest.

I thought of Serena caged in that concrete cell, pictured her pacing the tiny space, and knew I walked a tightrope of pending disaster. I only needed to take one false step.

Rupert lead me up the elegant curved staircase, past illuminated niches containing vases, marble statues, and even a gilded Buddha.

"You have such a stunning collection of so many diverse items, Rupert. I presume all are genuine?"

"But, of course, Phoebe. I do abhor fakes of any kind."

"Yes, but don't you appreciate a bit of pretense once in a while, especially when absolutely necessary to reach the desired end?"

"There are always exceptions, of course, providing the desired end is desired by all involved."

"My thoughts exactly. By the way, have you a collection of Russian icons here? I only ask because Yaggie is such a fan, and I understand you outbid him at an auction once."

"Indeed, more than once, in truth, for I am the more intrepid auction maestro. I do keep a small collection on the premises."

"Maybe I could see them?"

"Perhaps some other time."

"Sure. Anyway, I look forward to seeing Having Castle at the ball," I said quickly. "I imagine it being very large, with copious rooms for displaying your collections, or do you keep them in vaults?"

"Vaults do have their place, as does displaying ones treasures to enjoy on a daily basis."

"Do you prefer to keep all your precious collections displayed openly, then?"

"In some cases. However, there are exceptions, based upon the delicacy of the items, and their need for climate-controlled environments, not to mention protection against moths and thieves."

How in hell would I find a good excuse for requesting a blueprint of his damned estate?

I followed him down a marble hall lined with grand orientalist paintings, including an exquisitely detailed John Frederick Lewis oil featuring two Moroccan women swathed in silk. Finally I caught up with Rupert standing beside a pedestaled bust of an imperious Roman at the end of the hall.

"Caesar?" I asked.

"Claudius," he replied.

"I knew he had to be an emperor."

"That is a given; however, I am not above a great philosopher or two. In any case, now you have seen the second floor and, I assure you, the opposite end of the hall is more of the same. This admittedly brief tour must suffice for now, for sock knitting is the order of the day." He spread one hand, an indication that I was to proceed him back towards the stairs.

"Maybe I could see inside the actual rooms?"

"Some other time, perhaps. We are a little pressed for time."

"Of course, but maybe you let me see a blueprint of Having Castle, then? I've never been there, either, and I understand it's quite large."

Rupert paused, gazing across at me. "A blueprint, you ask?"

"A floor plan, yes. Just so I can get an idea of the space and where you house your yarn. Just curious. When I finally visit Having, it will be on the eve of the ball, and you'll be far too busy to show me around. You must keep a drawing here somewhere."

"In point of fact, I do not. My only blueprints are at Having itself. However, two of my staff will be making a short trip there later today to deliver my costume, and I will ask them to bring a blueprint back here for your perusal. You will be dropping by again tomorrow for another knitting session, I presume?"

"Of course," I said, heartened.

"Very well. In the meantime, may I suggest we return to the library to resume your lesson."

Hopefully, returning to Arkhangelsky empty-handed wouldn't result in more retributions.

We returned to the library, sipped more tea, this time accompanied by delectable sandwiches, and sat side by side by the fire while Rupert illustrated how to set up a toe on three double-pointed needles. Tiresome. When I suggested the addition of a small heart on each ankle to express my regard for Yaggie, Rupert accidentally poked my finger with one of the needles.

"Terribly clumsy of me," he muttered, not looking up. "Do forgive. Now watch as I work around the tee-pee of needles to form the toe. Phoebe, do pay attention."

At 3:45, the approximate time we ended our knitting sessions, Sloane entered the library carrying my carpet bag. "Excuse me for the delay, madam, but I wished to thoroughly dry it in the laundry room. I trust you are pleased?"

I gazed at my carpet bag with its deep reds and sultry indigos restored to their original luster. "It's been transformed. Thank you, Sloane." I clutched my bag closer like the old friend it was. "Oh, before I forget," I plucked out the sheaf of photos and passed them to Rupert. "Ivan and Anastasia, as promised."

Rupert gave only a cursory glance. "As expected, one bears too great a presence, whereas the other none at all. I did hope you would come as a queen of note, Phoebe. Nevertheless, I shall add them to our roster. Here you go, dear chap," he said, passing the photos to Sloane. "And what will your friends attend as?"

"Um, I hope to tell you tomorrow. I know, I know—time is running out, but the shop has been so busy lately that we haven't given it much thought."

"I can make an excellent suggestion for Max, if he is interested."

"I'll tell him. Well, I guess I'd best go. See you tomorrow, Rupert, and thank you for your help." Oh, my, didn't I sound so formal? I began to pack the sock apparatus into my bag.

Rupert stopped me. "One moment, please, Phoebe. Since you will be having further lessons, and have yet many inches before working on your own volition, do leave your emerging gift with me."

"Oh, of course," I laid the triple-needled toe scaffolding back on the seat. "I doubt I'll have much time to work on it tonight, anyway."

Rupert hastened down the hall while Sloane helped me into my coat. I stepped into the foyer to check through the glass sidebar.

"The Mercedes has not yet arrived," Sloane said behind me. "Would you care to wait in the library, and I shall alert you to its arrival?"

"No, thanks. I think I'll step outside and enjoy the snow for a bit."

Though the flakes had melted as soon as
they hit the pavement, a dusting of white
clung to the grass and bushes inside
Rupert's tiny but perfectly manicured yard.
Standing beside the wrought iron gate with
no Mercedes in sight, I fished inside my bag
for my iPhone and pulled it free.

I held the thing in my hand for a
moment, sensing something different, but not
grasping what. I studied my background
screen—the Mermaid & Baker gallery sign
remained the same, only different. I peered
down at it, finally spying something amiss.
Where once my screen photo had shown the
gilded sign glowing in the sun, now a small
squiggle had been added to the Mermaid's
tail. Pinching the photo wider revealed a
tiny golden "F." Then I understood: Rupert
had cleaned whatever Arkhangelsky had
installed, and re-secured my phone. Smiling,
I opened up the device, tapped the message
feature, and texted Max: GATHER MARCO AND
JENNIFER TOGETHER AND TELL THEM TO MEET US
AT YOUR PLACE TONIGHT. MARCO'S ON MATINEE
DUTY TODAY SO THAT SHOULD WORK. I briefly
considered texting Rupert, but decided
against it. I'd leave that for later. I
still wasn't positive the phone was clean.

After hitting SEND, I fished out the
second phone, my "Foxy" phone, realizing in
an instant that that, too, had changed. Then
I saw the Mercedes slipping up to the curb.
Dropping both phones into my bag, I stepped
through the gate to the car. "Well, Yaggie,
I'm well on my way to making you a Christmas
present."

17

"I'll have the blueprints in hand by tomorrow. I hope you're pleased," I said, sliding in beside Arkhangelsky. He stared at me with narrowed eyes as the car pulled away from the curb. "What?" I said. Did he somehow realize the phones had been switched? He hadn't searched my bag yet so how could he?

"Fox suspicious. You do not act like lover," he said.

"I don't? I mean, I think I do—knitting my boyfriend socks. How smitten is that?"

"He hears no words of passion."

"I called you 'Yaggie'."

"Pha!" He threw one hand up in disgust. "What is 'Yaggie'? Foolish, no passion. Yaggie like name of dog. Also, I say you show me place and walk around."

"I did walk around," I said, panic increasing. "The camera shows rare paintings and sculptures worth thousands. I even asked to see his icon collection. Surely you saw all that?"

"You did not get into rooms."

"I tried."

"Try is not enough. Where is Roman collection, the gold jewelry?"

"How should I know—Having Castle, maybe?"

"Your job to find out. You find out things. Sources say he keeps in London house. Pass over camera."

"Pardon?" I stared at him uncomprehending.

"The necklace—pass over."

I fumbled with the intricate clasp until he shoved my head forward and unfastened it himself. Pulling back, I saw him holding the Faberge pendent before his eyes. "I watch again, but will see nothing new. You failed."

"I didn't fail. I couldn't have. I did everything you asked: got you into the ball, arranged for the blueprints—everything."

"Not everything. I ask for pictures inside house; I ask you act like girlfriend. You do not behave like girlfriend, you do not give pictures of house." He flipped open the laptop sitting on his thighs and turned the screen to face me.

I swallowed hard. "No, please, no."

Rena was sitting wrapped in a blanket on a steel chair inside her concrete cube. I searched frantically for details of her cage but saw nothing.

"Please don't hurt her."

"You fail, Rena suffers." He spoke into his phone. A man strode into the room, Parka Boy from the garage. Rena turned as he entered, and was just about to rise, when he shoved her back down and slapped her hard across the face.

"No!" I cried.

The man wrenched the blanket from Rena's shoulders and struck her again, knocking her sideways off the chair.

I screamed. "Stop it! Tell him to stop! I'll do anything you say! I'll try harder! Please!"

Arkhangelsky barked an order into his phone and the man backed away, leaving Rena climbing to her feet, spewing a stream of Italian. Rena wouldn't beg. She'd never beg, unless it was to protect another. She'd never fail, either. Whether her shivering was in outrage or pain or fear, I couldn't tell, but I trembled in rage. And guilt.

"Let me speak to her, just one word," I cried.

Arkhangelsky slammed the screen closed. "No. Tomorrow you film Fox collections or Rena suffers more."

"You're such a bastard," I said. "The only passion you provoke is hate."

He grabbed my coat collar and yanked me closer.

"Go on, hit me," I said. "That's who you really are, isn't it, Arkhangelsky—a slimy little devil in fine tailoring? You're nothing more than a vicious street-scrapper with deep pockets. Does anybody love you for real, or do you have to pay for all of it?"

I expected another blow, maybe even wanted it in guilt over Rena's suffering, but he only clenched his jaw and flung me back against the door. I knew my words struck close to the bone. I just hoped they drew blood. Moments later, we were outside Baker & Mermaid.

"Tomorrow same time. Do not fail again. Next time my man enjoys more."

I bolted from the car, shoving past the driver and heading for the door. I thought of all the times Rena had waited for me there, ready to comfort, to make me laugh, to share her day with mine. Not this time, maybe never again. God, no! I couldn't let the last time be the last time. I had to do better. I had to get Rena back. This was all my fault!

I caught site of the closed sign and stopped. Closed at 4:30, two weeks before Christmas? Unlocking the door, I stepped inside, my heart in my throat. "Max?" I called out.

Jennifer rushed towards me through the darkened gallery. "Max's upstairs, Phoebe. You okay?"

"Forget about me, Jenn, are you all right? Why are you back here so soon?"

"I'm good. Like, nobody's going to knock me off my game, ever. We stick together, right? Look," she shoved back her sleeve to reveal her bandaged arm, "my war wounds. Not cool in short sleeved-shirts, but maybe I'll get tattoos like Tom Ford."

"You're not traumatized?"

"I'm, like, really, really pissed. No one's going to do this shit to me and get away with it."

"Do you mean …?" I was afraid to say more in case we were being monitored. "Why is the shop closed?"

"Max thought it better not to operate shorthanded. My classes don't end until tomorrow, and Rena's—well, anyway, Mr. Arkhangelsky bought up all our best carpets. Economically we're super-fine," she said, gazing at me pointedly.

"Super-fine. Right." She knew everything, including that we weren't super-fine.

"Stock's low, Phoebe," I heard Max say from the top of the stairs. "We'll just operate half days until the new orders arrive. Maybe I'll even shut her down until after the holidays. No worries, the coffers are full. Come upstairs. We've got the kettle on to boil."

I followed him up, Jennifer dashing up ahead. The only kettle we owned upstairs was in my apartment, and Max never entered my private space without an invitation. Something was way up.

Reaching the top, I turned towards Max's office. A little man sat with his head down over our security equipment. He nodded to me, and I recognized the same guy who'd sold me the burner phone months ago—one of Max's old associates, Ivan somebody. He'd be Ivan the Helpful, in my books forever more. I waved and he waved back.

"Come on, Phoebe," Max urged.

Inside my flat, I sensed that the atmosphere had shifted, but didn't know how. Every object appeared to be exactly where I'd left it, and yet …

Max stood studying me. "Where's that lovely present Yagar gave you?"

"Um, he took it back temporarily," I said, scanning my apartment.

"And your phones?"

"He returned them. That's why I texted you from Foxy's house." I rarely referred to Rupert as "Foxy" unless furious with him, which I wasn't. "Sloane cleaned my bag after I dropped it on the step."

Max relaxed as if air had been let out of him.

"Tea or coffee, Phoebe?" Jennifer called from my kitchen.

"Tea, please. Herbal."

"Chamomile okay?"

"That's fine," I called back. I didn't care that someone else was in charge of the domestic operations in my kitchen. "What's going on?"

"Ivan's swept the apartment and found two cameras and four microphones," Max said. "Crafty little bugger's rigged it up so that dummy footage plays through the camera feed, both up here and in the gallery. Ditto for the audio. If Arkhangelsky's paying attention, he might notice, but I'm betting he's focused elsewhere. He only needed to monitor us until you agreed to do his bidding. Now that he's got a hostage, he thinks he's got us where he wants. How's Rena, do you know?"

I slumped into a chair. "Not good. He's set me up to fail no matter what I do. Every time I fulfill a demand, he comes up with something more impossible. Today he let me see Rena on his laptop." I pressed a hand to my mouth, forcing back tears. "He's got her in some concrete box of a room, and had his goon hit her because I didn't bring back footage of all of Rupert's collections. How am I supposed to walk through every room in Rupert's house without him noticing? Tomorrow, it'll be something different, and Rena will suffer again. It's like I'm cornered—damned if I do, damned if I don't. It's all my fault."

"It's not all your fault. Why do you think that?"

"Because if I'd played his girlfriend properly from the beginning, he'd never have taken Rena, but I didn't try hard enough—too much pride, or anger, or something. Not enough smarts."

"Oh, come on, Phoebe, darlin'. You're not to blame because some criminal dropkick got it into his skull to hold Serena hostage and try to rob another weasel. That's on him, not you."

"I can't help it. Maybe if I played him more, Rena wouldn't be tied up and knocked around. He got one of his bullyboys to hit her, Max, hard." Hell, I just wanted to howl.

"Bastard's like the devil incarnate," Max said along with calling him other things a whole lot worse.

"Anyway, I have a plan—a long shot, but a shot. Did you arrange for us all to meet at your house?"

"Not my house, in case he's watching or he's bugged me, too. I've asked everyone to gather at 9:00 tonight. The location has been texted to everybody on the guest list."

"Jennifer knows, doesn't she?"

"She does, and so does Marco, and everybody who can help. We need all the help we can get, darlin'."

"Tea's served," I heard a voice call.

Turning, I expected Jennifer to come bearing the tray and mugs, but it was Brenda Higgins. "Surprised?" she asked as she set the tray down with a rattle.

"Well, yes," I said.

"What, didn't know I serve tea as well as teach self-defense to rug salespeople who get themselves in a boatload of trouble? That's me." She set the tray down with a clank. "Drink up, McCabe. Baker only told me half the story but I expect you to spill the rest."

* * *

Max chose the private function room of a tiny pub off a pedestrian-only lane near Neal's Yard. The moment I stepped into the Keyhole's narrow space, I knew it was perfect. The proprietor, another one of Max's old colleagues, was outwardly jolly, but looked as though he could crack a skull open in a millisecond. Visitors had to go past his muscled person to reach the narrow stairs leading up to our room, and nobody could park anywhere near. We were in a mini-fortress with our own private bouncer.

We all arrived about the same time, filing wearily upstairs. A motley crew—Max, Jennifer, Brenda Higgins, Marco, and Jake, Baker & Mermaid's van driver and delivery person—each sitting at a large round table gazing grimly at me. Nobody had had a decent night's sleep in days.

"We look like a bunch of rejects from a zombie apocalypse movie," Jennifer said as she sipped a glass of ginger ale.

"Just get my mother back safely and I promise not to look as though I could eat somebody for lunch," Marco said to me. The toque he wore to mask the sideburns and Regency coif did little to hide his arresting face.

Max thumped his palm on the table. "Let's get to work. Each of you will have a

184

role to play in what's to come, so listen up. It'll be a tricky op but I think we can pull it off."

I got to my feet. "Arkhangelsky has Rena held at some unknown place and intends to keep her hostage until after the ball."

"Is he really going to let her go if you do what he says?" Marco asked.

"Probably not. Keeping up appearances is all the collateral we have. We have to outsmart him," I said.

"How?" he asked.

I dreaded that question. "I have an idea."

"Great, so let's hear it." Marco leaned forward. All eyes were on me.

"Phoebe's going to find out where Rena's hidden and we're going to bust her out," Max added, climbing to his feet.

"Right, but using subterfuge."

"I know how these bastards work, Phoebe," Max said. "They understand force, so we'll force them."

"We don't know where he's holding her," I pointed out.

"So, you find out, then we launch a SWAT rescue," he said.

I stared at him, forcing him to meet my eyes. "We agreed that we need to outsmart the bastard."

"For once, she's talking sense," Brenda said, also leaping to her feet. "If you're going to launch some bumbling operative with your crime-gang friends, Baker, you may as well call in the police and do it properly. Use a trained SWAT team."

"What do you mean 'bumbling operatives'? My former colleagues are professionals," Max said, glowering down at her. "A couple of them have pulled off some pretty impressive ops in their time."

Brenda took a step towards him, hands on hips. "Like what, bank robberies?"

"Don't insult me, Ms. Ex-copper. I—"

"Stop both of you." I held up my hand. "Max sit down," I pointed to the chair. "You, too, Higgins. We don't have time for this. We have a ball to prepare for."

"What?" They all turned to me.

"We're talking about my mother's life and you're talking about a bloody ball?" Marco said.

"I am because that ball is key to your mother staying alive. I have an idea."

"I can't wait to hear your ideas," Higgins said. "but an idea isn't a plan, McCabe."

"The plan is a work in progress and I'll explain why."

"Comforting. Just remember that statistics aren't high for kidnapping victims to emerge alive," she said.

"I know that, too," I countered, shooting a quick glance at Marco, who stared grimly ahead. "Now, sit down and listen. As long as I play Arkhangelsky's game, Rena stays alive. I have to keep playing while finding out more information from both sides. Meanwhile, Sir Rupert knows something's up and he'll be doing his usual machinations in the background."

"How do you know Foxy's onto you?" Max asked, taking his seat, Brenda following.

"Because he knows me, and because I dropped so many hints, I probably cracked his marble floor."

"Arkhangelsky listened in on all your conversations, so how the hell could you drop hints without him cluing in? Yagar's no fool," Max pointed out.

"Neither is Rupert," I said. "Neither am I, for that matter. I used things like changing up my tea order and asked him to teach me how to knit socks. He knows I abhor sock knitting. And tea is a ritual for Rupert. Believe me, he noticed the change, yet didn't remark on it. Rupert remarks on everything. He's a detail person. Besides," I continued, "he knows I'd never fall for a lug like Arkhangelsky, even if I weren't already in love with another. And Arkhangelsky's such an egomaniac, he can't imagine some financially challenged female not seeing him as a prize worthy of any sacrifice."

"Is Yagar onto Foxy's suspicions, then?" Max asked.

"I don't think so," I said, "though he's afraid my lack of passion might give it away. But Foxy knows something's going on, like I said. Rupert even swapped out my cell phones. Evan, his high-tech former spy maestro, only had to give them the once-over to know Arkhangelsky's tampered with them. I tell you, Rupert knows I'm being strong-armed into getting Arkhangelsky to the ball, but he doesn't know what that bastard's got on me."

"Then he probably knows that Yagar's got something up his sleeve," Max said.

"Oh, yes, Rupert probably suspected something from the start," I said. "Those two are rival collectors, and I gather Rupert's bested Arkhangelsky more than once at auctions. He might think the Russian's after his icon collection, but he's really after everything he's got."

"How much is everything?" Higgins asked.

No way was I telling her how Rupert came by some of his magnificent collections. Besides, technically I didn't know. "Sir Rupert Fox has inherited a historical home, Having Castle, with some of the pieces kept as part of the estate for centuries. I'm talking important art and sculptures, not to mention the prize pieces Rupert has acquired as an antiques dealer. It's a significant collection, probably multiple collections."

"So this oligarch of yours is planning a heist to steal some of his goods?" she asked.

"All of it, or as much as he can," I said. "He's planning to pull it off during the ball, when Rupert presumably is busy with hundreds of guests in full regalia. It's a costume ball, Higgins. That's part of the challenge. We have to attend the ball while enacting our own counterplan and playing dress-up besides—we being me, Max, Jennifer, and Marco. You're not invited, I'm afraid. You, either, Jake."

"I'm broken-hearted." Brenda turned to Jake. "How about you, lad?"

"I'm just trying to figure out what role I'm supposed to play in this caper," he said. "I'm just a lowly serf."

"Driver," I told him. "If we're going to transport four people in full costume to a ball an hour's drive from here, we need transportation. Oh, and a guard." I looked pointedly at Higgins, then Jake. "Are you two in?"

"Sure," Jake shrugged. "Sounds like a good night out, even if it does mean I miss me football reruns."

"So, we're really going to this ball?" Jennifer asked before Higgins could reply.

"Yes, we really are, but not quite under the delightful circumstances you originally dreamed of," I said. "You'll all need to look as though we're merry party guests totally unaware that anything's going down."

"We'll be the best-dressed operatives there," Jennifer said, turning to Marco.

"We still need men who know their way around a situation," Max insisted.

"Like the police," Higgins said.

"No police, not yet, anyway," I repeated, "and no hired guns, either. Besides, neither have been invited, remember? We're the ones in the position to infiltrate the ball."

Marco slammed his palm of the table so hard the glasses clinked. "My mother's life's at stake here! We've got to do whatever it takes to bring her home safely." He turned to me. "What is this plan of yours, Phoebe?"

Damn. Here we go again. "Well, that's the problem," I said, getting to my feet. "We need more information before we can construct a detailed plan, and it's going to be doubly complicated from the start. Rupert is a master of playing underhanded games, even at the best of times. So, if he's doing his machinations while we're carrying out our plan, all without being able to speak openly with one another, well, you can guess the complications."

"Are you saying you don't even have a bloody plan?" Marco said, staring at me aghast.

I leaned over the table, fixing him in my gaze. "*Yet*, I said. I'm saying I need to get more information. I have to figure out what Rupert's got up his sleeve, while simultaneously learning the details of this Arkhangelsky heist, plus where Rena's being held. How am I supposed to do that, you ask? By being more underhanded than the master crook, by winning the Russian's trust, and doing it all while communicating in tongues to Rupert. Does it sound impossible? It isn't, it can't be, because we've got to win this game. We've got to be smarter than Arkhangelsky, and we've got to work together to bring your mom home safe, and send the oligarch to prison. It all starts with the ball. You'll need costumes adapted after famous portraits, that includes Jennifer, Marco, and Max. Arkhangelsky is going as Ivan the Terrible and I'm to be his first wife. So, we start there."

"I can help with the costumes," Jennifer piped up. "The studios are all empty after tomorrow for the hols. I can whip up something for me, and Marco, at least. I've got a few ideas."

"And what about my mom?" Marco demanded, eyes still fixed on me. "What's she going to be doing while we're getting ready for a merry ball?"

I swallowed hard. "Waiting for us to break her out, which we will."

"How? When?"

I kept my eyes on him. "On the night of the ball, Arkhangelsky will need to pull most of his goons away from guard duty in order to pull off his heist. By then, I'll know where she's at. Arkhangelsky will have a skeleton crew guarding Serena, maybe even just one guy. That's when we'll break your mom out."

"How exactly?" he asked.

"I haven't worked out the details yet. First, I need to find out just where she's being held. Don't worry." God, I can't believe I said that. *Don't worry?*

"And in the meantime is my mom supposed to just stay in the hands of these brutes? What if they hurt her?" he asked.

"She'll be fine as long as I behave myself." And I prayed that was true. I'd do anything to keep her from being brutalized one more time. I just had to get better at appeasing the beast. "Are you all on board so far?"

Everybody nodded. "So far," Higgins replied, "but let's see how well this information reconnaissance goes. You've got a non-plan consisting of nothing but maybes, McCabe."

"When we meet next, I'll have more details. Just hold tight until then," I said.

Everybody got to their feet, muttering but nodding their assent. Marco held back.

"Marco, I'm sorry I can't give you more assurances—" I began.

"I don't need your bloody assurances— they're worthless under the circumstances." He gripped my shoulders. "I need you to promise me you'll do anything it takes to keep mom safe, anything."

I nodded. "I will do anything."

"You have to act, Phoebe. Dig deep, understand me? Make it real. Tap into something true and give it all you have. Promise me."

"I promise," I said, gazing up at him.

"Good." And he released me, nodded to Jennifer, and headed downstairs.

I turned to Max. "What have I done?"

He gave me a smile of encouragement. "Nothing compared to what you've yet to do, darlin'. You up for this?"

"Yes and no. That's the truest answer I have."

He, at least, could see the terror below my bravado, "I believe my idea of knocking their lights out is more direct, but what do I know?" He shrugged. "This one's on you, kid. Now how in hell are you going to get the details of both Foxy's and Yagar's plans?"

I sighed. "I'll start by presenting something credible while lying through my teeth."

18

The next morning, I stared through the glass door onto the street waiting for Arkhangelsky, asking myself what would a man like him believe of a woman like me. As much of an egomaniac as Arkhangelsky was, he wouldn't buy a sudden transformation from the woman he thought he knew into someone else entirely. On the other hand, he didn't really know me. That gave me a little wiggle room in the deception department. He knew I was a business woman. That was where I'd start.

Still, some things I could never pull off. I couldn't play a sugar daddy hunter, for instance. My mother used to call them "gold-diggers", though I figured those women were only acting on an age-old instinct to partner with the dominant male. I got that, understood the need to survive any way possible, only that wasn't me, either. That was Maggie's territory. Thoughts of my pseudo-aunt made we wince.

Maybe it wasn't so much about thinking outside the box as imagining how to think *inside* another.

"Are you okay, Phoebe?" Max asked from behind me.

I shook myself from my reverie. "I think so. I'm just trying to prepare myself."

"How are you going to approach this?"

"Trust me, I'm not going to prostitute myself to anyone." I turned to look up at him. "I have another idea. Oh, damn." The black Mercedes pulled up to the curb. "I can't explain now."

"At least give me a hint."

"I'm going to mix in a little truth with a whole lot of deception."

"*What*?"

"I'll explain later. Wish me luck." I scuttled out the door to the waiting car. The driver stood by as I slid into the back seat beside Arkhangelsky.

"Morning," I said to Yagar. Maybe it was my imagination, but he seemed to be sagging around the shoulders today, his eyes heavily bagged. No sleep for him, either. Had he been anyone else, I would have felt sorry for him.

He glanced at me before staring straight ahead. "Today you do not fail."

"I won't fail," I said. "You want to know why?"

"You do not want more pain for Rena."

"Of course I don't—that's a given—but I won't fail because you're going to give me a big fat incentive."

He turned to me. "You waste time by joking?"

"No joke. See, Max and I have been thinking of just how useful I could be to you, and you to us. You knew that from the beginning, of course, but maybe not to the full extent."

He shrugged. "I listen."

"First, here's what I can do for you: you know that Sir Rupert has vault after vault of rare and priceless artifacts, but you don't know the extent, or have the necessary details—like how his collections are arranged by time period and/or medium, not only in his London house, but in his gallery and Having Castle, too."

"So?"

"So, you don't know the half of it, Yagar—like the collection of priceless Etruscan funerary objects, mostly gold. He trusts me, obviously, and I've been with him on a couple of his acquisition-hunting expeditions. He's told me things he's never told anyone else, because he thinks I'm naive and easily used. I give off that impression for a reason. You fell for it, didn't you?"

He smiled then, though this version seemed more predatory. "You say you are smart woman, yet nothing I see so far is smart."

I shrugged. "I've been playing you. I know you're not planning to let Rena go. I figured that out long ago." I counted the silence in seconds before continuing. "Because of that, among other things, I had no intention of following through for you, either. I intended to shaft you."

The mud-brown eyes widened then quickly narrowed. "Shaft how?"

"By helping you rob some of Fox's stash, but not everything; by blocking every move you made with more of my own; and by telling you half-truths at every opportunity. Like I've been doing up until now."

"I don't believe."

"Well, believe this: the best incentive to make someone like me do what someone like you wants isn't to take something away, but to give her something more valuable in return, and I don't mean marriage."

He laughed then, shooting Russian orders to his driver, who suddenly took a hard right and darted down a side street. *Oh, God, he's going to bump me off!* "What I give is your life," he said.

I kept an eye on the passing scenery. Was it my imagination or were we heading towards the Thames? "And what do you think you'll get in return if you bump me off? Not what you want. I can get you a fortune in art and rare collectibles, more than you can imagine. Foxy's got a Hermitage worth of loot in his vaults. I can help you access it all, but for a price," I said.

"Your price is Rena lives, maybe you, too."

"But you're not planning to let Rena live, so stop lying. I'm not stupid. How shortsighted are you? Give Max and me fifty percent of the cut and you'll buy our complete and utter cooperation, plus a whole lot more. Max wants to run the London operation, while I want to be the one who helps you identify and acquire rare objects worldwide." I may as well be bungee-jumping minus the rope. It was as if I stared down into a dizzying void knowing I could break my back at any moment. "Turkey's prime picking right now. The government is preoccupied with Syria and the ISIS crises.

We could go in and pick her bones clean. I have contacts."

Yagar barked an order and the car squealed to the curb. We were on a narrow street lined with apartment buildings. "Fifty percent? This crazy!" He turned to me, one arm sliding over the back of the seat, the other shaking a finger at me.

"Forty-five percent then. How much is world domination of the art and artifacts trade worth to you?"

"You say no before."

"I said no to marriage and servitude, and still do. Unless you turn out to be a helluva lot more lovable than you are now, marriage isn't part of the deal," I said. "What do you really want, Yagar Arkhangelsky—another girl to push around and cower before you? I'll give you something much more interesting—a real partner who can help you reach your business goals, somebody with stuffing instead of some half-baked piece of arm candy. If love grows along the way, so be it. But you will never hit me again, and you won't hurt my friends, either. You'll release Rena, and I'll bring her into the business. She'll do anything for me. If you do what I ask and give me forty-five percent of the Fox cut, you'll get what you want and more. That's the deal." *I was going to die, die!*

He laughed again, only there was real excitement percolating there. "You are in no position to bargain, Phoebe."

"Yes, I am. It's the old 'lead a horse to water' thing. You can make me do some things, but not others. You can't get me to work hard by force. That's just good psychology. If you push me, I can make things very hard for you. You know I can. I already have."

He stared at me. I could sense his thoughts punching the air around us. "Ten percent," he said finally.

I leaned towards him and straightened his tie. "Thirty. Who dresses you in the mornings, Yagar? An important man like you has to look the part."

He slapped a hand on my wrist, not hard but firm. "Fifteen percent."

"Twenty-five. I've got to pay my staff and buy off a few people, remember," I said, watching as he flipped my hand over to study my palm.

"Twenty." He began to massage my palm. "You have star in palm, star of fortune." I don't know what he saw there but my guess is it had more to do with filthy lucre than constellations.

I smiled. "Twenty it is. By the way, I want all Foxy's Pre-Raphaelite paintings. Oh, and the yarn."

"Yarn? You wish to steal yarn?"

"Sure, why not?I like yarn and he has lots, far more than I do."

He smiled, tightening his hand over mine. "If this is truth, today you steal for me, something I want—an icon. Make me believe."

19

I bolted from the car and hurried through the gate towards Rupert's mansion. Today that enormous wreath on the door reminded me of a bullseye with me hurling towards the target. How could I steal from a man who fortified his houses with every electronic gizmo imaginable, and some as yet unknown? Memories of the Orvieto hideaway drilled holes into my brain—the hidden cameras, the discrete alarms, the explosives. If I touched anything in his unhumble abode, I'd probably detonate on the spot.

The door swung open before my finger hit the doorbell.

"Good afternoon, Ms. Phoebe," Sloane greeted. "Sir Rupert has disengaged the bell until such time as the chords have been properly adjusted. It has been rather discordant of late. Please do come in. May I take your coat?"

I allowed him to take my coat so that I stood in the hall in my favorite and most fulsome green cowl, one which fell so far over my shoulders that it could easily conceal some small pilfered object. Arkhangelsky had agreed to forgo a little camera footage from the necklace to facilitate the theft. We were now getting along splendidly.

"Are you quite all right, Madam?" Sloane inquired.

I turned. "Why yes, Sloane. Why do you ask?"

"It is just that you seem a bit peaked today."

"I'm fine."

"Most happy to hear it. May I take your wrap? I'm afraid you will find it frightfully warm."

"No, thanks. I do feel a bit chilly so I'll keep wearing it, thanks."

"Very well then, please follow me. Sir Rupert requested that I show you to the library, where he will join you shortly. I have already provided tea. May I pour it for you?"

"No, thanks. I'll just help myself."

I trailed after Sloane into the library, taking a seat by the fire as the door clicked shut behind him. Immediately, I dropped my carpet bag onto the floor and stood up, taking a quick reconnaissance around the magnificent room with its tall, sweeping bookcases. Besides the occasional first edition and small collectibles like pens and paperweights, this was not the place to find icons.

I hesitated before a first edition of Tolstoy which looked to be in Russian, but I knew only an icon would prove my allegiance, something, in fact, that Rupert would secure under lock and artillery upstairs.

Rupert entered just as I was about to lift *War and Peace* from it's cabinet for closer inspection.

"We use the gloves provided before touching aged leather bindings, Phoebe."

I hadn't noticed the white gloves folded neatly beside the case. I withdrew my hands. "Oh, sorry. I only wanted to check if that was a first edition, but of course it is."

"Indeed it is."

"So," I said, turning towards my host, resplendent today in a burgundy velvet smoking jacket with charcoal satin trousers, causing me to feel mangy in my highly textured wrap. "Thanks for offering to help me with the sock knitting today, Rupert. I so appreciate it. I mean, you must have so much to do with the ball coming up and everything."

"In truth, I did not offer to assist you, so much as you had asked for my assistance, and, really, how can I refuse you anything? The timing is a trifle inconvenient, I admit, and occasionally I must excuse myself to attend to one matter or another, but otherwise, I am at your disposal. At any other time I would leap for the opportunity to introduce you to sock knitting, which must surely be the pinnacle of the knitter's art. Fortunately, I do have staff attending to most of the ball details, and I need only to orchestrate the particulars where necessary."

"In other words, you found the time. Thanks again."

"Indeed, shall we begin? Tea, Phoebe?"

"Yes, please, Rupert."

"Sugar with milk?"

"Three spoonfuls with just a drop of milk."

We took our seats beside the fire and I
studied Rupert as he attended the tea
ministrations. He performed every move with
his usual careful deliberation, pouring the
tea into the delicate china cups, stirring
with the tiny silver spoons without so much
as a clink of metal on porcelain. If he
sensed something amiss, he hid it well.

My gaze slipped from the cup he offered
to the knitting project folded on the chair
arm beside him. It blended so well with the
dark background of the crewel-work
upholstery, I hadn't noticed it earlier. I
blinked and took my first sip. The sock was
already half-complete, with only a few more
inches left before launching the heel. My
eyes met Rupert's over our respective cups.

"I made good progress yesterday on my
sock and hope to do at least as well today,"
I said.

"I trust you will," he replied. "You
are mastering the technique admirably. Do
continue, and while you are about it, pray
tell me what costumes your friends have
chosen for the ball." He picked up his own
project, which appeared to be one of his
gorgeous linen stitch scarves.

My fingers stopped mid-row. "I'm sorry,
Rupert, but they're still deciding. Jennifer
is only just finishing the term, but plans
to get working on hers and Marco's today."

"I really must know now—yesterday, in
point of fact. Whilst you dally, time goes
rushing by."

"I'll email their portrait selections
today, I promise. As for Max, how about you
prepare his costume, as you so kindly
offered? Max isn't good at that sort of

thing, and I'm afraid he'll only throw something together at the last moment."

"I have just the portrait in mind for him, quite perfect, in fact. Let it be a surprise. Your party can use one of my designated dressing rooms I'm making available at Having upon the night of the event."

"He'll be thrilled." Actually, he'd be quite the opposite.

"And Serena?"

"Serena will not be able to make it to the ball," I said, keeping my eyes on my knitting.

"Why ever not?"

"I'm sorry to say she's all tied up."

"Tied up right up until the ball?"

"I'm afraid so. Parties, lunches, her whole Italian family threatening to arrive right on the day of the ball. She says she'll be cooking nonstop for the next week, but sends her regrets."

"What a great shame," he said.

"Yes, isn't it?" I said as breezily as possible. "Anyway—"

At that moment, in came Sloane bearing a tray of the usual finger sandwiches and tasty morsels. My mouth watered as the butler lowered the tray to the table, removed our empty cups, and dashed away while notifying us of his intent to freshen the tea.

"Would you excuse me for a moment, Phoebe?" Rupert asked, standing up.

"Certainly, and if it's all right, I need to use the facilities," I said, rising also. I reached down to slip my cell phone from my bag to my sleeve.

"But of course. Down the hall, third door to the left."

I allowed him to escort me to the washroom, slipped in, and shut the door. I counted 15 seconds before I poked my head out. Finding the hall empty, I bolted for the grand staircase. Exquisite vases and statues flew by, some seeming to watch me in disapproval.

Soon I found myself standing in the long tiled hall stretching in either direction—empty, yet strangely unnerving. One end, the one Rupert had taken me through the day before, was well-lit. I thought I heard voices coming from a room on that end, so I swung around in the opposite direction towards the darker half of the long corridor.

What would I say if someone found me up here? That I was looking for someone, Rupert perhaps? I carried onward in my stockinged feet, trying doors as I went. Most were locked, but as soon as I found one that wasn't, I slipped inside. I expelled my breath and blinked. I was in a room filled with statuary. The light washing through the sheer curtains sent the ancient figures into silhouette. Twisting figures drew bows, wrestled, or stood frozen in time. Roman, maybe Greek—I couldn't risk turning on the light to find out. I had to find those icons before Rupert noticed my absence.

Moments later, I was tiptoeing down the hall again. Every door was locked. And yet, I sensed movement ahead. I paused, listening. Definite clicking sounds like a lock being turned somewhere, yet no lights. A shiver hit my spine. Why would anyone in Rupert's household sneak around in the dark, besides me, of course? I carried on, trying the knobs. Finally, one turned in my hand. I bolted inside, my heart pounding. This one looked much more promising. A smaller room, I could make out the shapes of little objects on the walls. Paintings? I fumbled for the light switch.

All four walls bore a cluster of artfully arranged icons hung against white walls among old sepia-tinted photos and paintings. Some icons were gilded and gleamed in the halogen glow, while others hung dark and worn, their painted surfaces rubbed by hundreds of years of prayer and tears. Some were tiny playing-card-sized pictures of the Madonna and Christ in the Byzantine style, while others were shaped like small books and as richly ornate as illuminated manuscripts. Still others appeared to be painted upon irregular scraps of old wood, like pieces of doors or signage. Whether they were all Russian, I didn't know, but it didn't take an expert to recognize their value. And how fortuitous that the only unlocked room on this section held icons. Too fortuitous.

I scanned for hidden cameras, seeing nothing obvious. I didn't care if this room seemed mysteriously available to my scrutiny. I needed to choose a prize and get back downstairs pronto. But which one? I tried a tiny icon on the nearest wall—a gilded Byzantine piece—and found it firmly fixed. Nails, maybe? I guessed that Sir Rupert Fox didn't do nails, but how he affixed his treasures to the walls was beyond me. I traveled around the room, testing each icon, finding each equally secured. Well, damn.

Then my gaze fell on an old photograph of Anastasia Romanov, daughter of Czar Nicholas the Second. She hung in the midst of a gathering of the larger icons, looking beautiful, lost, and doomed. My heart always lurched when I saw her photo. Maybe she had been the original owner of my necklace. I followed her gaze to the opposite wall, where a collection of ten small icons was arranged in an oblong shape. Desperate as I was, I took the photo to be a sign, and tentatively touched one. It shifted slightly at my touch. With excruciating care, I lifted this tiny painting of the Madonna and Christ from its bracket. Though not Catholic, stealing a religious icon hit me as a travesty. I imagined a wail of *Hail Mary's* in the background as I tucked the credit-card sized piece of brass-sheeted wood under my cowl and inside my bra.

No screeching alarms, no cries of *Thief! Thief!* I took a deep breath, turned off the light, and slipped out the door, banging right into the standing form of Mrs. Montgomery.

"Oh," I said. "I was just looking for Sir Rupert."

She smiled. "He is upstairs in the office."

"Is he?"

"He is," she said, her eyes studying me intently. "The third floor, in fact."

We stared at one another for mere seconds before she excused herself and relocked the door. "Sir Rupert prefers to keep all the doors locked in this wing."

And yet this one had been opened. For me. *She had to be a mole working for Arkhangelsky!*

"Well, I'll just head up to see him, shall I?" I said.

"Most certainly." And with that, she turned and hurried away down the corridor towards the stairs, leaving me to proceed to Rupert on my own. I spied a door ajar at the top of the stairs and dove inside to what turned out to be a washroom. In seconds, I was readjusting the icon more snugly into my bra.

I also slipped out my phone to check for messages. Skimming all until landing on one from Jennifer:

I think I have Marco and my portraits picked out. I'm going as Cecilia Gallerani and Marco's going as Ludovico Maria Sforza, Duke of Milan, when he was young and handsome, of course. She was his mistress so we'll be a couple. I'm sending pics to you from my phone. Will get larger ones 4 u ASAP. Super perfect! Still working on one 4 u. XXX J

I was just about to replace my phone in my bag when something on the screen caught my eye. I studied it intently, scanning app after app. What was different this time? I'd known from the start that Rupert had swapped this phone with my original, probably to deactivate any surveillance devices Arkhangelsky had installed, and to apply his own. I didn't care if Rupert listened in to everything I said. In fact, I hoped he did, under the circumstances. Otherwise, I hadn't given the phone much thought until now. There it was, a new app shaped like a red eye, but I still didn't have time to investigate further. I shoved the phone into my shirt pocket and stepped into the hall, back to the staircase, and up to the next level.

Another long hall, not as grand as the first two, and with wooden floors instead of marble. This floor seemed more lived-in, cozier. A Christmas tree sat twinkling at the opposite end and someone was playing a symphonic version of *Swan Lake* very loudly. I took off down the hall calling for Rupert, thinking that the only justification for me being on that floor was to be looking for him.

I only got halfway before somebody tackled me from behind.

20

I landed heavily on my front, and felt the icon dislodge from my bra at the same time as the phone slid to the floor. Thank God for cowls. "Get off me!" I said, bucking the weight pressing down on my back. He shifted slightly, allowing me to flip onto my back while he still straddled me. That left me staring up into Evan's face with his body pressing down on mine. "Do you mind?" I said, watching the pulse on his temple. The man had a great Adam's apple, too.

"My apologies, I thought you might be an intruder, Madam."

"Really?" He'd probably frisk me if he could, and I probably wouldn't mind, under different circumstances. "I said, get off me."

"Evan, old chap, whatever is going on?" Rupert's voice sounded overhead.

Evan kept me in an eye lock. "I thought I heard somebody sneaking down the hall, Sir," he said.

"Sneaking?" I put my hand on his chest and pushed him away. The icon slid further

towards my waistband. "How is calling out
for Rupert *sneaking*?"

"Evan, get up immediately," Rupert
ordered.

Evan slowly shifted his weight,
swinging one leg over as if dismounting a
horse, and stood, offering me his hand. But
if I got to my feet at that very moment, the
pilfered icon would clatter to the floor.

I clutched my stomach. "I think I'm
hurt," I said rolling over. "I'd better go
to the washroom."

"Dear, dear, Phoebe, are you all right?
I am deeply distressed, but we do have tight
security here, I'm sure you understand,"
Rupert said while helping me up.

"Sure, sure." I said, gripping my
stomach. Rupert steered me three doors down
to another washroom, where I darted in and
shut the door before he could investigate
for injuries. I leaned there for a few
minutes, waiting for my heart to settle.
Evan had to know I'd hidden something under
my shirt. He could have felt the hard object
under my clothes.

A knock on the door. "Phoebe, are you
all right?" Rupert asked.

"Fine. I'll be out in a minute."

"Very well. We'll be nearby."

I made a show of running the water and
flushing the toilet. By the time I's
resecured the icon and opened the door, the
hall was empty. I wandered back in the
direction I'd come, seeking my host.

Music filled the air, growing louder as
I approached. Finally, I stood in the
doorway of a large studio where a broad
celestial window emitted cool light. A long
table anchored the center, with Rupert and

Evan bent opposite each other studying a map or something. They didn't see me at first.

"Hello," I pitched my voice over the violins.

Rupert shot around. "Phoebe, have you quite recovered?"

"I quite have," I said.

Evan turned down the volume with a remote control. "Madam, please forgive me for the, er, um, incident earlier."

"Forgiven," I said, stepping inside. "What's this?"

Evan slipped smoothly in front of me still holding the remote. "It was really just an error. Oh, and I believe this is your phone."

I took my cell from his proffered hand. "Right." I tried peering over his shoulder. "It's almost time for me to go, and Jennifer messaged me with her and Marco's costume choice, which I thought you'd want to know about ASAP, Rupert." I stepped around Evan, my eyes fixed on the table and on Rupert, who had begun rolling up the paper they had been scrutinizing. "That wouldn't happen to be the blueprint you promised me?"

"No, Phoebe, it is not, but rest assured we have that document at the ready. Evan, old chap?"

"One moment, sir," and the driver-cum-bodyguard-cum-everything quickly strode to another table and returned with a long mailing tube. "The blueprints are within, Madam."

"Oh, wonderful." I tucked the tube under my arm. "And, Rupert, Jennifer said she will arrange for copies of the portraits of Cecilia Gallerani and Ludovico Maria Sforza to be sent to you."

"Jennifer is going as a Da Vinci as in the Lady and the Ermine?" he said, clapping his hands together.

"Apparently. I don't know if she plans on carrying a stuffed ermine around with her but I'm sure she'll make a striking Cecilia."

I glanced at the grandfather clock as it gonged with self-importance. "Time to go. Yaggie will be waiting outside."

"Ah, yes. Yaggie," Rupert sighed.

"Look, Rupert, I know you don't like him, but I so appreciate the effort you're making for me."

"One must keep an open mind concerning any individual, Phoebe."

"And I appreciate that, really. So, is tomorrow at the same time all right for our next sock session?" I asked him.

"Indeed."

"Excellent."

I was politely ushered down the main stairs to the foyer where Sloane stood waiting, holding both my bag and coat. I couldn't believe I'd just stolen something and was about to exit unscathed. It would take a few hours before Rupert realized what I'd done, if he didn't already know.

Moments later, I was outside, breathing deeply the damp air and thinking what a good little bad girl I was. The Mercedes pulled up at the appointed time and I climbed in beside Arkhangelsky.

"Well," I said. "I have a treat for you, two treats for you, actually. First, the blueprint." I passed him the tube.

"Very good." He plucked it from my hand. "You have something special?"

I slipped my hand down into my shirt, pulling out the icon, *voila*-style, and passed it to Arkhangelsky in the palm of my hand.

He took it carefully, stroking it like a small bird before scrutinizing every detail while I held my breath. Another thought hit hard: maybe it was fake. Maybe Rupert through Mrs. Montgomery had planted that particular piece for that reason? Suddenly I couldn't imagine Rupert relinquishing one of his collections for anything or anyone, and if Arkhangelsky recognized it as a forgery …

"Romanov," Arkhangelsky said.

"Pardon?"

"This piece Romanov," he repeated. He turned to me. "How many in collection?"

I calculated. "Twenty, maybe twenty-five."

"I want all."

I took a deep breath. "Sure, we'll work on that. So, why didn't you mention that you had someone on the inside, Mrs. Montgomery?" I think your mole helped me."

He smiled. "She watches you, reports to me. Yagar has eyes everywhere."

"Aren't we on the same side now? I'm keeping up my side of the bargain, now you honor yours."

"Yes. You do well. Tonight, you come to supper and I show you Rena."

★★★

"I just stole one of Rupert's icons," I told Max after we closed the gallery for the evening. We were closing early every day but tomorrow would be the last opening before the holidays.

"Seriously?"

"It's true."

"Fill me in on the details."

I followed him into our back room and slumped down on the table, finally allowing my shoulders to relax. "It went too easily. Rupert handed me the blueprints on a silver platter, and Arkhangelsky's mole steered me to a room so I could steal an icon—I mean a genuine Russian icon."

"Sure that icon's not a repro?"

I waved away the question. "That worried me, too, but Arkhangelsky is an expert, and he declared the piece to be from the Romanov family. He was obviously pleased, says he wants Rupert's whole collection."

"I just bet he does. One's as greedy as the other. And you're sure Foxy knows what's going on?"

"He knows, all right—maybe not the details, but he knows I've been sent in to steal something and, after today, I'm pretty sure he even knows why. I spoke in code."

"Since when did you learn code?" he asked. At 72, he was as robust as ever, but fatigue had grooved deep lines around his eyes and mouth. For the first time, I realized he'd lost weight, too much weight. Rena's vest would hang off him if she ever got to give it to him. I slipped into that line of thinking before I could stop myself.

"Not that kind of code, the code that exists between two people who know each other well. He realizes that Rena is 'all tied up', for instance."

"That's an idiosyncratic phrase that might be taken literally to anyone who doesn't speak English as a first language," he pointed out. "Yagar might clue in."

"Yeah, it was risky, but Yagar didn't flinch. And, Max, I played the line about you and me wanting to go in with him for world domination of the art and antiques trade. I'm stunned at how easy that was—me talking like a big wheeler and dealer, only interested in money and power."

"He didn't come on to you?" He stood suspended before the kettle while it boiled into a shriek.

"No," I said as he finally pulled himself away long enough to pour water into our big brown teapot. "I don't think he sees me that way anymore. I'm not decorative enough."

"Too much trouble, you mean." He smiled grimly as he sat down across from me.

"He doesn't know the half of it," I said.

"Look, the deeper you wade, the stickier it gets." He rubbed his stubbled chin. "I don't like it, I don't like any of it—you doing stuff alone while I twiddle my thumbs."

"Like you said, this one's on me."

"I know, I know, but it still burns my craw. Did you get a glimpse of the blueprints?"

"No time. Rupert practically shoved me out the door."

"How are you going to get information out of Yagar by Saturday night?"

"The ball is really only four days away?" I kept thinking we had more time.

"'Fraid so, darlin'. Will Rena last that long?"

"Don't talk like that. Of course she will. She's tough." I began playing with a piece of string. "Besides, he's happy with me for the moment and promises I'll see her tonight."

"Tonight?"

"I'm going to supper with him."

"No bloody way!"

"Stop it. You know I have to. I'll go as deep into his organization and mind as possible in the time left. I have to know where Rena is."

He grabbed my hand and held it tight. "Watch your step. It's dangerous, he's dangerous. You shouldn't be going in alone."

I squeezed back. "Don't worry about me. Seems I was born under a lucky star. Says so right in my palm, according to Arkhangelsky."

And then my phone buzzed from my pocket. I plucked it out to read the text aloud. "Jennifer says she needs to work tonight on her and Marco's costumes. Wants to know if we need her here for anything?"

"Tell her we're closing the gallery for the holidays, starting tonight. I'm moving it up a day. Make those bloody costumes her priority. What am I going as, anyway?"

I kept my head down while typing my response. "I left that to Rupert. He has a slew of minions working on stuff like that."

"Hell, no."

I looked at him. "Why not? You need a costume and Rupert will arrange one. He said he'd done it before."

"At his fairytale ball. I remember it well. He was pissed at me at the time so I ended up going as Peter Bloody Pan."

I laughed. "Peter Pan?"

"In green tights. Where he found green tights for a six-foot man, I'll never know. Anyway, I'd rather let Jennifer handle it."

I patted his hand. "Jennifer has enough on her plate right now. Besides, Rupert's trying to get back into your good graces, so maybe he'll find you a costume that better preserves your masculine pride."

"Masculine pride be damed. Pompous little guinea fowl Brit."

I leaned towards him. "It's not the guinea fowl Brit we have to worry about but the Russian raptor."

The doorbell rang.

"Who's that this time of day?" Max asked. "Our sign says CLOSED FOR THE HOLIDAYS."

"It's Higgins. I forgot to tell her not to come." I got to my feet. "I'll just go upstairs and let her throw me around for a bit. It's an ideal predate activity."

An hour later, I lay winded on the mat in my living room after attempting to best my instructor a few times. I did manage to block a a lunge or two. "I'm improving," I said, once I finally caught my breath. "But that's enough for now. I have a date with Arkhangelsky."

Brenda stood over me, hands on hips. "You think a few arm blocks and knee jabs make you a good match for the Russian mafia?"

I got to my feet. "Is that what he is?"

"Depends on how you define 'mafia'. I hear this Arkhangel nob runs a complex crime organization in Russia. Fits my description. Anyway, you need the police right now. Either you call them or I will. I've stood by long enough."

"You're not calling anybody until I give the word." I faced her. "You were brought into this operation—"

"More like a fumble and a pitch, if you ask me."

"I'm not asking you, that's the point." I faced her eye-to-eye, hands on hips, too. "If you bring the police in too early, it could ruin everything, and get my friend killed, not to mention me. I know an Interpol agent who gets the complexity of my various, er, relationships. I plan to contact him after I get the necessary details tonight. Don't mess this up, Higgins. I appreciate your help and willingness to lend a hand for the ball, but I have to handle it my way."

She shook her head. "You have guts, I'll say that much for you—no brains, maybe, but guts."

"Thanks, I appreciate the show of confidence. Do you want a sandwich while I make fresh tea? I have until 8 o'clock before the car picks me up and I plan to fortify myself in case we eat late, or not at all." I strolled into the kitchen, determined to get some food into me before I tackled what lay ahead.

Brenda dropped her hands and grinned. "I never turn down a brew or a snack. Are you really going out with this monster, then?"

"Yes, but not as a date." I briefly filled her in on my ploy while I fished out a hunk of Cheshire cheddar and sliced a loaf of bread Max bought me. He's also stocked my fridge with water and chardonnay, not that I had time to savor the latter.

"I don't believe it. I'd never have thought you could pull that off," she said. "Want me to make the brew? I know my way around your digs."

I sliced the bread. "Do you know where I keep the tea?"

"Right over the sink. Must be 20 varieties in here."

"I like options."

"I'm pulling out the pedestrian orange pekoe, saving the 'Jasmine Green Tea Delight' types for another day. Got a problem with that?"

"Nope."

Minutes later we sat opposite one another, eating and sipping, my body feeling oddly refortified.

"So, do you have a real boyfriend?" Brenda asked, while studying me from across the table. With her hair pulled away from her face in that tight ponytail she favored, her blue eyes seemed to pop. For the first time I noticed she wore mascara, which struck me as incongruous with her tough-woman swagger.

"Sort of."

"What does that mean?"

"It means that he doesn't live around here. He's a gypsy traveling all over. Are you attached?"

"Divorced, and my ex is a putz. I'm seeing a bloke, though. I like him well enough. So, what's this sort-of boyfriend of yours like?"

I paused with my sandwich halfway to my mouth. "He's hard to describe," I said, placing the food back on my plate, "but, to summarize: he's intelligent, funny, passionate, strong in all the ways that matter, brave, and sexy as hell. Oh, and he's also really good-looking, if you go for the tall, dark, and swarthy type."

"So why is this paragon only a 'sort of' boyfriend?"

"He's never around, that's the problem—well, one of the problems, anyway."

"Where is he?"

"I have no idea."

"You mean, he doesn't phone or text or something?'

"No. It's complicated."

"Everything is complicated with you—I get that now—but you sound head over heels for this bloke. Does he treat you well?"

I gazed down at the remains of my sandwich, smiling as if I eyed the most delicious edible on earth. "Really well."

"And he's into you, too?"

"I think so. I mean, he must be, seeing as he's risked his neck to save mine on a few occasions. He's there when I need him, providing he finds out in time." He wouldn't this time. No matter how many people surrounded me, I still felt as lonely as hell.

Brenda whistled through her teeth. "Sounds too good to be true."

"I neglected to mention that he's a thief on the run, and once shot a person before my very eyes. That bastard was trying to kill me, so I categorize it as a defensive move." I shrugged. "Anyway, nobody's perfect."

She stared at me. "This guy's a thief and a killer?"

"Don't do the label game, Higgins. Haven't you ever shot somebody in the line of duty?"

"British police aren't as gun-happy as Americans."

"I'm not American, but Canadian police carry firearms, too. Answer the question."

"No, but I kicked the stuffing out of a bloke during a robbery attempt and got demoted for my troubles. Ended up on traffic duty for awhile."

"Ah, so bad tempered, hey?"

"Let's just say I learned from my mistake. Do you have any Marmite around?" She looked over her shoulder at my cupboards as if expecting to see a jar of the yeast spread leap off a shelf.

"Don't change the topic."

"That's the end of the topic. I haven't shot anybody but your paragon boyfriend did."

"You can be a real pain sometimes," I said. "Look, my sort-of boyfriend's not a bad person just because he's done bad things, and neither are you. The world just isn't that black and white. Why all the questions about my love life, anyway?"

"I'm trying to figure out what kind of woman gets into a mess like this, who she hangs with, what she's after."

"I want the same things as most women— love, family, friends, a job worth doing— only the circles I find myself in keep snarling me up in dangerous situations." Talk about understatement. I chewed on my last bite of sandwich.

"It's the company you keep."

"Probably." I checked the time on my phone. "I'd better get dressed. Can I count on you to keep all this quiet?"

"For now."

It bugged me that she wouldn't commit, but I understood. She was still checking me out, still wondering what the hell I'd gotten myself into, and whether I landed on the side of good and legal, or bad and criminal. Fair enough. Some days I didn't know myself.

I left her to make herself another sandwich while I slipped into my room to dress. My look that night had to be sleek and businesslike, which meant my black suit and copper silk blouse with the big patch pockets. Those pockets were critical, since I planned to keep my phone on me at all times—camera, texts, calls for help.

Plucking my phone from the bed, I studied that little eye app again. Why had Rupert installed that, and how did he even manage such a maneuver, considering all apps had to be vetted by Apple? I couldn't worry about the how, so much as the what. That app did something and I needed to know the specifics.

I tapped the icon and peered down as it opened onto the camera screen. The outline of a red eye had been positioned in the center of a gridlike net. When I held the phone eye level, I could see my bedroom through the grid. Every time I moved the phone, the eye icon brightened or darkened, depending on how close I brought it to my face. When positioned directly before my own eye, the red intensified and the icon pulsed. I positioned the phone directly before my right eye, at its brightest point,

and a message appeared: TAKE PICTURE OF
IRIS.

What was Foxy up to? This had to be
some covert weapon of some kind. Hell, like
I had time to figure this out. I pressed the
picture button and the screen pulsed blue.
IRIS IMPRINT SECURED. ALIGN TARGET WITH EYE
AND PRESS BUTTON TO ACTIVATE flashed across
the screen. Target? I dropped the phone on
the bed and backed away. Was it a bomb? Had
Foxy really installed a *bomb* on my phone?
Wait, it couldn't be a bomb. There was no
countdown feature or anything indicating an
imminent explosion. I relaxed a little, but
only a little, and dropped the phone back
into my pocket.

No time left for further study, anyway.
Only ten minutes before Arkhangelsky picked
me up. All I could do is pray I could figure
that thing out before I really needed it.

21

Arkhangelsky was in a congenial mood that evening. I sat back in my seat, crossed my legs, and played it cool. "Max and I are both excited about our new partnership," I said.

"For now, good. I check video again and have questions."

"Fire away." Poor choice of words, under the circumstances.

"Colors of walls. I see white, only white."

I studied him in the sweeps of street light illuminating the back seat. Was this a trick? "Do you mean in Rupert's house?"

"Yes, Rupert's house."

"Ah, yes, the walls are mostly white," I said slowly. "He keeps them neutral to better show off his art. I hope to get more footage tomorrow."

"Interesting," he said. "I see fresh flowers, many flowers."

"Rupert adores fresh flowers. They're everywhere in his houses and gallery. He has a florist deliver them weekly. Where are we going?" We seemed to be following signs to the M25.

"To supper."

"At the Goring?"

"Not Goring."

"At a restaurant?" I looked behind me, not recognizing the road.

"Not restaurant."

He's going to knock me off!

"We go to new house." He was smiling.

"New house?"

"I bought house. Sit back, I show. We know each other better for long ride now. I begin." And, as the car turned onto a motorway, he began telling me about his childhood in Russia, how he grew up poor, dressed in hand-me-downs, struggling to find enough to eat.

"We didn't have much money, either," I told him, as the road stretched into miles of roadway, "but we always had food on the table."

"For us, never fresh, everything rotted. Do you know eating rotted food, Phoebe?"

"No. We didn't have much but it was always edible."

"Edible!" He slapped his hand on the seat and laughed. "You would not eat what we ate, Phoebe. Cabbage only thing green. Sometimes meat, but not often. We line up for rations, but never enough. Always end of line."

Sympathy for the devil? Nothing excused his actions. "What did your parents' do?" I asked.

"My father worked in factory until hurt leg, then no more work. My mother died when I was boy."

"Did you have brothers and sisters?"

"One brother. He is twin, works for me in Russia." Hell, there were two of them? "We both said never live poor again. We saw rich people, very rich people, even in Soviet Russia. We say: 'Why do some eat, stay warm, have nice clothes, but others starve, dress in rags? The world is for strong men, Phoebe. Weak men fail." He turned to stare out the window. "Today we are strong. We win."

His driver said something and Arkhangelsky turned to me. "Time for blindfold."

"Blindfold? But I—"

"You wear blindfold. Bend head."

I did as he demanded in case resistance infuriated him. Above all, I had to keep him in a good mood, find where he held Rena, and discover his heist plans. Even when he tied that thick black cloth around my eyes and tugged it tight, I didn't utter a complaint, at least not right away.

"I untie when we arrive. Still many minutes."

"Aren't we on the same side?"

"After theft, I show all."

Because by then I'd be culpable, too, meaning all his secrets would be safe. If I failed, if we failed, would I be doomed to play handmaiden to this brute forever?

"Tell me about brother," Arkhangelsky said.

"My brother?" I asked touching the binding. I couldn't even see the headlights from the oncoming traffic. I hated this.

"Your brother. He is thief, yes? Talented forger?"

So, he did his homework. "Toby is an artist. Forgery was a mistake, something he began after a love affair went south. Now he's on the run. Why do you ask?"

"My brother also forger, also thief."

So they were kindred spirits now? "How nice."

"Your brother joins my business."

"Toby's on the run. I doubt he's in the position to join anybody's business."

"I protect. Your brother safe with Yagar Arkhangelsky. We talk later. Now we go."

I held my breath as the car turned. We were driving more slowly now, as if on a back road or lane. The car eased along, stopping, slowing, then picking up speed. Yagar and the driver spoke Russian while I strained to understand, but it was useless. Unlike French or Italian, nothing sounded familiar in Russian. Finally, the car stopped. I gripped my carpet bag as the driver opened the door and helped me to my feet. The motorway traffic sounded far away.

"We take boat now," Arkhangelsky said.

"Are we in a field or something?" I asked.

Arkhangelsky didn't answer, only steered me by the arm across the uneven ground, my boots crunching on the frosty earth. "Careful. Step up," he said.

I stepped up, Yagar hoisting me by the arm. Here the ground evened and I heard wood planking beneath my feet and water lapping nearby—fresh water, not briny. I was liking this less and less.

Someone, presumably the driver, took my
other arm as I climbed a set of clinking
metal stairs. A boat, now I was on the deck
of a gently rocking boat. My senses picked
up rustling grass, the heavy scent of oil.
This was no pleasure craft. Someone wrapped
a blanket around my shoulders and eased me
onto a bench. It seemed that we were to
remain topside in the frigid air.

A motor rumbled to life and the boat
began chugging along. I clutched the blanket
tighter against the wind. By the sounds of
the wash on either side, I guessed we were
on a flat-bottomed boat, like a barge, on a
small river. Also, this waterway appeared
deserted, not that many people went boating
in England on December evenings. So, why
were we? Why didn't Arkhangelsky use a road
like everybody else?

*Because, wherever we were heading, he
obviously doesn't trust me enough to
disclose its location—a secret location.
Okay, Phoebe, act like you mean it.* "I've
always wanted to own property in England," I
said, pitching my voice over the engine. I
share a business with Max but not property."

"I have property now."

"Is this where you have Rena? When can
I see her?" I asked.

"Forget Rena."

Forget Rena? Was he crazy? I kept quiet
after that, my stomach churning like the
engine beneath my feet. Maybe I'd blown it,
maybe all my tough talk had only sealed
Rena's fate. I couldn't bear the thought.

By the time the boat slid to its
mooring, my teeth were rattling, and my
heart aching from a different kind of cold.

Arkhangelsky steered me from the boat to a jetty.

"Watch step," he said.

"I can't watch anything until this blindfold comes off," I said.

"In time."

We walked for a few minutes over stony ground, weaving through rushes and thorns. Then I heard voices, all in Russian, calls of greeting, I presumed. Arkhangelsky barked orders back. Soon I was stepping inside a building and steered along for a minute before Arkhangelsky instructed someone to remove my blindfold.

I blinked. Four battery-operated lamps illuminated what looked to be a massive hall, very old, with a huge empty fire place anchoring the shadows at one end. Overhead, I could just make out the shadowy shapes of beams crossing over a patch of open sky. I could detect the outline of centuries-old paint that had once decorated the ceiling beams—shield motifs, I thought. Piles of lumber were stacked everywhere and scaffolding was suspended against one wall. Arkhangelsky had bought a ruin?

"Wow," I said. "This place is amazing."

Arkhangelsky's retinue of driver and henchman nodded their approval.

"How old is it?" I asked.

"Built 1510, destroyed by fire 1536," Arkhangelsky said, grinning around the vacuous space. "Once hunting lodge. Not castle, but I make grand like castle. Come, I show."

"Couldn't get a castle, hey? Britain keeps them in the National Trust, right?" I asked as casually as possible. Too bad.

Castles were easier to identify than a moldering old hunting lodge.

Arkhangelsky only grunted. I followed him into a wide hallway where men were busy painting the walls lit by stacks of high-beam lights. No rest for the wicked, apparently. It had to be at least 8:30 P.M.

"They paint white," Arkhangelsky said over his shoulder as we crossed into another room. He swept his flashlight across the moldering walls. "I hang art here and here." He pointed to imaginary spaces, including a ragged hole where a wall might one day be.

The tour continued. I glimpsed a barricaded staircase climbing up into the darkness, sensed the weight of this heap of mouldering stone bearing down around me. Every window had been either boarded up or covered over in black fabric. We passed through room after ruined room until arriving at a warmer section with working lights and intact walls. One room, in particular, caught my attention. It appeared to have just received a new steel door which still hung half-open as a man soldered away at its hinges.

I stopped and pointed. "What's this?"

Yagar turned on his heels, his retinue halting also. "Vault. Come."

"Vault? Does this mean you're not returning to Russia?"

He laughed again, a big booming howl, his two companions hooting along with him. "Of course, I return to Russia! Russia my home, but I have houses many places. This my English castle. Come."

His English castle? I cast one more longing glance at the vault, trying to see through the opening, but only caught a glimpse of boxes and crates before hurrying on. I had to get back there somehow, see what he chose to keep so carefully guarded. We passed plenty of items mounded under drop cloths. Baker & Mermaid's logo marked the carpets he purchased from us still stacked in one corner.

At last, we entered a large room where a long table dressed in a white tablecloth and a vase of red roses had been positioned next to a monstrous crackling fireplace. Chairs clustered together around small tables here and there, and stacks of books sat on the floor beside walls of empty shelves. The scent of paint permeated the air along with fresh lumber and wax.

"This library," Arkhangelsky announced. "Here we talk and dine. Take seat." He instructed the two minions in Russian and they scooted through a beautifully restored oak door.

I pretended to study the oak paneling between the empty shelves, seeking identification of its prior owner. Sometimes the mighty would embed a carved seal throughout their master crafted properties. He or she had once claimed a heraldic shield and a hunting lodge, so they had to be bigwigs. I was betting on a king or queen.

"Sit, Phoebe."

I turned. Arkhangelsky was sitting at one end of the table before a bottle of vodka and two glasses. "We drink toast to new partnership."

I grinned. "Sure." I sauntered over, dropped my carpet bag to the floor, and sat down across from him, watching as he poured the clear liquid into two little shot glasses.

"To king and queen of world antiques market," Arkhangelsky stood up, glass raised.

"To the queen and king of world antiques market." I jumped up and clinked my glass with his, replicating his down-the-hatch drinking style—gone in one gulp. The liquor seared my throat, tears burned my eyes, and I silently swore.

He laughed. "I like you, Phoebe. Drink more."

I held out my glass, his eyes studying me across the table as he poured. "Maybe you learn to drink like Russian," he said.

"That will take practice."

"So practice."

"Let me see Rena, first."

"You see her when I say. Drink."

"I'd want to see her now, so I know that you're keeping your end of the bargain." I held my breath, thinking I'd just kicked his good mood all to hell.

"You make demands in my house? No position to demand, Phoebe," he warned.

"If you still want to go to the ball, I still hold some chips. There's still three days to go, Yaggie. Better play nice."

He stared at me hard and then threw back his head and laughed. "I show you Rena!"

He yelled and a servant came running through the oak door. Arkhangelsky gave instructions in Russian and soon the man left, returning in seconds, talking into a phone while holding an open laptop. Facetime? Skype? After a few minutes bent over the table, the man stood back.

I leaned forward, watching as the screen bounced along a dark corridor lit by flashlight beam. I heard clinking keys, saw a door grate open, and held my breath. Rena sat in some dark, dungeon-like room, much different from where she'd been held before. She sat, head in her arms, on a table with no light other than a feeble lantern. I almost cried out. "She looks asleep or sick. Let me see if she's is okay," I said.

Arkhangelsky yanked the phone from the minion and barked into it. Now I saw a hand roughly shaking Rena. She lifted her head and gazed blearily at the man before her. Swollen eyes, gaunt face, bruise on one cheek. I heard a male voice say in perfect English: "Say something to your friend. Go on."

"Phoebe?" Her voice came out in a croak.

"Let me talk to her!" I reached for Yagar's phone.

He shoved it at me. "Speak. Seconds only."

I took the phone frantically. "Rena, it's me, Phoebe. I'm going to get you out of there, I promise. Hang on, do what they say." Then I caught myself and proceeded more measuredly. "Yaggie and I are going into business together. You'll join us, too. We'll make lots of money and get really rich. Stay—"

The phone was wrenched from my grip. Arkhangelsky flipped the laptop screen closed and ordered the minion out. I stood breathing deeply, struggling to stay calm. She looked so weak. "Tell me that you're feeding her well, providing fresh food and blankets. I'm doing my part, you do yours."

"Ha!" more laughter from Yagar Arkhangelsky. The world was such a funny place to him. "You do what Yagar says and Rena lives, you live, too. Now drink."

Arkhangelsky had no intention of letting Rena live, and maybe not me, either. I knew that already but that knowledge suddenly hit me in a rush. After the ball, he didn't need any of us. This partnership could be as much a sham to him as it was to me. "I'm doing everything just as you instruct but, in the spirit of true partnership, let's talk about the plan first, while I'm still sober," I said, holding the glass up to study it as if it were fine wine instead of the corrosive acid it tasted like.

"First drink and eat, then drink and talk. Drink."

"Promise to get me home safely tonight?" I grinned.

"You go home tonight," he assured me.

"I see you left off the 'safely' part." I shot back another glass, blessing my foresight to eat before coming. This time the vodka burned less but still hit my gut like napalm. "Well," I said, dropping back to my chair. "Let's get this party started."

Arkhangelsky shouted orders. In seconds, minions burst through the door carrying platters of food, most only vaguely familiar to me—lots of fish and stuffed things, lots of pickled this and pickled that. By then, the specifics didn't matter.

"Delicious," I announced, diving into the beet soup before stabbing a fork at the fish. Water appeared in lovely crystal goblets and baskets of warm bread dropped on the table by themselves. Clearly I was missing the details. I needed to sober up fast.

Sometimes I glimpsed a servant darting about, but only the main server hung around, a shifty-looking creature who reminded me of a rat in a tux.

Though things had began to blur, at least my stomach felt marginally better now that it had something to do besides churn with anxiety. I glanced down at the table, surprised to see my vodka glass was on automatic refill. I knew I couldn't drink one more drop and live to tell the story, and yet the success of tonight's endeavor seemed to depend on me drinking like a Russian.

"Drink, drink!" Arkhangelsky insisted while shooting back another glass between multiple heaps of food. Was he trying to get me drunk so that everything I saw became mangled images?

I took my glass in hand and waited until the rat server had his back turned, busily refilling Arkhangelsky's glass. It only took seconds to pour my vodka into a beaker of salad dressing and replace the liquor in my glass with water. Jumping to my feet, I held up my glass. "Another toast!"

Arkhangelsky lurched to his feet, his glass raised, too. A toast!" he boomed. "You enjoy vodka?"

"Like a Russian! I toast world domination with Arkhangelsky and Mermaid!" I cried.

My host clinked glasses with me. "What is this 'mermaid'?" he asked.

"My code name," I said. "My tattoo. Maybe I'll show you sometime."

"You say 'Mermaid' but where is Max?"

I grinned. "Max who?" and watched Arkhangelsky collapse into laughter.

"So," I said, "what do you say we get down to business?"

"To business!" Yagar snapped his fingers to Rat Man and soon the food was swept up, the dishes removed, another bottle of vodka brought to the table.

"Keep the water, please," I said to Rat, who left the water bottle on the table beside the liquor. So, somebody else spoke English here. He was about to remove the flowers, too. "No wait, bring them here." I patted the empty table to my right. "They're too beautiful to hide."

"You like flowers?" Arkhangelsky asked.

"Red roses are a favorite." Actually, they weren't but, hell, lie a little, lie a lot.

Arkhangelsky snapped his fingers. "Leave flowers."

The waiter complied, delivering the vase to my right. By now, another minion was unfolding a large sheet of paper down at the opposite end. "Is that the blueprint of Having Castle?", I asked.

"Yes, I study and make plan. Come." He picked up his glass and the vodka bottle and headed to the other end, me trailing behind. Along the way I tipped my latest vodka refill into the roses, and brought the water bottle along, refilling my glass as I went.

The blueprint, secured flat by glasses on all four corners, was nothing but a large printout with countless notes and side-bar comments inked in Rupert's elegant script.

"Ball held here," Arkhangelsky said, tapping the paper. "Vault here, here, and here."

I leaned over, rubbing my eyes. The first thing that registered was the sheer size of the property, which appeared to have five wings branching off from what looked to be a Norman keep. Each wing had been subdivided and labeled in block letters. I read BALLROOM and ROMAN GALLERY, EAST WING BEDROOMS, and MAIN SALON, plus multiple others. I pulled back. "Mind if I take … a picture? I don't have a copy."

Arkhangelsky pointed to a tube leaning against one of the shelves. "Fox provided extra. You take home to show Max."

I nodded. "Okay, but the place is so…huge. Um, how do you know which rooms to target?" And then I giggled for effect. Let him think I was drunk.

"Simple," he said. "Most valuable objects in vaults. Vault 1 is jewelry and gems; Vault 2 is gold; and Vault 3, is new, so is mystery. Together, worth fortune. We hit all."

I followed his finger around to the back of the property where three comparatively small rooms had been labeled in Roman numerals, I,II,III. Squiggly lines indicated water nearby. I shoved a finger between my eyes as if to reset my brain. "He'll have extra guards … um, on duty there that … night." I gripped the table as if keeping myself up.

He looked up. "Not feel good?"

"Just the vodka."

"Vodka health drink. Drink more." He made to refill my glass but I waved him away.

"My glass is half-empty" I giggled. "I mean half-full. Your waiter took good, um, care of me." I covered my mouth with my hand and snickered.

"So drink."

I tossed back another shot of water, wiped my mouth with the back of my hand and swayed. "Um, ah, think I'd better sit down for a minute." Arkhangelsky hauled a chair from the table and I collapsed into it. "Just need to rest," I told him.

"You rest." He patted my head like a dog.

I closed my eyes, my head lolling backward against the chair seat. "Not Russian … yet."

"Take second."

Moments passed. I heard him leave the room, his footsteps echoing on the wooden floor. My eyes shot open. I was alone. Springing from the chair, I dashed down to the other end of the room where we'd entered. In the corridor beyond, men still painted by the lamplight. I waved to them as I passed, heading back towards the steel-doored room. Turn left, turn right. Ah, there it was, but where were the dungeons? That had to be where Rena was held.

The vault was still open and I could hear voices inside. I slipped in.

A conversation was going on behind a mound of crates sitting in the center of a large freshly painted white room. Empty glass cases lined one wall and I could just make out doorways to other rooms opening on either side.

Hunkering down, I lifted one of the cloths. What looked to be paintings leaned against one crate. Too fortified to welcome a casual peek, each piece sat encased in a wooded frame sheeted in thick plastic. The label on the first was visible, the writing in Italian, with one recognizable word: *Raphael*. I stiffened.

An argument erupted behind the mound—
two men's voices, both Russian. I slipped my
phone from my pocket and took a photo of the
painting's label, plus a quick video sweep
of my part of room. I heard Arkhangelsky
bellowing from far down the hall as I bolted
for the door. In seconds, I was on my hands
and knees, gripping my stomach as footsteps
pounded down the hall toward me.

A minion yanked me to my feet by the
arm. I shook him off. "I need the bathroom.
Where is the damn bathroom?"

Arkhangelsky arrived, barking orders.
In seconds I was being half-dragged down the
hall towards the back of the building. A
cavernous kitchen flew by before I was
shoved into a tiny, recently installed
bathroom, with a toilet and sink so new,
they still bore price tags. As soon as the
door slammed behind me, I launched retching
noises so convincing, I almost vomited for
real. I flushed the toilet and moaned. After
splashing my face with cold water, I finally
opened the door and smiled sheepishly.
"Coffee?"

Arkhangelsky stood arms crossed flanked
by two henchmen. Behind him I could see two
women working at the stove, one of whom shot
me furtive glances over her shoulder—blond
hair, extraordinarily pretty. Yagar snapped
his fingers at her, and she hurried to the
counter to pour a dark brew into a mug. She
stepped towards me, holding the mug while
smoothing her apron with her other hand. As
I reached for the mug, our eyes met, her
beautiful blues silently pleading, or
possibly apologetic, I couldn't tell which,
but what struck me most was her perfume,
that perfume.

"This Katia. She real Russian woman," Arkhangelsky said, one arm grasping Katia's waist and drawing her near. He whispered something into her ear, while she studied the floor.

Minutes later, I was back in the library and sitting at the table while Arkhangelsky glowered over me.

"So, I'm not a Russian yet," I shrugged.

"You never be Russian." He almost spat his disgust.

"Where were we?" I left my seat and swayed down to the blueprint. "My head's still a little fuzzy, but I'll try to pay attention."

He joined me, propping his feet on the table while swigging directly from the vodka bottle.

"You've got this great big space here and you plan to steal whatever Rupert's got in those three vaults? What about the guards? He'll have lots of them on duty that night."

"Guards no problem. We kill," Arkhangelsky said.

"Oh, right. Easy."

"Easy, yes. At 11:35, big explosion, another in ballroom." He paused to down more vodka. "Same time we blow vaults. Everyone run, scream. People killed. We break into vaults and steal contents, transport to vehicles, disappear. No one sees, no one hears. Everyone sees Arkhangelsky, who runs and screams, too. It is beautiful plan."

I looked at him in amazement. "Beautiful?"

He pounded the table with his fist. "Beautiful!"

"But how will that work exactly?"

"Do not be stupid girl! You know nothing."

"That's the point. Aren't I part of this deal? Besides, that's no way to speak to a partner." I straightened and held up my hands. "Whatever happened to respect?"

"You earn respect," he said through his teeth. "Then Yagar Arkhangelsky makes you partner. First you prove worthy."

"Okay, okay. So, how do I do that?"

"Kill Rupert Fox."

22

I sat in my kitchen sipping some
concoction that Max insisted eased
hangovers. I didn't want to know the
contents, just downed the stuff with two
Advil and slumped back in my chair. "Max,
did you hear what I said? He wants me to
kill Rupert at the ball. He hasn't said how,
just that I'd know when the time was right."
        "I heard."
        "And he's got this plan to create an
explosion at the ball as a diversion while
he blows up the vaults."
        "Figures."
        "He's trying to kill us all," I said..
        "Nothing about this is new, darlin'.
Are you ready for battle?"
        "Just waiting for the pain killers to
work." I buried my head in my arms.
        Max sat down at the table across from
me and handed me a glass of water. When I
had arrived home at two A.M., he'd been
waiting up for me, camped out on the living
room couch, intending to call the police if
I hadn't shown. After the driver had dropped
me off, I'd lurched past him into my bedroom
to flop on the bed in a semistupor. Though I
hadn't swilled half the vodka Arkhangelsky

believed I had, I'd still downed enough to leave me feeling like roadkill.

Hours later, I'd stumbled into the kitchen to find Max poring over the blueprint I'd brought home. It spread before us on the table now as I gazed across at my godfather's ravaged face.

"I need you to get your brain back and tell me every damn thing that bastard said and did last night, got that?" he said. "Coffee's on the brew and I'm going to fix you some toast. After that, we talk and think."

I nodded. I desperately needed to muster my brain cells before I could drag myself free from the quagmire.

Following coffee and breakfast, I recounted everything that happened in the order in which it occurred, while Max listened and jotted notes.

"Max," I said finally, "Arkhangelsky doesn't want to just steal Rupert's treasures and murder him, he wants to *be* him. Rupert is his idea of the height of success as he defines it—rich, privileged, an owner of estates worldwide, possessor of a castle—"

"The linchpin of the London artifacts and priceless antiques trade, right on the damn cusp of everything rare being smuggled in and out of Europe."

I stared. "He is?"

"Thought you knew that."

"I knew Rupert was powerful, well-connected, and filthy rich, but I never grasped the extent of his influence."

Max freshened his coffee. "Foxy doesn't just have influence, he has power," he said. "In order for Yagar to be at the epicenter

of the black market in London—in Europe, for
that matter—he has to get rid of Foxy, or
the bear will be forever dancing to the
Fox."

"Well, this bear is ruthless." My gaze
dropped to the blueprint. I leaned over to
study it more closely. "He says he's going
to create a diversion the night of the ball,
something that results in death and chaos,
while simultaneously breaking into the
vaults at the rear of the castle, here and
here." I pointed out the vaults.

Max peered down at my finger. "Yeah,
those are new."

"Have you been to Having Castle?"

"Sure, many times, back when Foxy and I
did business together. In those days, he
kept most of his treasures—the smuggled
antiquities, anyway—down in the dungeon
vaults, but he had expansion plans. Most of
this blueprint is how I remembered, except
those vaults."

I looked up at him. "Arkhangelsky's got
a huge vault of his own waiting for new
acquisitions to arrive, and it's not empty.
I saw a painting—well, I couldn't actually
see it, but I read the label on the crate.
Here, I have it on my phone." I brought up
the picture of the label and the video
sweep. "See, the label says *Raphael*. Do you
think that could be what I think it is?"

"Bloody hell. Raphael's missing self-
portrait?"

"The portrait of a young man they
believe to be the artist himself? That's
what I thought, too."

"Worth a fortune. Went missing when the
Nazis occupied Italy."

"And the Monuments Men rescued so many believed to belong to the same Nazi thief, except that one. So maybe now we know where it ended up," I said.

"If that's true, that Russkie bastard's pulled off one of the greatest acquisitions of the art world. Foxy would give his eye teeth to get his paws on that."

"Only Arkhangelsky plans to steal his treasure, first. He's planning a massive transportation of Rupert's treasures into his heap of a castle. The only way he could possibly think he could get away with that is if he expected to blow up every scrap of evidence left behind at Having, human and otherwise. There's no way he intends to leave any of us alive. How could he? We all know too much. He'll hit the ballroom for maximum damage. I have to warn Rupert."

"How can you do that without risking everything?"

"I'll find a way. It's Mrs. Montgomery, the mole, that worries me now. With her on the inside, she's finding out stuff even I don't know. Anyway, we need another meeting. We'll beat this bastard yet."

* * *

It's not like the phrase *easier said than done* had no meaning for me. I left Max searching for hunting lodges on the Cole River, along with seeking boat rentals, while I scrambled down the street. We needed to muster the forces; we needed to pull the pieces together; and we needed to do it all while ensuring Rena and Foxy—all of us—got

out alive. Easier said than done,
considering the ball was only two days away.

I had less than 30 minutes before
Arkhangelsky picked me up for Rupert's
house, and I intended to make every minute
count. Bolting down the street, I darted
around the corner to a take-out restaurant
where we'd all become regulars.

"Hi, Tiki. Mind if I use the phone?"

"Cell phone busted?" she asked.

"Battery dead, and I'm in a bit of a
rush." I had my secure Foxy phone, plus the
rejiggered iPhone, but I still didn't trust
either. It felt like my very clothes were
bugged.

Tiki, who remained on cash for the sole
purpose of funding her next world trip,
nodded. I ducked behind the counter and into
the little back room. In seconds I had
dialed the cell number I memorized and
waited—waited unbearably long—as the ring
buzzed in my ear. I counted ten seconds,
fifteen …

"Sam Walker."

Thank God. "Sam, Phoebe McCabe here."

"Ms. McCabe? Am I hallucinating? What's
it been, a whole six weeks since you blew up
that house in Orvieto and returned to
London?"

I squeezed my eyes shut. "I did not
blow up that house—not exactly. Anyway, I'm
trying to prevent a bigger disaster. Listen,
I know of a criminal who's planning to blow
up Having Castle to steal Sir Rupert Fox's
art collection. I'm talking major heist
here. He also intends to murder Sir Rupert,
me, and countless innocent citizens."

"You're like a disaster magnet."

"Look, this disaster magnet helped Interpol crack a Camora smuggling ring, and break up a nest of antiquities thieves in Turkey. Show some respect. Besides, I don't look for trouble, it has me on speed dial. Can you help or not? This is big."

"This is a job for Scotland Yard. It's way beyond my jurisdiction."

"If I call the Yard, they'll start poking around and asking questions, which could tip the criminal off, and get us all killed. I figure you'd understand the complexity of my circumstances, and might help."

"By complexity, do you mean the vast number of criminal elements you get wrapped up in, including your brother and boyfriend? I can't help you here, I said. I specialize in tracking smuggling operations internationally, not running a counter-op to a major heist on British soil. Get Scotland Yard and do it now. I'm serious. Besides, I'm not even in London, but Rome."

"You can help if it involves stolen art from another country, right?"

"As much as I've long suspected Sir Rupert to be a smuggler, I'm still not in the position to deal with crime of this magnitude."

"Does a missing painting by Raphael in the possession of one Yagar Arkhangelsky fit your jurisdiction?" I counted the seconds of his stunned silence. "I thought so. Can you be back on London by tonight?"

Moments later, I was on the street, hoofing it back to the shop, when a black Bentley slid to the curb. I leaned toward the open driver's window. "Evan?"

"Madam? May I offer you a lift?" Evan asked.

I peered in at him. "But I'm only a block away from my place."

"I would be pleased to drive you to Sir Rupert's house, Madam, as in the old days." He was staring at me intensely.

I swallowed and tried to laugh. "The 'old days'? You make that sound like it was in another century. I'm sure things will get back to normal after the …" At that moment, a black Mercedes slid up to the curb behind us. Arkhangelsky's car. If anything angered him—like me having an unauthorized conversation with one of Rupert's employees—Rena would pay. "I have to go. Hope to catch you later."

I walked towards the Mercedes. Though I couldn't see the back seat through the smoked glass, the driver was visible, and it wasn't the usual guy, but the Rat.

"You're five minutes early," I told him. "I was just going to run back to the shop and get something."

"You get in now," he replied, his narrow face and pointed chin looking particularly rat-like in the daylight. "Am very busy man today."

Very busy? Usually Arkhangelsky gave the orders. I hesitated, but climbed into the back seat anyway, surprised to find it empty. "Where's the boss?" I asked as the car peeled away.

"Busy. He will not be happy to hear you talk to M16 agent," he said.

I leaned forward. "Do you mean Sir Rupert's driver? He's a *former* MI6 agent, and why do you care what he used to do for a living?"

"I care because I know this man. I was KGB."

I sat back in my seat. So that's it: Rupert had a former MI6 agent, so Arkhangelsky had to get himself a former KGB. How sweet.

"Put on necklace and wire," Rat ordered.

I found them in a box on the seat beside me, and put them on without a word.

A few minutes later, the Rat delivered me to Rupert's, though he made no move to open the door for me. I exited the car and shot through the gate up the walkway, suddenly on the verge of tears. All the festive decorations on the streets we passed hit me hard and, when Rupert's doorbell played *We Wish You a Merry Christmas* in the tinkle of silver bells, I almost came undone.

The door opened and there stood Sloane. "Good afternoon, Ms. Phoebe. Please do enter. Are you well today?"

"Fine, thank you. Just allergic to the air freshener in Yaggie's car," I said, wiping my eyes. I stared. Suitcases and boxes of all sizes and shapes stood piled neatly against one wall. "Are you going somewhere?"

"Yes, indeed," said Sloane, taking my coat. "Today Sir Rupert's household retires to Having Castle until after the holidays, and for the grand fete, of course. We will not return until the New Year."

"Oh." I stood there feeling unaccountably bereft, which made no sense at all, except that the season of jollity felt so dismal and frightening, and I knew Rupert was not going to have a merry time in the days to come. That is, unless I could avert the pending disaster.

Sloane took my coat and I followed him into the library. The sight of tea and fresh scones lifted my spirits slightly, but not enough to fend off the overwhelming sense of doom.

"Sir Rupert will be with you shortly. Please do make yourself at home," and with that, Sloan exited the room.

I sat down immediately, not caring whether Arkhangelsky expected me to spy more or not. I wasn't doing it and that was final. With the big date looming and him in possession of the blueprint, I figured he had everything he needed to plan his disaster. Rupert may know that something was amiss, but whether he understood the full extent was the issue. How could I tell him the details without detonating Arkhangelsky's wrath?

Rupert interrupted my pondering moments later. "Phoebe! How delightful to have you visit this fine day. I see you have not touched your scones, which won't do it all. Sloane made them especially for you with his own sugar plum jam. Do try. Shall I pour the tea?" He perched on the chair opposite mine, decked out in a tweed traveling suit with leather-trimmed pockets. No doubt matching gloves were in the waiting somewhere, too.

"Yes, please," I said, reaching for a scone. The scent of the warm biscuits hit me with all the nostalgia of a letter from home, my real home. "Two sugars and no milk, thanks. You look ready to exit at any moment," I said as I buttered the treat.

"Yes, we must leave this morning. We've delayed long enough."

I bit into my scone, allowing ten seconds of pure bliss before responding. "Because of me?"

"Well, yes, we had to complete your gift to Yaggie, didn't we? Today, the stockings will be complete, after which my retinue will retire to the country to ensure the final details are in place for both the grand fete and the holidays. What fun!"

The scone stuck in my throat. He seemed unaccountably jubilant for a man with suspicions of a heist in the works. I sipped my tea and swallowed hard.

"How is your beau of late?"

"My beau? Oh, you mean Yaggie? Oh, fine," I said, my mouth still full.

"Let us finish up the last of his present, shall we? Only a few remaining touches and you are done." He passed me a bundle of yarn that had been sitting out of sight beside his chair. One finished sock sat neatly folded in the pile along with the second, now hanging from the needles, with only a few rows left until completion.

I held up the work in progress. "It's turning out rather well, isn't it?"

"Indeed it is. You shall become a maestro sock knitter, after all," he said.

I mouthed the words *not likely* before dropping my head and knitting a circular row. In moments, Rupert was on his feet again, heading for the door. "I shall return directly." Minutes later, he was back, two ornate boxes in his arms. He sat one—a large box decorated in foil stars—onto the ottoman between us and put the smaller glove-sized one aside. "Oh, excellent. You are almost done." I was? I hadn't even bound off yet.

"Do set your stocking down for a moment, Phoebe, and open the box."

I did as he asked, removing the ornate lid with a flourish, and lifting a single incredible boot from amid the tissue paper. "Oh," was all I could say at first. It was magnificent, a perfect little calf-high brown velvet boot trimmed in mink, just my size. "It's exquisite."

"And so is its mate. It took me awhile to source, I must say, but I do have my connections. I thought them the perfect addition to your Anastasia costume. I'm sure Yaggie has provided footwear with the outfit, but hopefully will indulge me enough to allow you to wear these as my Christmas gift to you. There are matching gloves inside the box, too."

"Why, thank you, Rupert," I said. "I will treasure them forever."

"I doubt they will last that long. Nevertheless, the pleasure is mine." He reached over and retrieved the second box, holding it to the right, out of view of my necklace camera. "And this one is for your gift to your beau, in the event you do not have a suitable receptacle handy, you understand."

"How thoughtful." I took the box and the hint, keeping everything out of camera range. It was surprisingly heavy.

At that moment, in walked Sloane with a tray of fresh tea. As unobtrusive as ever, he collected the plates, poured the tea, and exited, my sock-in-progress grasped under the tray as he left.

I stared at Rupert. He stared back.

"Thank you again for the gift, and for providing the box for my sock present," I said. So formal.

"You are most welcome. Of course, I cannot be with you when you dress for the event, but I trust you can tie those laces without difficulty. They are a bit tricky, thus you'll find a discrete zipper on the sides. Russian royalty did have the benefit of servants to tie laces and such but we do not."

"I'm sure I can manage. What about Max's costume? He has been asking."

"I am certain he has, being such an impatient chap. Let us keep it a little surprise. The costume awaits him at Having Castle, in the dressing room I have assigned your party on the second floor. When you arrive Saturday night, you will be escorted to the aforementioned room where you can dress in privacy. Naturally, there are both male and female sections."

"You think of everything." If the costume was a surprise to Max, it would be likewise a surprise to Arkhangelsky. My plan began to feel increasingly more doable.

"I do try." He climbed to his feet. "Do pardon me, Phoebe, but I really must attend to the finishing details of my wardrobe. Evan has already proceeded to Having, and the rest of us will depart shortly in a little motorcade of sorts. Would you mind terribly continuing without me? I will look forward to seeing you at Having."

"Of course, Rupert." I stood up, too, and almost gasped when he took me in his arms and gave me a big hug, patting me on the back in the process.

"Try to keep your tension even when completing that last row, Phoebe, and do follow the directions accordingly," he said in my ear.

"I will." I almost said "what directions?" but kept my mouth shut as he strode across the room, pausing by the door only long enough to wave before exiting.

I sat back down and made as if working on something in my lap, out of the camera's range, when really I was literally twiddling my thumbs. Almost an hour later, Sloane appeared to tell me my ride had arrived. Bundling up my packages, I followed him out, donned my coat, and said my goodbyes. Rupert had disappeared by then, but other servants were busy depositing luggage and boxes on the pile against the wall.

Back in the Mercedes, the Rat was still the driver and Arkhangelsky still hadn't made an appearance. The car peeled away from the car to stop at the opposite side of the square.

"I check bag first," the Rat said, holding out his hand for my carpet bag. I passed it over, watching as he dug around in the contents before tossing back at me. "Now boxes."

I handed him the big box first.

He held up one of the boots and made a face. "This no Russian woman wear."

"They're made for a queen."

"All Russian queens dead," he remarked.

"Maybe it's time one of them lived long enough to kick some ass."

The rat actually rolled his eyes and shoved the boot box over the seat. "Hand over small box."

I was still carefully repacking my boots in the tissue paper when I heard him snort. I looked up to see him holding up a single perfectly executed sock between his nicotine-stained fingers. "What is this?"

"What does it look like? I knit it myself. It's my Christmas present to your boss, and you'd better not get it dirty."

"Mr. Arkhangelsky has many socks." He tossed them back at me, box and all, sending the tissue paper flying.

"You're a pig," I told him as I replaced everything. "I bet nobody ever made you anything, except maybe a Molotov cocktail."

The look he gave me in the rearview mirror then sent chills down my spine. I kept my eyes averted and zipped my lips after that. Never taunt a vicious dog.

Because of increased Christmas traffic, the drive home took longer than usual. I sat glowering out the window as the minutes ground by. Finally, the car pulled to the curb outside of Baker & Mermaid.

"Tomorrow, I arrive here at 4:00 P.M. for drive to country. You will dress there and leave with Mr. Arkhangelsky for ball."

"No, I mean, I can't. I've arranged for my godfather and my guests to travel together to Having. I can meet Yagar there."

"That is not plan. Tomorrow, here at 4:00 P.M. or friend pays, I warn you."

"Listen Rat Man, or whatever the hell your name is, you tell your boss this for me: when I get to his 'castle', on the night of the ball, I expect to see Rena alive and well or the deal's off, got that?"

"Ha!" he laughed. "You do not threaten Mr. Arkhangelsky, Mr. Arkhangelsky threatens you. And I am Oleg."

23

"I checked it out," Max said, "and King Henry the Eighth had a hunting lodge on the Cole River, now a ruin. While Phoebe went to Foxy's this afternoon, Jake and I took off for a drive and, sure enough, the heap is just upstream from Having Castle."

"It looks a right wreck," Jake added.

"No one would know from the road or river that anything's going on in there, unless you chanced to notice the electric fence," Max continued. "It's stuck slam dunk in the middle of hayfield that used to be a forest centuries back."

"There's even a bloody cow or two hanging around," Jake said. "I stepped in a meadow muffin."

Max, Jennifer, Jake, Higgins, and I stood around the table upstairs in the Keyhole Pub, the blueprint of Having Castle spread across the table in front of us. Marco was on stage that night, so Jennifer was recording the conversation for his benefit on a standard tape deck. Nobody trusted anything digital.

"So you intend to, what, just cruise by and pick up Rena on the way to the ball, like you were fetching yourself an order of fish and chips?" Brenda asked.

"Don't give me grief, Higgins. I'm not in the mood," Max said. "But, yeah, something like that. Phoebe will keep that Russkie bastard busy while I do the deed."

Brenda crossed her arms and stared hard at Max. "Really? Planning on tackling all of the Russkie bastards, including the former KGB he's got working for him? Where there's one, there's more. And are you thinking of taking these guards on single-handedly, one by one, while the others watch? You have a death wish or something?"

"What's your point?" Max said, turning towards her.

"My point is that I'm going in with you. At least I know my way around a dangerous situation."

"Why, because you used to be a traffic cop?" My godfather pulled himself up to his full height and glared down at the much shorter Higgins.

"I wasn't always a traffic cop, you big nob, and I sure as hell know how to fight."

"No thanks. I work better alone," Max began, "I—"

"Max, *think*," I interrupted. "She's right: you do need help, we all do. We're in this as a team from here on in, and it's time we start acting like one. No more pissing matches." I turned to her with a smile. "Thanks, Higgins, we need all the help we can get."

"Got that right," she replied, slightly mollified.

"Marco's going in, too," Jennifer said.

We all turned towards her, standing there like some example of a glossy magazine's feature on how to stay gorgeous in a tweedy jacket and leggings, December edition.

"Marco?" Max erupted. "Marco will be trussed up like a Renaissance bludger in breeches and hose."

"He's going in with you," she said, enunciating every word. "He *insists*. He's got this understudy playing Darcy that night and, like, Rena's his mom, you know? He'll be in costume, sure, but Renaissance men carried swords, and Marco knows how to use one. He trained for *Romeo and Juliet*, remember?"

Max frowned. "I understand why he wants to be involved, but Marco's a hothead, Jenn."

"And you're not?" I said, laughing. "Look, Max, Marco's young and strong, and he can be a huge help. He goes in with you, too, okay?"

Max stared at me in silence.

"Okay?" I pressed.

"Okay, okay," he conceded.

"Good," I sighed. "That makes three of you to rescue Rena. You'll have only a few minutes to overcome the guard or guards, and do it without sounding the alarm topside, where I'll be entertaining Arkhangelsky. You'll rescue Rena, make a dash for the boat, and zip on down to where Jake and Jenn will be waiting in the van."

"Easy-peasey," Higgins said.

"Well, that's what we've got to work with," I said. "And, Arkhangelsky's men will be crawling around the place getting ready for the heist, so hopefully they'll be preoccupied. Also, there will probably be a couple of barges moored on the Cole, so you'll have to get around them without being seen or heard."

"No worries," Max said. "I've rented a little skiff with a sail and an engine, just in case. Plus, I tossed in a kayak or two for good measure."

"Great, we'll do a getaway paddle," Higgins said.

I glared at her. "So," I went on, "if Rena's in bad shape, somebody's got to take her to a hospital ASAP, and carry on to Having afterward."

"Marco won't leave her side," Jenn said.

"No, of course not."

"But I'll carry on to Having, one way or the other, to help you get dressed," she continued.

"That's not necessary," I said.

"It is," she insisted. "Those period costumes are, like, super-challenging to get into. You'll need help. Clothes are my specialty, so I'll, like, be there."

"Okay, great. Thanks, Jenn," I said, relieved to know somebody else was handling the details I'd glossed over. With so much to think about, so much I didn't know, I had to be missing lots of things, and the costumes had gone to the back of the line.

"So, after Max, Marco, and I whip in to rescue Rena, zip downstream back to the van, then Jake and I are to wait in the van outside Having Castle like a taxi cab or something?" Higgins asked.

"No, I need you to wait by the river where we believe they plan to load the stuff. As soon as you see signs of trouble,

call Max or me. We'll be on the inside
trying to nail Arkhangelsky and warn
Rupert."

"Give us a challenge, why don't you?"
Higgins said with a grin.

"Look, this entire balls-up sounds
impossible, but we've got to find a way.
Like Phoebe said, we'll need all hands on
deck," Max said.

"Don't get your knickers in a twist,
Baker. We'll figure out a way to be useful,
won't we lad?" Higgins looked over at Jake
who shrugged and nodded. "But what do you
plan to do once you're moving around inside,
Phoebe? You're the linchpin here." she
asked.

I took a deep breath. "Warn Rupert,
foil Arkhangelsky's plans—not that I know
the exact details of those plans—make life
hell for him any way I can. He plans to harm
Rupert, and I'll do whatever it takes to
stop him. I'll improvise, fly by the seat of
my pants, while hoping Walker pulls through
with the backup team."

"Doing a lot of seat-of-our-pantsing,
aren't we?" she pressed.

"Yeah, but what choice do we have?"

"Right then. We'll figure out
something," Higgins assured me.

"We will, too," Jennifer added. "Marco
wants to make that bastard pay for what they
did to me and his mom—once she's okay, I
mean."

I nodded. When I stopped riding my wave
of bravado, the whole crazy nonplan sounded
suicidal.

"Should be so easy—*not*," Higgins said,
shaking her head. "And, of course, your

Arkhangel bloke will be watching you like a hawk."

"Yeah, that's going to be a problem, but I have to get to Rupert somehow. I'll try phoning him, of course. Anyway, Rupert has a dressing room designated for us. I'll arrive with Arkhangelsky and escape his company as soon as I can while you guys change into your costumes."

"So, that's settled then," Max said. "And I suppose Foxy still hasn't revealed whether he's decking me out as the Pied Piper of Hamlin?"

"What does it matter? What does any of it matter as long as you're unrecognizable? What matters is us all getting out of this alive."

Nobody argued with me there.

"So, that slimy little Russian bastard is picking you up at what time tomorrow?" Max asked.

"Four o'clock," I said. "It takes nearly an hour to get to his heap by car and boat, so I'm presuming he wants to give himself lots of time."

"You going in alone is so damn risky at this stage," he pointed out.

"While everything else is a piece of cake?" Higgins said.

I threw up my hands. "Actually, it's perfect, inasmuch as anything in this horrible situation is perfect. I'll be there to distract Arkhangelsky while you break Rena out. I'll cause a commotion myself." I pressed my hands against my mouth. My God, how was I going to do that, exactly? "Anyway, we have no choice. This is the best we can do with what we have to work with, and the rest will fall into place at the

time. There's so much we don't know yet—like
what Rupert has up his sleeve, the details
of Arkhangelsky's plan, just everything. We
have to get in and be prepared to respond to
whatever happens next."

"What about this Interpol friend of
yours?" Higgin's asked.

"I wouldn't call him a friend, exactly—
more like a colleague on the opposite side,
if that makes any sense—and he won't commit
himself. I'm not even sure he'll show, but
he knows Arkhangelsky by reputation. He
became pretty damn interested when I
mentioned that our resident oligarch might
have a lost Raphael in his possession. I
suggested he could sweep into Arkhangelsky's
pseudocastle after helping us to foil the
Having heist, and maybe walk away as an
Interpol star with a fortune in missing art
under his belt. I'm betting that he's going
to show up somehow."

"That's comforting, that 'somehow'
bit," Higgins said. "For a minute there, I
actually thought you planned to take on this
Russian gang leader and his men with a posse
of trained ops, rather than go in as a bunch
of amateurs. Should have known better."

"Higgins, will you just stop," I said,
beyond exasperated. "We need positive energy
around this. That's the only way we're going
to pull through. If everyone goes in
believing it's impossible, it will be."

24

On the day of the ball, I was in a mental spin. I'd get up, take myself for a walk—either by circling my flat or dashing around the block—always thinking *if this happens, I'll do that, or maybe that*, each scenario fevering my brain. There were so many possible outcomes, so many things that could go wrong, I thought I'd go crazy. Nothing could go as planned, since we had no solid plan. I may as well go skydiving without a parachute.

We had no weapons, no serious counter-ops. What if Max, Marco, and Higgins were injured, or worse? What if Rena didn't make it, or that bastard decided to kill her early? What if Arkhangelsky planned to have Rupert murdered as soon as we arrived and, if I wouldn't do the deed, took care of the matter another way? Wait, I reasoned, he'd want Rupert to know he'd been bested first. He'd want the satisfaction of seeing Rupert's face at the moment of catastrophe. No, we'd have a bit of time to foul up the Russian.

And how I missed Noel, remembering him by my side during the last two times disaster hit. I needed him now, wanted him, was so damned tired of being solo that I wanted to cry. I hated this.

After one frantic dash around the block, I returned to my flat and kicked the couch in frustration. Downstairs the gallery hung strangely empty, as if holding its breath—no Rena, no Max, no customers. For one terrible moment, I wondered if it would always be that way, if the results of this night would end all life as I knew it. Maybe I'd end up more alone than ever before, or simply dead.

We needed help, we so needed help. I tried contacting Walker again, to beg for his assistance, but ended up blabbering into his message recording, instead. I even tried texting Rupert, but thought better of it. Even though I was 75% positive that Rupert had secured the phone, Arkhangelsky ran the dark web in Russian, so could have the smarts to bypass anything Rupert may have installed. I couldn't risk it, couldn't risk Rena's neck. Her life hung on a thread as it was.

I tried to settle my mind, think strategically. I laid out the boot and sock box by the door, and packed and repacked my carpet bag. My carpet bag was to be taken to Having in care of Max, since I knew my phone would never pass Arkhangelsky's scrutiny. The only thing I was taking with me were the boots and gloves from Rupert, and the woolly sock present for Ivan the Terrible. He'd be sure to strip me of everything else, certainly any communication devices.

Staring down at my carpet bag, I remembered Rupert's enigmatic eye app and plucked the phone from the side pocket. I was scanning the room with the phone at eye level when Max burst in carrying a package.

"Oh, Phoebe, darlin', there you are. What are you doing?"

"Rupert had this weird little app installed on my phone, which I'd forgotten to mention. I'm pretty sure it's a weapon of some kind, but I have no idea how to work it."

In two strides he was by my side, dumping the packages on the couch en route. He slipped the phone from my hand and held it up to study. "It's a bloomin' detonator, one of Boy Friday's inventions. You have to line the bomb up in your sights and then push the picture button."

"I figured that much, but what bomb, what's it I'm supposed to detonate?"

"Foxy will expect you to think like him and figure this out, brilliant little conniving weasel that he is. He forgets that most people don't process information in that way. What else has he given you lately?"

I pointed to the boot box. "He gave me those boots to go with the Anastasia costume."

"Hold one up and stand over there," Max said.

I walked toward the window, one boot dangling from my fingers. Turning, I extended my arm as Max held up the phone. "I've already imprinted my iris with the app."

"Yup, the eye is flashing red, but the detonate button is blacked out, which means it won't detonate for my iris, only yours," Max said. "Bloody brilliant!"

"Bloody brilliant? Max, are you saying those boots are bombs?" I stared at the beautifully crafted boot in horror.

"Yes, they are, luv. The perfect weapon. Here, let's try the second one."

We did, and the eye icon again turned red.

"The crafty little ferret. You now have two weapons at your disposal."

But I still hadn't adjusted to the boots-equals-bombs equation. "Foxy was going to have me wear explosives to the ball?"

"They won't detonate while you're wearing them, darlin'. That slimy limey MI6 agent of his must have lined the soles with some kind of undetectable explosive. He expects you to use this app as a detonator, but they'll be perfectly safe before then, or I bloody hope so. All you need do is remove the boots, line them up with the eye icon, and then push the *kaboom!* button."

"Oh, my God." I covered my face with my eyes. "I don't believe this." But I did, of course. This was Rupert Fox, after all. I dropped my hands. "But I can't risk taking my phone with me in case Arkhangelsky snatches it."

"We'll take it upstairs to the Having dressing room with your other costume. Now, what else as he given you lately?"

"Matching gloves."

In moments, we were both scrutinizing the long kid leather, fur-lined gloves, each with the gorgeous embroidered scrolls curving around the tops. I spied the tiny hand-stitching between the fur and the leather first. "Here." One tug released the stitching, revealing a tiny packet of white powder. "Poison?"

"Or a drug of some kind. Either will be useful. Slip a little into the Russkie's drink, that sort of thing. Both gloves are the same, but looks like one powder is a different color—two different concoctions, maybe. Sprinkle a little in all of their drinks to make them dopey or sick."

I stared at him. "You make it sound so easy."

He enveloped me in a huge hug. "Oh, hell, Phoebe. Since when did you do easy? Look, I've brought you something else."

While he dumped the contents of his bag onto the couch, I tied a little knot in the glove's stitching and buried it beneath the fur. When I looked up, Max was holding what looked to be a miniature walkie-talkie. "Is that what I think it is?"

"We have to communicate with one another while you're inside Arkhangelsky's heap somehow. Ivan may not be as brilliant as Evan at electronics, but the bloke's a master at piecing together something from nothing. He tells me this used to be some sort of hearing aid, one of the kind that transmits sounds through wireless. I keep the transmitter on me and you stick this thing in your ear the moment you get a chance. It will only work when we're within 500 feet of one another, and may not be too effective through stone, but it's worth a shot. You'll be able to hear me but not talk back—that'll be a nice change." He grinned. "Stick it somewhere on your body—down your bra, or something."

"They made me strip to my underwear before."

He handed it to me. "Do the best you can. That's all any of us can do, darlin'."

"Max, I'm terrified."

"Of course, you are—so am I—but one of the many things I admire about you is that you never let fear stop you." He checked his watch. "Nearly 2:00. I have to pick up Jake and Higgins in a few minutes to get ready for tonight. We plan to reach the heap at 7:00 PM, when it's dark. Marco and Jenn are meeting us at the rendezvous spot at 6:30 where I have the boat moored. The ball starts at 8:30, so that gives us plenty of time. Give me a hug." He spread his arms and I dove into them, burying my face in his shoulder, inhaling his cologne, thinking how much I couldn't bear to lose him, lose anyone.

"Promise me you'll be safe," I murmured into his leather jacket.

"I promise. You promise me, too."

"I promise."

"Don't try to call me on any phone from here on in. We don't know who might be listening."

"I know," I said.

He gave me one last squeeze, picked up my carpet bag, dropped the phone back into it, and left. I listened to his feet beating down the steps, heard the alarm reset, and let myself cry for five whole minutes. That's all I could afford before getting up, taking a shower, and dressing in my black leggings and tight silk tee-shirt. I planned on wearing the leggings under my gowns so that when I ripped off the skirt of my second costume, I could move freely.

By 3:35, I was standing in the kitchen sucking back a smoothie while gazing down at the blueprint of Having Castle. Max claimed he'd memorized the crucial bits while

everyone else seemed more interested on the
vaults, the ballroom, the location of the
dressing rooms, and such. Today for some
reason, all I saw was Rupert's multiple
sidebar notes, the little comments like
Paint the upper salon deep moody red. We'd
all assumed that these were notes to staff,
part of one of Rupert's massive decorating
schemes, but something occurred to me now
that hadn't before. Why the teeny-tiny
writing? Wouldn't Rupert want notes to
staff—especially a master plan aimed at one
of his house maestros, like Sloane or even
Mrs. Montgomery the Mole, neither of whom
had teenage vision—to be more legible? There
was plenty of room for block letters.

With one of my crafter magnifying
glasses in hand, I dove down for a closer
look, running the glass up and down every
square inch of blueprint. Midway along,
positioned just above the back vault labeled
Jewellry, I found a tiny symbol that all but
a certain group might take for a
measurement: 3YO,K0. Only a knitter would
recognize that as a stitch. A yarn over was
a double-cross.

I pulled back. This wasn't the true
floor plan of Having Castle, but a decoy.

25

The original driver was back at the
wheel with no Arkhangelsky to accompany us
as we drove along the motorway towards what
I now referred to as 'the heap.' This guy
either didn't speak English or preferred not
to talk, period, but at least didn't insist
I wear a blindfold. That was worrisome. If
Arkhangelsky didn't care whether I knew the
way or not, maybe he didn't plan on me
living long enough to give anyone
directions. And no boat trip, either, just a
straight drive along the motorway, followed
by a cross-country trek through villages
linked by medieval lanes and tunnels of
hedgerows.

I stared out of the window, my hands
clasped in my lap, watching cottages pass by
as we slipped through a village sparkling
with Christmas cheer—a magnificent decorated
fir in the town square, couples and families
holding hands on the cobbled streets, a pub
alight with multicolored twinklers. If this
was to be my last night on earth, I wanted
to suck up every bit of light possible, to
hold in my heart for all the days, years,
eons, to come.

Finally, the Mercedes eased across a narrow stone bridge and down a tiny lane hemmed in on either side by hedges so tall, they all but obscured the view. I imagined stars riding overhead with a sliver moon on the rise. The night was cold and clear—perfect for heists, murder plots, and all manner of festive cheer.

When the car lurched to a stop, the driver leapt to open the door. I climbed out clutching my boxes, gaping at the blackened ruin before me. A huge chunk of crumbling stone rose ahead, all empty windows and jagged edges, of what must once have been a beautiful Tudor beam and stucco building. Now blackened and caving in on one side, a fire must have struck the first blow centuries ago, and time had done the rest.

The driver beckoned for me to follow. We crossed under the ruined doorway and stepped into a courtyard. I stopped. A newly restored exterior rose in the Tudor style ahead. I gazed at the mullioned windows before turning to look behind me. The front was only a facade, and Max was right: no one would even know what was happening here.

Inside, everything was just as I remembered—blacked-out windows with work in progress everywhere, minus the workers. The halls were deserted. The driver led me past the stepladders and rolls of wallpaper to the library, where a fire burned in the grate and many more books now occupied the shelves than before, but no Arkhangelsky. Without a word, the driver left me.

I carefully placed the boxes on the table and waited. A few minutes later, in came Katia bearing a tray with bread and cheese. The master had decked her out like a

servant girl in a long black gown complete
with a starched white mop hat and apron, her
blond hair braided down her back.

"Wrong century," I told her. "He has
you dressed up like a Victorian parlor maid
instead of a Tudor servant, or even a
Russian handmaid. Do you understand
English?"

She cast me a shy smile before lowering
the tray to the table. "You eat."

"You were the one hiding in Yagar's
hotel bedroom, weren't you? I recognize the
perfume."

Before she could answer, in swept
Arkhangelsky, resplendent in a long brocade
robe trimmed in ermine, holding aloft a
gilded scepter, the perfect representation
of his Ivan the Terrible portrait, right
down to the gray/black beard and the built-
in glower.

"You are like Ivan's doppelganger!" I
exclaimed, determined to act as though I
suspected nothing, believed we were partners
in crime.

"What is doppelganger?" He asked,
gazing at me with a convincing fierceness.

"It means double in German. You look
like Ivan the Terrible's double."

"Ah, yes, I am Ivan tonight, and you
Anastasia."

"And your key into Rupert Fox's domain
but, first, I want to see Rena. I know
you're keeping her here somewhere—in the
dungeons, maybe?"

"After theft."

"I need to see her now, just to make
sure she's all right. That was our deal."

"Our deal? Our deal is you go to ball
with me and I let Rena live."

"I just want to see her," I pleaded. "I just want to know she's all right."

"She is alive." His gaze fell to the table. "What is in boxes?" he asked.

I picked up the smaller of the two. "My present to you. These are the socks I knit for you while at Rupert's."

"I have socks, have many socks." He took the box anyway, flicked away the lovely silk ribbon Rupert had provided, and held up a pair of long black stockings, expertly knit on excruciatingly small needles with far more expertise than I possessed. "You knit?"

"Yes, for you. They are like boyfriend stockings. I wanted Rupert to think we were a couple. Do you like them?"

"I have socks," he repeated.

"I know you have socks but Rupert will ask to see these on. He always does. Will you wear them tonight?"

"Phaw! I will wear stupid socks," and he tossed the socks on the table and picked up the larger box. "This?"

"Those are a present from Rupert to complement my Anastasia costume."

I watched as he opened the box and frowned down at the contents, finally lifting one boot in his hand and inspecting every inch. "Very fine workmanship. Like Russian."

"They are a special present," I said. "I can't wait to wear them. There are matching gloves at the bottom."

"I give you boots, gloves. No need for these." He tossed the boot across the room, where it slid to a stop inches away from the fire.

I almost dove for cover but stopped
myself. Slowly expelling my breath, I turned
to him. "What did you do that for?"

"You don't wear boots and gloves from
Rupert, you wear boots and gloves from
Yagar," he thumbed his chest, the ferocity
not feigned. Here was the beast in tzar's
clothing.

"Are you crazy? Rupert will expect to
see me wearing those tonight. If I show up
without them, he'll get suspicious. He'll
want to know why my supposed date would
prevent me from wearing his gift to his
ball. Do you want to piss him off before we
get our plan initialized?"

He pulled out a golden chain from his
pocket and peered down at an ornate watch.
"Our plan?" He asked without looking at me.

"Well, it is our plan, isn't it? Aren't
we going to best Sir Rupert Fox so that we
can rule the antiquities market together? I
just need more information so I can help."

"You help when I say." He was studying
the watch, checking it against the
grandfather clock. "Katia, take her to
dress. Search her. Take boots. Keep eye on
her," and finished off in Russian.

I had forgotten about Katia, who had
sunk into the background against the
bookcases. She jumped into action now,
gathering the tossed boot and putting it
back into the box, tucking the box under one
arm, and taking my hand. As she tugged me
through the oak doors, I called back to
Arkhangelsky. "Don't forget to wear my socks
or Rupert will be suspicious."

We were heading towards the kitchen and
all I could think of was Rena. Why wouldn't
he let me see her? Without my phone, I had

no way of counting the minutes before we left for Having. It was now 7:00—not long before the rescue team arrived. I had to do something.

I caught a glimpse of a man dashing down a corridor laden with bags, and another calling to someone in Russian. Lots must be happening behind the scenes.

Katia delivered me to the deserted kitchen. I gazed around at the stove, now cold, everything cleaned and packed away for the night. On a long counter sat two trays, one stacked with a hearty sandwich, pickles, potato chips, and a clean beer glass, while the other plate bore nothing but a piece of bread, a slice of cheese, and a bottle of water. "Are they going to the prisoner and her guard?" I asked.

"No talking," Katia said. "Must dress." She emerged from a side room, her arms full of rich fabrics—a gold embroidered gown with a firm-trimmed red velvet cloak. "Take off clothes."

"Here?"

"Yes, here. Hurry."

"I want to wear my leggings under the dress—no slips and corsets." The gown appeared loose enough to accommodate my own bra. I saw a cloak, a cream satin long-sleeved underdress, plus the lampshade crown. Apparently, even if I had enough hair, it wouldn't show beneath the headgear.

"Yagar says you wear all," Katia said, still not meeting my eyes.

"I want to wear as much of my own clothes as possible under there." I caught her by the wrist. "Katia, do you do everything Yagar tells you to do? I saw the way he looks at you. You're like his slave, aren't you? Is that what you want?"

She tugged away her hand and held up the clothing. "Put on dress."

I removed my black tee-shirt and let her help me into the satin shift. It fit snugly but I could still breath—just. Next came the gold overdress, almost a surplice style, with loose sleeves and a skirt that fell straight from the shoulders. Next, Katia fastened on the crown with its veil-like extensions, and it weighed me down with its paste jewels and glittering trim. If I dipped my head a certain way, the whole thing would go flying.

The final touch was the thick velvet cloak fastened around my shoulders. "How did they move in those days? I guess that was the point: keep us all imprisoned in our skirts. Are you a prisoner, Katia?"

"Sit. I put on boots."

I eased myself into a wooden chair and watched as she untied the laces. "There's a zip on the side," I said. "But be careful. They are, um, valuable."

She nodded as she unzipped the hidden zipper.

"Look, Katia, when Arkhangelsky leaves tonight, my friend, Rena, will die. You know that don't you? You've been taking food to her, haven't you?"

Her blue eyes met mine. "He will not kill. He promises."

"Really? Does Arkhangelsky keep all his promises to you? He'll kill her. She serves no purpose to him after tonight, and neither will I. Is that what you came to England for, to participate in murder?"

She flung the boot aside. "I do not murder!"

"Be careful with those," I said as I gripped her wrist. "Did he promise that you'd live well and have this great new life in England?"

She tried to jerk her wrist away but I held tight.

"I live well."

"You're a slave! He uses you for sex and to cook and clean, right? How is that a good life? Look, you help me and I'll help you. I can get you to safety, help you start a new life. Help me save my friend and I'll save you, please!"

"He'll kill me."

"No, he won't, because you're going to escape. Where is Rena?"

She looked over her shoulder to a half-door near the bathroom. I'd never paid attention to it before. "In there?" I asked.

"At bottom of stairs."

"Katia!" A man burst through the door, yelling in Russian.

I released her wrist and Katia jumped to her feet, pointed to me, and to the tossed boot and yelled back at him.

It was the shorter guy I'd seen back in the Islington garage, now dressed like a commando in black, and packing a machine gun. A machine gun!

Katia kept talking, her arms waving. Finally the man growled something, snatched the sandwich off the plate, and left.

"What was that about?" I whispered after he'd gone.

"He hears arguing, wants to know why."

"And you said?"

"I say boots too tight. You complain."
She crouched back down. "We finish now."

I sat still as she pulled each boot on
over my leggings. "Are they all as well-
armed as he is?" I asked.

She didn't seem to understand.

"Guns, do they all have big guns?" I
asked.

"Guns, yes." Our eyes met. "Many guns."

I lowered my voice even further. "I
have a drug to make them sleep."

She looked puzzled.

I mimicked stirring something into a
cup, drinking it, then placed my head on my
hands, eyes closed.

"In food!" she exclaimed.

"Yes! We put some in their drinks,
starting with the man guarding Rena."

She swung around to glance at the
trays. "Must hurry!"

She left me to zip up the second boot
while she dashed around the kitchen,
bringing out mugs from the cupboards, and
beer from the fridge. I tip-toed towards her
on my explosive boots, afraid to apply
normal pressure, but that was crazy—I had a
wild few hours to get through, and some of
it was bound to involve running.

"Here," I began picking at the threads
on the gloves. The seam of the left glove
was gaping open when another man stormed
into the kitchen yelling at Katia. She
yelled back, threw her hands in the air,
indicating the food, the drinks, me, all in
the classic *can't you see I'm hurrying as
fast as I can?* gestures. The man got the
message and left.

"He says men leave soon. Must have
food," she said.

In minutes, I had distributed the contents of one packet into eight mugs, pouring beer into each until the liquid foamed over, and adding an extra dose for the glass destined for Rena's guard. "Is this all there is, eight men?"

"No, more. Others gone."

Damn.

Katia replaced the stolen sandwich from a tray she removed from the fridge. She headed for the door, carrying the tray of beer. "I serve beer. You bring sandwiches."

"No, wait. First Rena's guard." I checked the kitchen clock. Only ten minutes before the rescue team was due to arrive. How could they take on machine guns?

"No, first men, then guard, or they come. Bring food."

"We only have a few minutes left," but I picked up the plate of sandwiches and followed her out.

We traveled along the darkened passages to the back of the building and down another hall. I worried that I walked on the equivalent of land mines. While trying to maneuver the gown while carrying a tray, I banged into walls, and nearly tripped several times.

"Careful!" Katia admonished.

Finally, we reached an open door, where two men crouched over a coil of wire and what I guessed to be boxes of explosives. Both were dressed commando-style. Through the door I could make out more black figures dashing down a walkway and caught a whiff of river breeze. That had to be the route I came in two days ago. Max would have to come that way, too. What if they saw him?

Katia spoke to the men while lowering the tray onto a box.

One guy, a new one to me, grinned up at her and jerked his head in my direction.

"You should bow to me," I told him, offering a sandwich. "I am your queen."

Katia translated and the man laughed, taking a sandwich in the process. This one was young and handsome, and clearly had eyes for the boss's woman.

"Let's go," I said to Katia.

Together we scurried back to the kitchen.

"Is there another way into the building besides those two entrances?" I asked as soon as we were alone.

"Many," she told me. "Many holes. They try to fill."

"Okay, let's get to Rena." I couldn't wait a single minute longer. Time was running out. Wherever Max's team entered, they had to encounter a drugged guard, and I had no idea how long the drug or poison would take effect.

"Stay," Katia said, sliding the two plates onto another tray. "I take, you wait."

"No way," I told her. "I'm coming with you."

"No, if guard sees …" She made a throat-slitting motion that required no translation.

I watched as she hiked her up skirt, balanced the tray in her right hand, and ducked under the doorway like an accomplished server. In seconds she was gone. I stood at the top of the stairs looking down. She had a point about me staying out of sight, but what if Max and

the others appeared before she could get the
guard to drink? What if he opened fire on my
friends? What if the whole game was lost
before it began? I shot one glance towards
the kitchen door, unfastened my cloak to
leave on a chair, took a deep breath, and
followed her down.

26

I heard Katia arguing with someone the moment I stepped into the stairwell, the volume increasing with each step. Then she screamed. Hiking my skirts, I plunged down the narrow stairs and, in seconds, was at the bottom, hurling forward over uneven ground. I could see light spilling into the corridor from an open door ahead, voices coming from inside.

About a yard away, I tripped, falling hard on the earthen floor directly in front of the doorway. My crown went flying. Winded, I hoisted myself to my knees. To my right, I saw the back of a man hunched over a writhing Katia, who was bent over a table, legs flailing. She pounded him on the back with one fist, while the other hand reached for a butter knife beside an empty plate.

I stumbled to my feet and into the room.

"Phoebe, watch out!" Rena's voice.

I swung around. Rena sat tied to a metal chair while another man stood nearby, chewing a sandwich and sipping a beer. He raised his glass in salute. "You come to watch show?" he asked, stepping forward. "Maybe I do you while friend watch?"

I dodged him, grabbed the empty plate, and crashed it down on the other guard's skull. Katia shoved him off and he fell to his knees. The standing guard tossed his beer to the ground and lunged towards me. Oh, God, he had a gun, too!

"You can't hurt me," I cried, falling back against the wall. "Your boss wants me alive and well for the ball."

"Maybe I don't care about boss," he sneered.

"Oh, yeah? Got a death wish?"

Katia stepped between us, speaking in Russian. I slid away from the wall and ran over to Rena. They had her handcuffed to the chair, the flesh beneath the shackles black with bruises. "Rena, I'm so sorry!," I whispered, crouching beside her. "We're going to get you out of here."

"Happy to see you, so happy," she said, tears in her eyes. "Beat these bastards!"

Sunken cheeks, puffy eyes, bruises everywhere. I stifled a sob. "They'll pay for this. Where do they keep the key?"

"Watch out!" she cried.

I turned. The second guard was lurching towards us, blood dribbling down his ear, rage in his eyes. Behind him, the other guy was slamming Katia against a wall. The guard grabbed me by the throat and started choking me while I tried to knee his groin, but couldn't get the thrust I needed in that damn skirt. Max's voice scratched in my ear. "*Coming, Phoebe. Just looking for the room now.*"

Then Katia was behind us, trying to yank the guard off me. He kept squeezing, Katia kept pounding until she snatched up a shard of beer glass and rammed it into his back. The man released me with a howl and struck Katia across the face. She fell to her knees while I shoved air in my lungs and coughed.

Pounding feet in the corridor. That had to be our rescuers but, no, two more black-garbed commandos burst into the room, shouting in Russian.

I panicked, desperately searching for a weapon. I spied the drinking guard now flat on his back on the floor, either dead or doped, with his gun still in its holster and a ring of keys on his belt. I needed that gun and those keys, but the other guard was blocking me, yanking Katia to her feet while reaching for me with his free hand. I tried to kick him but my legs were snarled in the gown. "You bastard! You're dead!" I cried. He barked at the two new commandos, both of whom had their guns pulled.

"Let my friend go," I cried, pointing to Rena.

One of commandos was talking into his phone, probably to Arkhangelsky. *Shit, shit, shit!* Katia could barely stand. The man holding us gripped tighter. The second new guard stepped over his comrade's body and pointed his gun at me, "You come." Then he jerked his pistol first to Rena and then Katia. "Those dead. Her first." *Rena!*

The guy holding me pushed me towards the gun guy. Lowering my head, I hurled towards him, bull-style, knocking him in the stomach back against the wall. A bullet pinged against the ceiling. I fell on top of him, floundering in my skirts. Face-down on top of a raging, gun-wielding bastard, at first I didn't see what made him yell. By the time I caught the flash of a sword, saw the fist punch him full in the face, he was already unconscious.

I rolled onto my side, and looked up.

"You okay, darlin?", Max asked, helping me up. "Sorry it took so long. Had to find a way in. Finally found a break in the foundations."

"I'm fine. Help … them."

But Higgins was busy kicking the second guard's gun from his hand, wrestling him into a neck lock, and calling to Max: "Let's tie the bastard up!" while Marco was unlocking Rena's shackles. Marco paused only long enough to slice at one of the guard's legs, in case he tried to get back up.

Footsteps pounded on the stairs. "Get out of here! They're coming," I cried.

"Come with us," Max said, holding Katia upright.

"No. He won't hurt me yet. He needs me. Take Rena and Katia and go, all of you!" I cried.

Marco scooped his mother into his arms and leapt for the door, Rena blowing me a kiss in passing. "You are kick-ass, Phoebe!" she called.

Max enveloped me in a huge squeeze. "I can't leave you, Phoebe."

I pushed him away. "Stick with the plan. Go!"

Higgins grabbed him by the arm, saluted me, and tugged him away. In seconds, I was alone, propped up against the wall, staring at the wounded men sprawled across the floor, and wondering how I'd explain that.

Ivan the Terrible arrived with three of his men 15 beats later—I counted every second.

* * *

At first, all he did was bellow in Russian, his face boiling, his eyes glittering like shiny black bugs burrowed into his sockets. Dropping my gaze, I tried rubbing the dust from my gold dress, hoping the bits of torn embroidery wouldn't show too much. The satin sleeves were ripped so badly, I'd have to keep them tucked away under the robe. The more he yelled, the busier I became, until finally he took me by the shoulders and shook me so ferociously, I thought my head would snap.

"What did you do?" he said, succumbing to English.

"I used … my self-defense training," I said, watching over his shoulder as his men began helping their fallen comrades.

"You expect …" he paused to take a deep breath before continuing—poor man couldn't afford to beat me to a pulp yet. "Where are others?"

"What others?"

"Do not lie!" He shook me again. "Where is Katia?"

"She's gone, plans on becoming an equal pay activist."

"Rena?" he snarled, dropping his hands.

"I let her go. I didn't trust you to play nice any longer."

"How?"

"I'm mightier than I look." I shrugged again. "You'd never know it to look at me, I know."

One of the men, the one who'd downed the beer, propped himself up on one elbow—doped then, not dead. A battery of Russian followed.

"You drugged beer!" Arkhangelsky accused me, stabbing his finger in the air. "You drugged beer! You drugged all men upstairs!"

I shrugged. "Probably just awful beer. Don't blame me—you bought it." I could see how badly he wanted to hit me then, but I couldn't stop goading the bastard. Besides, every wasted minute equaled more time for the others to escape, and they *had* to escape. Arkhangelsky didn't have the manpower to chase them down.

"No matter," Terrible Ivan suddenly dropped his hands. "You all die tonight. Main team already gone."

He wrenched my arm behind my back and steered me out the door, stopping only long enough to pick up my crown and slam it on my head. It almost covered my eyes. We tromped back up the stairs into the kitchen, Ivan twisting my arm at every opportunity. Like Higgins said, some abuse never shows.

Four commandos sat at the table drinking coffee. One's head lolled to one side, while another appeared to be sleeping, head in arms.

"My, what lazy slaves, you have, Ivan. How do you stand it?" Really, I should have kept my mouth shut, not that it would have made much difference at that point.

"Put on robe." Arkhangelsky tossed the red cloak at me.

I fastened the cape over my shoulders. "Why should I do your bidding now that Rena's gone?"

He bared his teeth at me through the fake mustache. "You think Yagar does not have backup plan? Yagar always has backup plan." He snapped his fingers and two of the men lurched to their feet and came stumbling over. Arkhangelsky spewed instructions in Russian and one of them hobbled away.

Before I knew what was happening, Terrible Ivan had me by one arm and his man by the other. I had this horrible thought that maybe he didn't need me to get into Having Castle, after all. Still, I didn't expect to have the cloak thrown over my head or be slammed against the wall, face-first. They still held me tight and, baffled, I just stood there as something was fastened around my waist. A gun belt? Did he really think that anything could convince me to shoot Rupert? I felt the belt twisted into position and tightened. In minutes, I was released, and turned around. Arkhangelsky straightened my crown, smoothed the cloak over my shoulders.

"You have beautiful belt now," he said.

I looked down. A leather belt deeply tooled in gold leaf and fake gems cinched my waist, but nothing about it felt right. It was far too thick, for one thing, especially at the back. My eyes met Arkhangelsky's. "Oh, my God," I whispered.

He laughed. "You understand. Now you are bomb. You cannot take belt off."

27

I could hardly breathe. As we zipped along the winding country roads towards Having Castle, I'd grip the seat every time we hit a bump. Arkhangelsky would catch my tension and chuckle. He didn't know the half of it: there was still the little matter of the boots. And how was I supposed to get upstairs to change costumes and retrieve my phone when I was riveted to a pack of explosives? I couldn't risk being anywhere near people—as if I had a choice.

Arkhangelsky must have the detonator in his pocket. Maybe it was part of his phone, like Rupert's eye app. Every ten minutes or so, he pulled out his cell and barked into it, presumably keeping in touch with the commando team that had gone ahead. We may have temporarily disabled some of his men, but he'd obviously entrusted the most delicate operation to another crew. Had Max and the others reached Having safely? Would Rupert be prepared for the chaos that was bound to follow?

Still, I reasoned, Arkhangelsky had no idea that Rupert had fed him a false blueprint. Presumably the commandos would attempt to penetrate the castle where presumably the vaults were located. On the other hand, Mrs. Montgomery may have fed him the correct information. Now I realized exactly how Ivan the Terrible planned to create a massive explosion and kill Rupert at the same time—me.

Soon the Mercedes slowed down. We were passing through an imposing stone gate in a long line of cars. Each car was being stopped by men dressed in knee-high boots, red velvet breeches, and green cloaks, the outfit topped off with a distinctive wide-brimmed hat to complement the long black curly hair—Cavaliers. Of course, Rupert as Charles the Second would require his retinue to don the fashion of the king's men. Under any other circumstance, I'd find it entertaining, but as it was, all I could think of was not exploding.

Down came the window on the driver's side and a man with the ubiquitous long curls and a face I didn't recognize peered into the car. "Invitation, if you please."

The driver handed him the card I had secured for Arkhangelsky what seemed like eons ago. The cavalier scrutinized it, swept it through a scanner, and briefly read the confirmation on his hand-held gizmo before passing it back. "Please leave the keys with the valet at the door. Enjoy the ball, Czar and Czarina." He bowed, indicating we move along with a sweep of his hand.

"Phah! Czar and Czarina?" Arkhangelsky scoffed. "Not proper greeting for ruler of all Russia!"

"What did you expect, trumpets and fanfare?" I asked.

We sounded like the worst kind of stereotypical married couple. In this case, we really did want to kill each other.

We followed the procession of automobiles along a bare-branched alee where fairy lights had been strung in every imaginable color. Ahead a Norman keep, flanked by multiple wings stretching away on either side, rose in a flood-lit expanse of ancient stone, with candle lights flickering in every window. I gasped.

Ivan the Terrible began muttering in Russian.

"That's what a real castle looks like," I said.

"Shut up!" he snarled.

By then, we were pulling into a curving drive, where the cars stopped to be waited on by more Cavaliers. We watched as a couple swathed in pink and blue satin and velvet in the eighteenth century style emerged from a Rolls Royce. Music poured out through the open doors as the attendees swept up the stairs laughing all the way. When our turn came, another Cavalier stepped up to open the door on my side.

"I am Ivan Vasilevich, ruler of all Russia," Arkhangelsky announced, leaning over me. "You open door for Tzar first, then woman."

The Cavalier grinned. "When in England, do as the English do. Madam." He offered me his hand, which I took, allowing him help me out. "Thank you so much," I gazed straight into Evan's face and added. "Could you show me where the bathrooms are? I feel like I'm going to explode."

Something flickered in his eyes but he only smiled and said. "At the top of the stairs, Madam."

The driver opened the door for Arkhangelsky, who shoved him aside and strode towards me. "Woman stays with me."

Evan stepped back. I could feel his eyes on me as Arkhangelsky took my arm and tromped up the curving stairs.

"I have to pee," I hissed.

"No pee. You hold."

We stepped into a phantasmagoria of light, color, and music. A huge foyer presided over by a giant sparkling fir tree had been festooned with holly and ivy, the air alive with strains of the *Nutcracker Suite*, but the true glory came from the costumed occupants who swept the floor in dance. Besides the procession of Cavaliers ushering us towards the double doors ahead, we were caught up in a myriad of personages from different ages in a dizzying array of outfits.

Each attendee was announced as they stepped into a magnificent ballroom which seemed to streaming color and fabric.

"Admiral Horatio Nelson and Lady Emma Hamilton," a voice boomed, followed by "Prince Leopold the First of Belgium and the Girl with the Pearl Earring." Not all couples matched, apparently.

Where were the dressing rooms? I couldn't see Max or the others anywhere. Panic stormed through me. I tried to break away from Arkhangelsky but he gripped my arm even harder.

"Czar Ivan the Terrible and Czarina Anastasia Romanova," the voice boomed. The herald, a man standing at a podium dressed like a town crier, held a scroll aloft. He had to be identifying the guests from a list.

Arkhangelsky shouted over him. "I am Ivan Vasilevich, ruler of all Russia!"

Everyone turned. Prince Leopold ahead of us looked him up over, and grinned. "Good show, old boy! A very convincing Ivan the Terrible behaving terribly."

Me, with my ruined gown, askew crown, and probable dirty face, elicited attention of another kind.

"Are you all right, Czarina?" The Girl with the Pearl Earring asked. She looked so much like Scarlet Johansson, I was taken aback.

"Oh, yes," I said. "I'm playing the poor, battered wife. I'm pretty certain Ivan knocked her around. Do I look convincing?"

"Totally," she said.

Terrible Ivan's fingers dug into my arm. "You speak again, I detonate," he hissed into my ear.

"You're going to detonate it anyway," I hissed back. I just didn't know where or when.

Where was Max? Why wasn't he talking into my ear?

The orchestra in the gallery above the dance floor suddenly stopped, replaced by a contingent of trumpeters dressed like seventeenth century courtiers who marched into the room from a far doorway. The dancing guests parted to make way for the procession. Ten feet away of us, the trumpeters stopped, turning to form two lines as they unfurled pennants from their gleaming instruments. At the end of the line stood King Charles the Second, resplendent in blue satin and an ermine cloak, his long curly hair draping over his shoulders in

glossy coils. As he struck a pose, Ivan the
Terrible growled.

"King Charles the Second of England!"
the crier announced. The guests cheered as
the king swept a graceful bow. More
Cavaliers began assembling around the king,
bowing to him as they ushered him forward.
King Charles the second now fixed his gaze
on Ivan the Terrible with such intensity, I
knew something was afoot. He planned to
restrain Arkhangelsky.

Arkhangelsky stiffened. He'd never
allow himself to be captured, and what a
perfect time to detonate my belt. All he'd
have to do is dive for cover while the
explosion took out Rupert, all these guests,
and create the commotion he required.

I hiked up my gown, jerked Ivan the
Terrible towards me, and kneed him in the
groin. Though his robes cushioned the
impact, he was startled enough to release my
arm, which was all I needed to break away,
and bolt for the door.

I ran blindly, thinking only that I had
to get away from these people, and from
Rupert, his target. Let me go up in flames
someplace safe. I plunged through the crowd,
pushing people aside as I aimed for the
front doors. "Excuse me, I'm about to
explode," I cried.

"Something you ate?" somebody called.

Outside, I had to get outside, away
from all these people. Reaching the foyer, I
pushed past the new arrivals, shoving
Cavaliers aside, and dashing down the
stairs.

I thought I heard someone call "Madam!"
behind me but paid no attention.

The castle went on and on as I bolted over the lawns and past the ornamental hedges. Maybe if I got around to the back and reached the river? I heard footsteps beating the ground behind me. I yelled over my shoulder. "Back off! I may explode!"

"Madame, it is me, Evan. I can deactivate explosives. Just … stop … running."

"Evan?" I stopped, bent over, panting. "Arkhangelsky … has explosives around my waist. Wants to … kill Rupert … steal his treasures."

"Yes, we know about that last part." He stepped in front of me. "We are containing the Tzar now. Would you mind moving into the light?"

"He's got lots of men and some of them must be already here somewhere." I took a few steps to the left until I stood beneath a lit window. "Is this good enough?"

"It will have to do."

I lifted my cloak and turned around, trying not to whimper. "I think the explosives are on the back."

"Yes, I believe I recognize the style."

"The style? Do you mean explosives come in a choice of styles?"

"In a manner of speaking. I will need you to remove your cloak and lay face-down upon the ground. It's critical that you remain very still."

I did as he said, using the cloak as a barrier between me and the frosty ground. "Can you deactivate it?" I asked.

"I believe so, Madam, but there is always a margin of error."

"Margins aren't comforting in these circumstances, Evan, and could you stop with the 'Madam' business, at least for now."

"You must lie still. Please."

But staying still was agony. These could be my last moments on earth, and there was so much I'd left unsaid and undone. Had I told enough people that I loved them, besides Noel, I mean? That was my biggest regret. At that moment, shivering on the ground dressed like some poor dead queen, all I wanted was to tell people I cared, starting with him.

"I don't hear any ticking," I said, really just wanting to make conversation in what could be my final minutes.

"It's not a time bomb, Madam," he said. "It's a more sophisticated explosive cell meant to be detonated by an external trigger. I can't risk attempting to deactivate it, but will cut it away from the belt. I need you to remain very still. In fact, if you could try to breathe shallowly and absolutely not speak, I will begin."

"Right." That meant no crying, no whimpering, no famous last words. I lay as still as death, trying not to shiver, my eyes focused on the plush red fabric beneath my face. Where were Max, Rena, and the others? The minutes and seconds ground on. I couldn't tell what Evan was doing but I felt the occasional tug on my belt accompanied by a definite sawing sound. An icy sweat drenched my body.

Suddenly, Evan sprung to his feet and dashed off amid the trees. I climbed to my feet, retrieved the cloak, and waited, shivering. In seconds he returned.

"I dropped it into the old well. Should it detonate, it will do minimum damage."

"Oh, Evan, how can I thank you?" I could think of several inappropriate possibilities but there was no time for any of them. "I have to find Max. They're going to try breaching the vaults!"

"Mr. Baker was upstairs dressing when last I saw him. Here, use these stairs." He led me to a green door tucked behind a flying buttress and released the lock panel with his thumb print. "Go straight up to the top. At the second window, enter the hall. Take two lefts, one right, and you're there."

A phone buzzed from inside his cloak and he answered it through Bluetooth. "Yes? What? Where? Secure the keep. I'll be there directly." Turning to me, he added, "Sorry, Madam, but I must leave. The Russian has escaped and we appear to be under attack."

"What? Really, I—"

But he dashed up the stairs ahead of me and was gone.

28

Go straight to the top. At the second window, enter the hall. Take two lefts, one right, and you're there. Why is it that the best-meant directions always lead me astray? I was somewhere on the castle's second floor, totally lost. A long corridor stretched into the distance, a dimly lit expanse of parquet flooring and locked rooms—obviously an unused wing.

It was Max's voice crackling in my ear that guided me. "We're up here in the dressing room…" cracklecrackle "Where are you, Phoebe? One of Foxy's blokes said you escaped the Russkie … cracklecrackle."

The faster I strode in one direction, the clearer the voice became, until I turned into another hallway sparkling with festive trees. A redheaded man with a bandaged ear stepped out of a room to my left.

"Oh, pardon me. Are you all right?" he asked, catching sight of my disheveled person. "You look a bit worse for wear, if you don't mind me saying so. Are you supposed to be from *Les Miserable*? Oh, wait— wrong ball, wrong year."

"It's a long story, Vincent. Just looking for a dressing room so I can fix myself up," I said. "Do you know where they are?"

He pointed down the hall. "There's a string of them down that way. They used to have Cavaliers standing on guard outside each, but they took off. Seems to be a spot of ruckus going on in the castle tonight, all part of Sir Rupert's stellar flair for showmanship, no doubt. Something afoot in Having. Our host is putting on quite a skull and dagger show."

And those daggers were real. "I have to go get cleaned up. Thanks!"

I hurried past multiple doors until I spied one with an embroidered ikat ribbon dangling from the knob. I peered in at a long room lined with multiple dressing screens, where several fifteenth century personages were clustered around a tall man in a red and gold striped doublet, red hose, and pointed shoes with jingling pom-poms on the toes.

"Max?"

"Phoebe! It's about time!" he said, pushing aside his attendants to stride towards me. He stopped two feet away. "What did that bastard do to you?"

"He strapped explosives on me but Evan cut it off," I told him. "Who are you supposed to be, anyway?" I asked, looking him over.

"The Ferrara Court Jester Gonella," he growled. "Foxy made a fool out of me again, literally."

"But he looks a smashing fool, doesn't he?" said the handsome Renaissance gent I recognized as Marco. Jennifer looked equally splendid with a stuffed toy cat made to look like a ferret fixed to her velvet shoulder, but the other woman gazing at me with love and admiration took my breath away.

"Rena?"

She took me in her arms as I clung to her, unable to stop the tears a moment longer. "Rena, why aren't you at a hospital?"

"I am fine. Nothing hurts me that time cannot heal. I eat, I drink, am fine. There is work to be done now, no? We must stop this Arkhangelsky monster. Look, I bring Katia."

A woman emerged from behind a screen and waved. "Changing clothes. I am glad you escape, we all escape."

"It's not over yet, but I feel the same way. Sir Rupert let you in?" I asked.

"Sir Rupert let us all in and brought us here," Rena said. "He is so wonderful. He tells me that you are to call him as soon as you can. He is ready for Ivan the Terrible."

"Maybe not ready enough. Looks like Ivan the Terrible has escaped Rupert's guards, and must be somewhere in Having plotting his catastrophe. And then there's all Arkangelesky's men. Even the doped ones must be rousing by now. Where's Higgins and Jake?"

"I told them to stay on the boat and watch for barges. By my calculation, the Russkie will be sending a couple of floaters down to the castle to ferry the goods back to the heap," Max said.

"Oh, good," I said.

"But Yagar has many men in costume, too," Katia said. "Some here in the castle."

"What? You mean they're not all dressed like those guys back at the heap?" I asked.

"No." Katia shook her head, looking stricken. "They dress like Sir Fox's men. No chance to tell you."

"You mean as Cavaliers?" Max asked. "How in hell did that Russian twat find out about that? We didn't even know Foxy planned to deck his guys up like a bunch of cocker spaniels."

"King Charles spaniels," I corrected.

"The spy," Katia told him. "Spy working for Sir Rupert."

"Mrs. Montgomery. I'm already on to her," I said. "I've got to warn Rupert." I pulled away. "And get cleaned up and use my bomb boots. Where's my phone?"

"We've already tried calling him a couple of times. He's not picking up," Max said. "I figured he was busy doing his grand entrance downstairs."

"Your phone's in the pocket of your new costume," Jennifer said, stepping forward. "You look, like, horrible, so It's a good thing Sir Rupert Fox has an alternative costume waiting for you here."

"He does?" I said.

"Yes, and it's, like, brilliant. Come, let's get you get dressed."

Jennifer tugged me by the hand down the wall of screens until we reached the bottom section. "Ta-da!"

Inside the enclosure stood a dress unlike any I had ever seen outside a painting or the Victoria & Albert Museum. A mass of pearl-encrusted cream satin embroidered all over in scrolling gold and pearls, it swept from the stand in textile majesty. Full sleeves layered in cream silk erupted in a flurry of lace at the cuffs, the same kind of lace that stiffened at the neck into to a high ruff. The total effect inspired awe, as did the woman who wore the original. A wig of tight red curls sat on a stand nearby, already wearing its crown of diamonds and pearls. Beside the wig, hung a portrait.

"Queen Elizabeth the First?" I cried. "Is Rupert nuts?"

Max appeared behind Jennifer. "Probably, but you'll make a great queen. Get dressed, darlin'. Marco and I are heading out to find Rupert. Use your phones to keep in touch, ladies. Consider this room our war room. Ready, lad?" he said turning to Marco.

"Forsooth, but let us depart."

"Be careful, both of you," Rena implored.

"We will, but you wait here," Max replied. "You're too weak to be trotting about tonight. Rest!"

"Yes sir!" she saluted him.

After they'd gone, Jennifer and Rena began washing my face and removing my cloak. "Is this the belt the bomb was fixed to?" Jennifer asked as she tugged at the thing.

"It is. Evan cut off the explosives but left the belt."

"But I can't get it unfastened. I can't see a buckle or anything," Jennifer said. "There's, like, no fastening."

"Let me." Katia nudged her aside. "It is Russian. Secret closure you twist like that." With a sharp tug, the belt released and fell to the floor, allowing me the deepest breath I'd managed in hours.

"I wear," Katia announced. "I go as Yagar's queen."

"That's dangerous," I said. "Arkhangelsky will be looking for me in that costume, thinking he still has a bomb to blow up."

"I will be decoy. Decoy is right word?" Katia asked.

I nodded. "Right word, maybe wrong idea."

"Not wrong idea," Katia said. "I have bones to pick, too. Bones to *break,*" she corrected.

"I get that. Okay, so let's get me dressed," I said.

"I think it's brilliant!" Jennifer exclaimed. "Two queens to kick butt. How cool is that?"

"We could still get our own butts blown off before the night is out, so no crowing until Ivan the Terrible is out of the picture, pun intended," I said.

Fifteen minutes later—far too long, but dressing like a former queen of England isn't exactly a snap—I stood trussed into a farthingale, encased in starched ruff around my neck, encrusted in pearls over every inch, and taking up enough floor space to accommodate three people, plus a couch.

"I'll never get through the door," I said.

"You will," Serena told me. "Wide doors in these old houses. In Italy, the doors can handle horses and cows."

"Well I'm at least cow-sized now, but I can hardly move."

"The skirt can be removed by pulling on this cord here. Look," Jennifer demonstrated the release mechanism. "Sir Rupert obviously

wanted you to have all the freedom you
need."

"He thinks of everything," I admitted,
patting the secret pocket tucked in the
gown's folds. "And as long as I have my
phone and can activate the boot app, I'll be
fine."

"What about the sock app?" Jennifer
asked from behind me. "That looks cool,
too."

"What sock app?" She was applying my
wig and tucking in the hair pearls.

"The one on your phone with the little
sock icon." She was now fastening pearls on
my ears, too, while Rena applied my makeup.
Directly in my line of sight, Katia pulled
on the ruined garb of Anastasia Romanova,
finishing it off with the belt. Somehow she
managed to look stunning, in a battered kind
of way.

It took me a minute to clue into what
Jennifer said. "Jenn, have you been going
through my phone?"

"Just a quick peek. I mean, Max said
Sir Rupert had installed a boot app, so I
just wanted to see it and, well, that's when
I saw the sock. Is that, like, a sock bomb?"

I pulled out my phone, thumbing past
several screens before seeing the little
sock icon. I'd missed it before. What the
hell was I supposed to do with that? There
was no iris, nothing but a flashing message:
PRESS SOCK WHEN FEET ARE WITHIN TEN METERS.
What feet? Then I knew. Pressing the speed
dial, I rang Rupert's number, but the line
rang and rang with no pickup. Baffled, I
dropped the phone back into my skirt.

"I have to get going. Are we ready?" I
asked.

"Yes, yes." Rena clapped her hands and stepped away. "You look magnifico!"

Jennifer nodded. "You really do. Like, *wow*. Oh, and you have a staff."

"A staff?"

She lifted a gilded staff with a golden orb on top.

"That's a scepter," I said.

"Seriously? It's so you, like a giant knitting needle or something," she said, passing it over.

A giant knitting needle? For some reason this scepter had a pointed end. "It's a weapon of sorts," I told her. "Sir Rupert again. Well, I'd better go. Who's coming?"

"The two girls," Rena said. "I'll stay behind to guard the fort, but, Phoebe, Sir Rupert, he left a map, a real blueprint. He said he sent it to you by email."

I sailed from the screened enclosure like a square-rigger plying the air. Katia watched me in wide-eyed wonder as I steamed around the corner and faced my reflection in the floor-length mirror. The sight rendered me speechless. Queen Elizabeth the First had been reborn in all her regalia, and her presence infused me with such a sense of empowerment, I thought I could launch a thousand ships—or, at least a couple of bombs.

I lifted my scepter and cried: "Off with his head!"
And then the floor shook under our feet.

29

"Where did the explosion come from?" Jennifer asked as we entered the corridor.

"Downstairs, I think, but I can't tell. This place is so huge," I said. "We'll spread out. You two try the third floor, and I'll go downstairs. That's where Arkhangelsky plans to kill a few dozen people, so I'll start there."

"Oh, you sound so commanding," Jennifer cooed. "Very queenly."

"Right." I straightened my shoulders. "Now, listen, if you see Arkhangelsky, don't let on that you recognize him, whatever you do. Call me and Max ASAP. And ditto for Russian-accented Cavaliers. They can disguise their clothes but not their accents. If you see somebody suspicious, get him to speak."

"Everyone looks suspicious here," Jennifer pointed out as they took off down the hall.

"Be careful, both of you," I called.

Lifting my abundant skirts, I dashed off in the other direction, heading towards the grand stairway and the sound of music. I'd had only a few seconds to study the map PDF Rupert had sent, enough to gain a general sense of layout. The main sections of the castle appeared to be the same as in the bogus blueprint, but the most of the treasure appeared to be secured in the keep. I had to find Rupert. All I needed was to locate one real Cavalier. Surely the king's men would know where their lord was located?

On the top of the sweeping curved staircase, I hesitated. Wearing a starched ruff, stuffed inside a huge gown, and carrying a scepter, maneuvering was tricky. And looking down was pointless—my feet had totally disappeared. How had Her Majesty managed?

Below, the guests were waltzing merrily away to Strauss, oblivious to the explosion. I gripped the banister and took the first step, managed two stairs, and then tripped on my hem, pitching downward. I flung my scepter away in an attempt to steady myself, and managed to remain upright long enough to plow into the waltzers at the bottom of the stairs, knocking over Napoleon and Josephine, and burying Rembrandt and Einstein beneath my royal person.

Had I been myself, I might have apologized, but Queen Elizabeth the First might tumble but never stooped. "Get me up at once!" I cried, staring down at Einstein's started face. Below me, the physicist bellowed: "Get the ef off me!"

Two Cavaliers appeared, lifting me up by the arms to set me back on my feet. "Fetch my scepter!" I ordered one. As he rushed off to retrieve it, I turned to his companion. "Where is the king?"

"Which one, um, Your Majesty?"

British accent. He was Rupert's. "*The* king, King Charles."

The man insisted upon being obtuse. "Which one? There are two, Bess. King Charles the First is also in attendance, though he only showed up briefly before taking off."

I yanked my arm from his clutches. "Oh, for heaven's sake! Where is Sir Rupert? And don't deign to call me *Bess*."

"He has taken off searching for Ivan the Terrible and instructed us to keep the party going," the other one said, returning with my scepter, which, except for a few dents, remained remarkably unscathed. I took this Cavalier by the arm and led him away from the glowering Einstein and Rembrandt.

"What is going on? Where did that explosion come from, and why is everyone partying as if everything is normal?" I asked." It feels like the Titanic around here."

"The explosion came from the third floor, east wing, near the keep, I believe. We were instructed to expect a big one and to tell guests that any such noise was all theater, while keeping them calm and enjoying themselves. Sir Rupert and the other Cavaliers are bringing Ivan to heel. That's all I know. My post is here."

And then my cell phone rang. Turning my back, I fished out my phone. "Hello?"

"Phoebe, it's Max. Yagar's got Jennifer." I could hardly hear him over the orchestra.

"What?"

"The Russians have Jennifer!" he bellowed.

"Where?"

"In the bloody keep! Shit, they heard me. I—" and then the phone went dead.

Dropping the phone back into my pocket, I turned to the Cavalier. "How do I reach the keep?"

Up the stairs to the third floor, turn right, and blah blah blah. I tried to commit his words to memory as I steamed towards the stairs.

Einstein and Rembrandt, stood arm in arm, blocking my way.

"Remove yourselves immediately. I am in a hurry!" I said.

"We demand an apology first," Rembrandt piped up.

"Oh, go paint a picture. I need to get up those stairs now!"

"Nevertheless …" Einstein began.

I brandished my scepter at them until they parted. "Perfect," I said, pushing past.

What had got into me? I was not typically brazen or imperious, and yet here I was both and loving it. If only all was right with the world, which it clearly was not. Jennifer!

There seemed to be many more stairs than I remembered. The stairway formed a graceful curve as far as the first and second floors, before narrowing into a steep stretch leading to the top. Occasional personages floated past on the way to and from the washrooms, nodding at me along the way. A Gainsborough lady—I couldn't remember whom—curtsied to me on the second landing. No time for niceties, I kept hurling upward.

At last I reached the third floor and took a moment to catch my breath while gazing down the long dimly lit corridor. This had to be the oldest part of the castle. Rupert kept the decor authentic with tapestries and wall sconces that mimicked candles. The effect might be atmospheric but it reduced visibility and imparted a sense of gloom.

I caught a whiff of smoke and voices as I carried my voluminous person down the hall. How could we rescue Jenn with a bomb as a weapon? I couldn't very well throw an exploding boot at her captors without harming her as well. Why, oh why, had I told them to go off by themselves? We should have stayed together. And what had happened to Max, Evan, the others?

The corridor ended with an iron-studded door which hung ajar on ancient hinges. I peered in at a narrow corridor at the end of which light flickered. The scent of smoke was stronger here. I crept inside, tiptoeing towards the light. As the walls fell away around me, I realized I was on a balcony looking out into a circular space framed by blocks of hand-hewn stone—the keep.

About twenty feet below, and against one side of a circular wall, Ivan the Terrible stood with a knife to Jennifer's throat, while Rupert, Evan, and two of Rupert's Cavaliers stood still as death watching him. On the wall closest to me, I could just see the top of Max and Marco's heads as they stood at gunpoint, the weapon held by another commando. Bodies of several men in both Cavalier and commando dress littered the floor, and a couple of unidentified men in costume stood with their backs toward me. One woman lay on her back in a mass of torn and bloodied clothing— Katia! I blinked and re-registered the scene exactly as first witnessed. Shit!

"Come, come," Rupert was saying. "You shan't get away with this monstrosity—entering a man's castle, plundering, terrorizing his guests. I shall bring you to heel, and promise you that I will make the rest of your days a living hell!"

"Ha!" sneered Terrible Ivan, "Words useless. Look around—men wounded, many treasures gone, big hole in keep. You are dead man, Rupert, dead! Back away or I stick pretty girl."

Rupert, still inflated with royal importance, didn't falter. "You will fail, Yagar, I say ..."

While he talked on, I pulled out my phone, brought up the sock app, and rose to my feet. "Behold!" Everyone looked up. To all but Rupert and Evan, Queen Elizabeth the First was about to take a selfie, which I hoped like hell wouldn't end up as a photo bomb. "Release her immediately or I shall blow you to smithereens!" The sock icon was flashing green as I pointed the camera in the direction of Ivan's feet.

Yagar Arkhangelsky gaped up at me, then laughed. "You joke! Blow up Yagar, blow up friend!"

"My dear Queen Elizabeth, I have been awaiting your arrival," Rupert called out. "Pray, do press the button at once."

But somebody fired at me first, the bullet zipping through my skirt inches from my legs. I lurched to the left, falling against the wall as the phone clattered to the floor. Damn. Another shot ricocheted against the wall nearby.

"Phoebe, watch out!" a man called.

Footsteps pounded up the stairway. I fumbled for the phone but snagged it too late. A black-clad commando dashed up the stairs, gun in hand. Dropping the phone, I whipped up my scepter and whacked his kneecaps before he could fire. He fell backwards down the stairs, but already another Russian Cavalier was shoving his comrade out of the way as he hurled towards my balcony. Five seconds was all it took to release my skirt. The Russian Cavalier arrived in time to receive a vicious kick in the groin followed by a shove that sent him flying backward. I grabbed the phone, hurling down the stairs behind him, kicking all the way. At the bottom, I froze.

Terrible Ivan had dragged Jennifer into the center of the room and now dug the knife so deep into her throat that blood trickled from the point. I heard her whimpering, sensed other men, other faces, tensely watching. I kept my eyes fixed on Jennifer.

"No, don't, I beg you!" Marco cried.

"For God's sakes, you bastard! Let her go," Max begged.

"Yagar, I implore you: Take my treasures, but release the girl," Rupert said. "You can have it all."

"No," Ivan said. "I take girl and your treasure. I go to boat now. If you follow, girl dies."

All eyes were fixed on that tight little circle, so I aimed the phone and fired the flashing sock icon at Yagar's feet. Nothing happened. I caught my breath, swore silently, and shoved the useless piece of shit under my farthingale into the top of my leggings.

"Let her go," I called. "I'll be your hostage."

30

"You?" Arkhangelsky said, turning.

"Yes, me." I stepped forward. "It's me you want, isn't it? Let her go."

His lips pulled away in a sneer. "Step closer."

"Phoebe!" Max's voice cried out from behind me, but I couldn't take my eyes off hostage and captor for a second.

I stepped forward, crossing the circular floor with its wounded men, rubble, and gaping hole opening into the darkness. So many eyes upon me. When I was within inches of Arkhangelsky, I spat in his face.

He tossed Jennifer to the side and grabbed me in a headlock so tight, I had to stand on my toes to breathe. The knife ripped through the ruff and dug into the skin above my jugular. "You, I want, yes," he sneered into my ear. He swung me around so I could see the watching faces. "Back off," he said to someone, "or I stick." Max froze midlunge.

With my head thrown back, I only saw eyes after that—worried eyes, eyes that loved me, eyes that feared for me. The knife dug deep enough to break the skin. I felt blood trickling down my neck.

"I go now. You follow, she dies," Arkhangelsky warned.

I wanted to tell them to follow anyway, that he'd kill me, regardless, but that knife rested too close to my mainline to risk speaking.

Arkhangelsky called out in Russian, giving his remaining men instructions. My eyes were fixed upward as he began hauling me through the opening and out of the keep. I stumbled, the knife digging deeper.

"You stand!" he shouted. I had to keep steady so that point wouldn't slip, but the frozen ground rose and fell underfoot, and it was all I could do to stay upright.

Overhead, I saw the stars spangling through the trees. *Let light be the last thing you see before you die.*

Then an explosion rocked the earth, the force reverberating beneath me. Fire inflamed the sky. Arkhangelsky fell back, the knife slipping away. "Your friends die!" he cried, falling on top of me. I kicked him off, got to my feet, and tried to run, but he grasped my ankle, and sent me hurling to the ground. The keep was ablaze. I heard people shouting from inside the keep, so much screaming.

Oh, God, no! Terror, pain, horror, crushed my chest with force of another kind. I couldn't bear to keep breathing. Surely to hell he hadn't just blown up the keep and everyone in it? Not Max, Rupert—everybody? I struggled to run towards the carnage, but Arkhangelsky and another one of his goons pinned me to the ground. One of them tied my wrists and hauled me to my feet.

"No!" I cried. I called out to Max, Jennifer, and Marco. The commando goon was shoving me towards the river while Arkhangelsky trotted behind, barking into his cell phone.

I could smell the river, heard voices, and something else far away—a plane, no a helicopter. I hoped to God that was Interpol, but by now, it was too late. I'd already lost everything, everyone. I'd been so stupid. I should have called Scotland Yard right away, should never have thought that I—we—could take on this murdering bastard and his gang by ourselves.

Who the hell did I think I was?

Arkhangelsky and his commando were now talking excitedly, the goon pointing to barges by the riverbank. I tried to focus: two barges—no three—two moored on the bank end to end, the other further upstream. A smaller, unmanned boat floated gently downstream. Dark figures loaded crates onto the nearest barge, while a man cried out in either surprise or pain from the other. I caught my breath when I realized hand-to-hand combat was in progress on boat number two.

Hope flared. Arkhangelsky's men were trying to load one of the barges, while their comrades fought intruders on the other? I saw the silhouettes of at least two figures fighting against four commandos. One of them looked to be Higgins, the other appeared to be a man in Cavalier dress. Beside me, the commando pulled his gun and took aim at the Cavalier, but I lunged at him, knocking him sideways, shouting out a warning.

Arkhangelsky pointed to the barge, ordering his minion to help his comrades while he came after me with the knife.

"You want me to yourself, Terrible Ivan? Well, come and get me," I taunted while backing away.

He lunged for me with his knife extended, but I kicked it out of his grasp before falling back on top of my bound hands. I rolled away as he came after me again but suddenly, inexplicably, he let out a howl.

Had someone shot the bastard? But no, he was stomping his boots as if putting out a fire. I watched transfixed as he sat down and began unlacing his boots, swearing and screaming. Off flew one boot and the exposed sock, the very one I gave as a present, appeared to be searing into his feet, blistering and blackening the skin.

Never had burning flesh smelled so sweet. I pushed myself upright and came after him, kicking away at his arms and legs, plus more vulnerable places. "You murderous bastard!" I screamed. I wanted him hurt. I wanted him dead.

He yelped, tried to grab my ankle, but he was in so much agony by then, he only shoved me away, and bolted for the river, calling out in Russian as he went. I barreled after him, head down, but tripped, falling heavily on my stomach. Damn, he was getting away!

Footsteps pounded the ground towards me. "Phoebe, is that you?" a man whispered.

I looked up. "Jake?" I croaked, shoving air into my lungs.

"I didn't recognize you. You look bloody awful."

"Undo my hands—quickly! Is that Higgins on that boat?"

"I'm such a cowardly ass. Brenda took on the Russians, but there were too many of them. I'm not cut out for this shit, so I hid," he said while slicing my bindings. "Sorry, Phoebe. I let you down."

"No you didn't," I said. Once my hands were free, I pushed myself to sitting and yanked off my boots. "Your part is yet to come. How's your aim?"

"Aim?" he said, looking confused.

I heard Arkhangelsky shouting to his men from the river. One glance told me they were untying the moorings of the first barge, getting ready to sail. "Aim," I said to Jake, "You play soccer, don't you?"

"Football? Sure."

"When I give you the signal, take this boot and hurl it at the first barge so that it lands on deck where I point. Got that?"

I tossed him the boot, took his utility knife, and left him standing there dumbfounded as I bolted in my stocking feet for the second barge, the other boot tucked under my arm. From far away near the castle, people were shouting. I glanced over my shoulder long enough to see silhouettes crowded before the blazing keep, while the sound of fire engines blared across the countryside. Overhead the helicopter circled, as if looking for a place to land. I kept on running.

Arkhangelsky had disappeared, presumably boarding the first barge, which was already several yards into the river by the time I reached the bank. Somebody fired at me but I ducked, my sites on the second barge. Damned if I was going to let Arkhangelsky get away with murder.

I sprang on deck, leaping over a wounded commando, and paused, listening— sounds of a skirmish were coming from below. I sprung for the rear of the deck, pulling out my cell phone while calling out to Jake. "The first barge," I yelled. "Hit the stern deck where I'm pointing. Got it?"

He was standing on the bank, peering through the shadows. "Which one's the stern?"

"The back. Look where I'm pointing."

"Okay, see it."

"Now!" I yelled.

He threw the boot as if it were a ball, and for a terrifying second, I thought it would flip straight into the river. It hit the pilot house, instead, landing nearly flat on the stern deck.

Oh, shit, shit, shit! Would the app get a signal in that position? I held up my phone, aiming the eye towards the deck while shifting it back and forth until the icon flashed green—not nearly as brightly as when in my flat, but still bright. I pushed the button.

An explosion flung me backwards against the pilothouse, sending the phone flying, the barge rocking. All I could see was a crackling blaze streaming straight up into the air, amassing in a plume of sooty smoke. Men screamed and hit the water. I lay with my back against the pilothouse, briefly stunned. Struggling to my feet, I stood leaning there, unable to remember what I planned to do next.

Footsteps beat the deck behind me. I turned, registering the snarling commando hurling forward—Rat Man. Something in his hand ready to strike me, but someone tackled his legs first, sending him sprawling onto the deck. I was leaning against the pilothouse watching King Charles the First pummel Rat Man with his fist, when another commando burst onto the scene behind him. He paused mere microseconds to gape at the burning barge, which was all the time I needed to brace myself against the wall and shove him overboard. He fell into the gap between the barge and the embankment.

A few yards away, a helicopter whipped the air as it maneuvered down into a clearing near the river. "Interpol!" I cried. "It's about time."

King Charles lifted his head, one hand still on Rat Man's neck. "That's not Interpol, Phoebe. That's Arkhangelsky's getaway." That voice—familiar, unexpected— almost knocked me sideways, but I couldn't stop now.

"What?" I swung around to look, seeing a wet figure hobbling across the bank towards the waiting copter. I grabbed my boot, retrieved my phone, and scrambled past the king. "Are you coming?"

I was just about to leap from the barge when I saw a fallen commando reaching for a gun just as Brenda Higgins knocked one of his comrades in the jaw, and flung him off the stern. I kicked the gun from his grip, sliding it towards Higgins. "We're not done yet," I called to her as I jumped onto the bank.

Once my now-frozen feet hit the ground, I hurled myself toward the helicopter, vaguely aware of people swarming towards the river from the castle.

Ahead, the helicopter beat its way upward—two meters, four meters. I dashed through the tiny windstorm and flung my boot up into the open cockpit, only it missed and draped over the copter legs, instead. I saw Arkhangelsky glowering down at me, registered the machine gun he held, but was too busy aiming my phone app at the shifting boot to care.

I slammed my thumb down on the detonator button just seconds before someone tackled me, jettisoning us into the bushes as a twosome.

31

I clung to King Charles the First as we watched the flaming mass of metal swerve towards the river. Two burning figures leapt out, screaming as they hurled into the water moments before the helicopter crashed into the second barge.

"Let me guess—Foxy's exploding boots," King Charles said mildly as he held me close in the flickering light.

"How'd you figure that out?" I asked as I leaned against his bloodstained waistcoat. All I wanted was those few precious seconds of comfort and peace, maybe even pretend that we were just an ordinary couple holding one another under ordinary circumstances—a fire down the street, fireworks, maybe.

"I've heard about them, but it looks as though Evan's honed his skills even further. I'd never seen his explosive devices detonated by a phone before."

I gazed up at him, letting my finger trace the fresh scar running beneath his long curly wig to his jaw. "That's from Orvieto, isn't it? And, despite everything, you came."

"Of course, I came," he said, holding me tighter. "Foxy told me that you were, as he put it, 'in a spot if trouble', and so was he. His message was cryptic—something about Ivan the Terrible attempting to snare my sovereign queen. How could I resist that?"

I laughed. "Some queen—but I guarantee you, Ivan truly was—is?—terrible." Still shielded by the bushes, we watched as a police team arrived, some of whom appeared to be fishing Arkhangelsky and his pilot from the river. Other men were apprehended the moment they climbed ashore. Firetrucks and sirens pierced the night and the crowd of watchers beside the river began to swell.

I could just make out the bald head of Agent Walker poking around the crates by the riverbank. "Late as usual," I muttered. Then, a sudden horrible realization struck. I gasped. "I've lost Max, Rupert—everyone!"

"No, you haven't," Noel said, stroking what was left of my hair. My wig had fallen off long ago. "They're all in the crowd. I see Max hunting for you by the river now, and the others are there, as well. The explosion in the keep was all pyrotechnics, Phoebe. Rupert and Evan swapped what was supposed to be the Russian's devices with their own, staying one step ahead of everyone, as usual."

"You mean, Foxy's okay?" I said, feeling stabs of alternating joy and fury.

"He's standing right over there talking to your Interpol friend," Noel said. "You're a bit shorter than I, so you're missing some of the action."

"I'll kill him," I said, pulling away. Pushing through the shrubbery, I stormed towards the scene, Noel on my heels, or so I thought.

Evan was bounding across the lawn towards me. "Madam!" he said, a grin lighting up his handsome face. "You saved the day again. Thanks to you, all is well."

I met him halfway. "Are you kidding me? All is not well! People got hurt here, terrorized, and I, for one, have just about had it up to here!" I pointed to my blood-stained ruff.

Evan seemed dumbfounded as I strode past him towards King Charles the Second, who stood by an open crate, talking to Agent Sam Walker.

"Agent Walker, I see you arrived too late, as usual," I said stepping between the two men.

Understandably, it took the man a few minutes to recognize me dressed in a farthingale and leggings. "Ms. McCabe?"

"Yes, it's me, and you," I pointed at Sir Rupert, "you could have stopped all this long ago. I couldn't because it risked Rena, but you could have alerted Scotland Yard the moment you knew that Arkhangelsky planned to rob you, using me as leverage."

"Why, my dear Queen, one cannot win a war by mere artillery alone," Rupert began. "What could these fine Interpol chaps have done without catching the thief red-handed, so to speak?" He was lifting his hands so that the frothy lace about his cuff—slightly blackened in places, but still elegant—cascaded around his wrists. "It was necessary for us to bait the trap, a process with which you participated skillfully, I must say. Together we lured the criminal to his ultimate denouement, and now will rest comfortably knowing he and his gang are behind bars," he paused as emergency personal carried two stretchers past us, "or in a more permanent resting place, whichever comes first."

"Speaking of catching criminals red-handed," Sam Walker said, "at the moment, I'm more interested in checking Sir Fox's crates. I understand Arkhangelsky was in the process of loading these onto the barge before Queen McCabe here launched her own Armada. Let's just take a look, shall we?"

"By all means," Rupert said.

I shot a quick glance at Rupert, who now stood steepling his fingers. He seemed remarkably nonplussed for a man about to have his secret art and antiquities collection exposed to the eyes of the law. Walker used a crowbar to pry open the first crate, holding the treasure to the light. We stood staring at a black velvet painting of Elvis, complete with pearly teeth.

"Not my usual taste, I deign to say," Rupert said with a sigh, "but rather an excellent rendition, do you not think? I particularly appreciate the detail on his jacket—the sequins and rhinestones, in particular."

Walker stared hard. "Is this your idea of a joke?"

"Now, now, Agent Walker, try not to judge another man's taste through your own, taste being a very subjective matter," Rupert admonished.

"Do you expect me to believe that Arkhangelsky launched an operation of this magnitude for a bunch of kitsch?" But the agent was already onto the next crate, practically hacking it open. This one, a much smaller box, contained nothing but an assortment of plush toys. He flung away the box in disgust and turned to Rupert. "You switched them. Where's the originals?"

"Surely you did not expect me to let the Russian plunder my family heirlooms? Perish the thought," Rupert said, looking affronted. "Of course, I took the necessary measures to secure my belongings through the setting decoys and deploying various sleights of hand. Rather than continue haranguing me, do ascertain the particulars from the criminals at hand rather than the intended victim." He indicated the several wet and wounded handcuffed commandos waiting to be taken away by either ambulance or police van. "Now, if you don't mind, I have guests to attend."

"Anyway, Agent Walker," I said. "I told you that Arkhangelsky had a probable Raphael in his possession upstream. That's where you should look for your art treasures."

"Don't worry, I'll be heading there next," Walker said before storming off to help his men sort out the wreckage.

"So everything in the barges was also worthless?" I asked Rupert, the moment Walker was out of earshot.

"There may have been a few items of worth destroyed. Nevertheless, we did conspire to make it appear as though we were in the process of upgrading our vaults, hence convincingly crated and labeled the valuables to await Arkhangelsky's arrival. Phoebe," he said, abruptly turning to lay a hand on my arm, "do forgive me if I permitted this all to get a bit out of hand. I would never, never want anything to harm you or those you care about. I admit to enjoying the thrill—"

"Terror," I corrected.

"*Thrill* of a little feint and parry, but perhaps the carnival atmosphere got a trifle out of hand. Am I forgiven?"

I gazed up at his slightly disheveled version of King Charles the Second. "You know, I was seriously planning to end our friendship before this, but now I realize that's not possible. They say you can't choose your family the way you can your friends, but that's not true. Sometimes your friends *are* your family. One way or another, I'm stuck with you, and you with me, but, just for the record, you drive me crazy."

Rupert clapped his hands together. "You cause my heart to sing! We must celebrate immediately! Where's that young man of yours? I asked him to come as my Christmas gift to you, though did not expect the gift to be wrapped so spectacularly." We both scanned the crowd looking for the tall bedraggled figure of the other King Charles, but he had melted into the crowd. I swallowed hard.

"Do not fear, Phoebe, dear," Rupert said, patting my arm. "He will be awaiting you somewhere."

"Interpol Agents tend to make him twitchy."

And suddenly I was being hugged ferociously by Max, followed by Jennifer, and then Rena. Jake waved at me and held up the sneakers I kept in the van for installation days. Brenda Higgins stood beside him, her arm in a sling, nodding.

"We were looking all over for you," Max said. "I got here just when the copter crashed. How are you, darlin'?"

"Fine," I said, laughing.

"Katia's okay," Jennifer said. "I mean not *okay* okay but she's just been knocked out, the paramedic said, and here's your skirt and the wig. You can't go back into the ball looking like that."

"Back into the ball?" I asked.

"But of course, Phoebe," Rupert said. "The night is but a pup. We must reengage the revelry and celebrate the season." And off he went to shepherd the crowd into the castle.

I fastened on my skirt, let Jennifer apply my wig, and watched as Jake put on my sneakers like I was some kind of Cinderella, all the while squeezing Rena's hand, and seeking Noel in the crowd. Where did he go?

"I am very tired," Rena said, giving my hand another squeeze. "Too much excitement. Sir Rupert has offered me one of his guest rooms for the night and one each for us. I will rest and see you at breakfast, yes?"

I nodded. "Shouldn't you see a paramedic? You've been through hell."

"Nothing a warm bath and a good bed won't cure. We will talk more tomorrow." She linked her arm into Jake's and let him escort her back to the castle.

"Ta-da, see you inside," Jennifer said as she took Marco's hand and followed the sounds of an orchestra warming from inside the castle.

"I'd better track down that boat, Phoebe," Max said. "One of the coppers said I could borrow his Zodiac and retrieve the thing downstream. See you later?"

"Sure," I said. I wanted to tell him that his son was here somewhere, but now didn't seem the time for a momentous meeting. Besides, his son had disappeared again.

The world was alight with red and orange, a brilliant phantasmagoria of fiery color with police milling about. Ahead I saw a couple of plainclothes officers disengage from their colleagues and make their way towards me. They'd have questions, a thousand questions, and I didn't feel like answering any of them that night.

I lifted my skirts, and flounced towards the castle. Where moments earlier, I'd been the center of attention, now I seemed caught in the wake of some kind of strange aftershock. Everything felt so unreal, *I* felt so unreal. My heart hung in my chest with a weightiness I couldn't shake.

I was just rounding a privet hedge when someone stepped up behind me and took my hand—him. I grinned. He grinned back.

"You know I can't stay," he whispered as we strolled across the frosty lawn.

"I know."

"All we need is for Walker to see us together to reach the right conclusion."

"Noel, I need to tell you something, about what you said in Orvieto."

"Hey, you there! Wait up!" A man shouted. We turned to see the police officers jogging towards us.

"Let's dance. Come."

Noel tugged me around to the front of the castle, past a handful of Cavaliers in the process of regrouping, past the fire trucks and the service vehicles, up the stairs, and into the ballroom alive with revelers. The orchestra was belting out *God Rest You Merry Gentlemen* with a definite rock edge, while one of the musicians ran guitar-like chords on his electric violin. All vestiges of decorum had been dosed under fevered celebrations. Bewigged servants wove through the crowd bearing trays of champagne, while King Charles the Second stood on the top of the landing and shook his royal booty. Rupert never looked more gleeful.

Noel and I plunged deep into the heaving crowd, laughing all the way. "Dance like there's no tomorrow, Phoebe!" he called.

"But there's always a tomorrow for somebody," I cried. "I want one for us!"

But he didn't hear me over the music. I couldn't take my eyes from him. Rogue, renegade, killer, thief—my heart belonged to him alone, whether he knew it or not. We bounced around for a while, until Noel pulled me closer, insisting on dancing slow despite the outburst of *We Wish you a Merry Christmas.*

"Noel," I said into his ear, "If you send me a postcard, I promise to answer this time."

"Pardon?"

"I said—"

He pulled me closer. "Don't look now, but Sam Walker just stepped into the ballroom looking for someone. My guess is it's you. I have to bolt."

"No, don't go," I said, hanging on to him. "I need to tell you something—"

But he gave me a quick kiss on the lips and slipped into the crowd, leaving me bereft.

"Who's that?" Agent Walker asked, pushing through a pair of tipsy Renaissance courtiers.

"King Charlie's dad, who else?" I said.

"Right. Pardon me for disturbing your fun, Ms. McCabe, but I'm commandeering you to help us find that Raphael. We're heading up to Arkhangelsky's place now. Care to come?"

As if it was a request. I cast one more longing glance in the direction Noel disappeared, took a deep breath, and said: "Sure. I'll take you there." As I followed him to the black sedan, I unfastened my skirt and left it spread over the snow like a fallen angel, all satin and pearls. One of the cavaliers slipped a cloak over my shoulders.

Thus, I got into the car with Agent Walker and his stern-looking colleagues, and drove through the icy countryside with a convoy of black vehicles on our tail. I gripped the cloak closed over my shoulders, thinking of Noel. Would we, could we, ever have a future together? I wanted so much more than these brief forays under extraordinary circumstances. I wanted him, all of him, every day of the year.

"Tell me everything you know about Yagar Arkhangelsky's operation in Britain," Walker asked beside me.

I forced my mind back to the here and now, recounting the salient details. I told him what I could, careful not to implicate Rupert. "Did you round all those bastards up?"

"We got most of them, but are still chasing down others. He had quite a troop of illegal immigrants running around, one in particular we've been chasing down for years, his second in command who got away—a former KGB agent. He's the one we're zeroing in on now."

"Oleg somebody, the Rat?"

"Oleg Stanislav—that's the one."

"And Mrs. Montgomery, the mole, did you get her?"

"Got animal names for all of them, do you? Sir Fox delivered her to us early on. And how have you fared, Ms. McCabe, all trussed up like Queen Elizabeth the First gone AWOL?" He turned to face me then, and in the shadows periodically flashed with light from the passing villages, I felt the intensity of his gaze. He almost looked handsome then.

I grinned. "Look at me, Walker—I'm a queen undone, traipsing about in leggings and a bloodied farthingale. What do you think? Right now, all I want is to get back to Having, have a hot bath, and sleep for days." *Sleep for days with the man I love by my side, which wasn't going to happen.*

"We'll get you back to Having as soon as possible. You can give us the rest of your statement tomorrow when we take Sir Rupert Fox and your godfather's."

Within ten minutes, we were pulling up the winding drive.

"This it?" Walker asked, gazing at the ruined facade.

"That's it. Follow me." I climbed out of the car and tramped across the rough ground towards the building. Inside, the place was empty, everything left just as I'd seen it hours before.

"Comb the property," one of the detectives said. As the officers spread out,

I led the men down the hall towards the new vault.

"They were just constructing it," I told them. "You'll probably have to use some kind of device to open it …" My words trailed away. The door hung on one hinge, a ragged hole where the lock had been. The vault itself, jumbled by broken crates and smashed glass, had obviously been plundered. It only took one glance to know the painting was gone.

I stared in disbelief. "But this place was full of stuff just a few hours ago. How could Arkhangelsky have removed his loot *and* launched that heist attempt on Rupert at the same time?" But even as I spoke, I knew he hadn't. Foxy had to be behind this. "Look, I swear is was full only hours ago, but clearly Arkhangelsky has moved it since. You'd better look even harder for your Oleg Stanislav. I'm guessing he just shafted his master. Meanwhile, could one of your officers drop me back to Having now? I'm freezing."

Walker didn't argue, being too absorbed in sorting through the remaining boxes, some of which were still intact. He nodded and called a plainclothes officer over to drive me back to the castle. Most of that brief trip passed in a blur. The moment the car stopped, I bolted for the stairs, pushing through the staff cleaning up after the party. Most were still in costume, though jackets had been removed and some had swapped boots for sneakers.

"Where's Sir Rupert?" I demanded of the first bedraggled Cavalier.

"I have no idea, miss. Probably upstairs somewhere." He indicated the stairs with a jerk of his head while continuing stacking glasses onto a tray. Is that how to treat a former queen? I launched for the stairs, taking them two at a time. On the way, I pulled out my phone and texted Rupert. *Where are you?*

The response came in an instant. *In the dressing room with Max.*

In seconds I was upstairs, throwing open the door to stand, stunned, looking over at Max and Rupert sitting side by side, a pot of tea between them. Rupert's wig was off, yet he remained in full kingly regalia, though his hose were muddy and his mustache askew. He also appeared surprisingly dejected. Max hunched over elbows on knees, still in the jester costume, though the pompoms appeared to have been ripped off his shoes and cap and now lay strewn on the floor. Both men rose to their stockinged feet. "Phoebe! Is everything all right?" Maxed asked.

"No, it's not, but glad to see you two are finally getting along." I slammed the door behind me and strode over to Rupert. "You stole Arkhangelsky's loot, didn't you? While chaos raged here, you sent a barge up river to clean out the heap."

Rupert pulled a sooty handkerchief from his pocket and mopped his brow, further smearing charcoal across his forehead. "Really, Phoebe. Hasn't there been enough drama for one evening? I admit to being rather exhausted and do resent your tone."

"I delivered Interpol and Scotland Yard to Arkhangelsky's heap a while ago, fully expecting to see a certain missing Raphael returned to the public where it belonged. Instead, the thief's vault had been plundered, the Raphael gone. Don't lie to me. You were involved, weren't you? I saw that barge waiting upstream."

Rupert straightened to kingly size, as if readying to blow more puffery into his reply, but stopped suddenly and sighed, as if letting the air out of his intention. He threw up his hands, charred lace falling around his wrists. "Indeed, I admit to arranging the retrieval of certain items belonging to me, with the intention of commandeering any interesting tidbit I might find along the way—as interest, you understand—specifically that Raphael, which I have long known Arkhangelsky possessed. However, matters did not go as planned."

"What do you mean?," I asked. "The painting is gone."

"I sent a trusted personage along to ensure my wishes were carried out whilst we were absorbed with matters here," he said, "but, alas, that individual absconded with the painting. I admit to having some difficulty processing this. I can hardly breathe. Oh, my. Why would he do such a thing?"

"What trusted personage would steal from you?" I asked, aghast. "Surely not Evan?"

"Not Evan," Max interjected, "Noel."

I turned to him in disbelief. "*Noel*? But Noel was with me."

"Only part of the time, darlin'. Seems my boy's gathered a skilled team of his own, and outmaneuvered old Foxy at his own game, Bloody brilliant!"

"It is not *bloody brilliant,* Max," Rupert said. "It is deceitful, even reprehensible, after all I have done for that young man. I shan't tolerate it. On the contrary."

I was only half-listening, my mind running over every detail of the past few hours. I first saw Noel on the barge, but he had to have been on site for hours earlier. He wasn't around during my bomb-belt incident, either. He had plenty of time to get up to the heap, steal the painting, and arrange for its transport. No wonder he didn't stick around when Walker appeared. "But why didn't he just leave it to Interpol if he wanted it returned to Italy?"

"Ah, there's the rub," Max said. "Why didn't he? Maybe because he didn't want it tied up in the courts for eons deciding who in Italy has the rights to it—Raphael's ancestors? The Uffizi? Rome? I'm guessing he'll whisk it off to Italy and see to it himself."

I straightened and turned to Rupert. "I have a few priceless pieces of Etruscan gold in my possession that require repatriating to Italy, too. Maybe it's time Noel and I made a joint deposit in the names of Italian heritage?"

THE END

DID YOU ENJOY *THE GREATER OF TWO EVILS?* If so, please leave a review and visit my website at http://www.janethornley.com/blog/

ABOUT THE AUTHOR

Jane Thornley has been writing her entire life. Stories weave through her life constantly in elements that arise in both her books and her fiber art. Learn more about Jane and her works at Janethornley.com.

Made in the USA
Monee, IL
15 October 2020